A Feast Fit For A King

"I am to go to Aquitaine," Eleanor said, "to raise arms and men and money for the Crusade. The Abbot will go to Germany to rally the Hun. Louis will stay here in France. And you—"

"And me?"

"Will come with me, darling. You will, won't you? It's truly a heaven-sent opportunity. I can show you Aquitaine, which is paradise on earth. We can be alone far from my husband. We can make love . . ."

"I don't know." Bernard frowned a mock frown. "I have heard that Aquitainians eat Gascons for breakfast."

"Only Aquitainian Queens," Eleanor assured him. "And you'll like that. Truly you will . . ."

THE COURTESANS

The Scarlet Raptures of Eleanor of Aquitaine

by Hillary Auteur

PINNACLE BOOKS   NEW YORK

The author of this work is a member of the National Writers Union.

Although many of the characters and events in this book are historical fact, the incidents described are the creation of the author and have no basis in historical fact.

THE COURTESANS: THE SCARLET RAPTURES OF ELEANOR OF AQUITAINE

Copyright © 1984 by Hillary Auteur

An original Pinnacle Books edition, published for the first time anywhere.

First printing/November 1984

ISBN: 0-523-42140-0

Can. ISBN: 0-523-43126-0

Cover art by Harry Burman

Printed in the United States of America

PINNACLE BOOKS, INC.
1430 Broadway
New York, New York 10018

9 8 7 6 5 4 3 2

The Scarlet Raptures
of Eleanor of Aquitaine

Chapter One

Lady beware!

Beware the sensual spankings of amorous Aquitainian uncles.

Beware inept deflowering by a loutish haymow lover.

Beware the disappointing droop of a royal French bridegroom.

Beware impalement on the horns of a unicorn.

Beware Gascon poets with Plutonic pricks.

Beware cunnilingus by priests with mouths like dragons breathing fire.

Beware performing fellatio on a Byzantine knight in tight armor.

Beware raping a handsome infidel; he'll never forget!

Beware anal intercourse in Antioch.

Beware Aegean pirates who are into leather.

Beware the Golden Shower of Sicily.

Beware bending over before a bowlegged Norman.

Beware the temptation to use naked thighs as a garrote.

And finally, lady, beware four fiery lovers in a royal English marriage bed!

Such are my cautions, Oh medieval ladies. Such is the advice that I, Eleanor, Duchess of Aquitaine, Queen of France and Queen of England, pass on to you in the divine wisdom decreed by my royal status. And I would add that although in this year of Our Lord 1155 I am scarce into my third decade of life upon this earth, nevertheless each piece of advice is based on that which I have myself personally experienced. Indeed, young as I still am, I have not only been twice crowned a Queen, but have lived through such amorous experiences with the greatest men of so many lands, near and far, European and Oriental, blasphemous and exotic, that I have no hesitation in deeming my hard-earned wisdom a boon to all women of my age and therefore here take liberty to set it down in print for the amorous edification of all my sisters, both noble and baseborn.

I shall begin at the beginning. I was born Eleanor, Duchess of Aquitaine, in 1122, anno Domini, a descendant of mighty Charlemagne, the granddaughter of Duke William IX—a composer and singer of romantic love songs who was known as William the Troubadour—and the oldest daughter of Duke William X, one of the most powerful and influential warrior-knights of his day. My younger sister, Petronilla, was born less than a year after I was. Our mother died when I was in my eighth year. After that, our father took it upon himself to personally bring up Petronilla and me. This meant that we traveled with him constantly over the realm of Aquitaine which he ruled.

Ah, Aquitaine! Opulent Aquitaine! My native land is a

verdant, rolling expanse sprawling between tiny France on the one side and Gascony and Spain on the other. To the west the Atlantic laps its sun-drenched shores and to the east lie the wooded hills of Burgundy. It is a rich land where every sort of crop flourishes. The sheep grow fat in our lush grasslands and our forests are filled with game. Vineyards are everywhere. The many rivers that wind through our fertile valleys are so thick with fish that hunger is an unknown phenomenon in Aquitaine. Indeed, Dame Fortune has smiled so generously on us that we have frequently been the target of expeditions by neighboring nations eager to plunder our abundance. For this reason, there are many castles and forts in Aquitaine where the people may rally round their rulers and fight off invaders.

My father, as Duke of Aquitaine, owed fealty to King Louis the Fat of France. That the Dukes of Aquitaine were bound to the Kings of France in this fashion was a tradition stretching back over many centuries. My father observed this tradition despite the fact that his realm of Aquitaine was four times as large as France, that his army was three times as powerful, and that he considered Louis the Fat the most inept of rulers.

"Blocks of wood must be wedged beside his bed to keep him from rolling out of it when he is with a woman," Papa would sneer.

Well, *mes amis*, this was Papa's measure of the French monarch, and I truly suppose that it will do as satisfactorily as any other. It says, I suppose, as much about Papa himself as it does about King Louis the Fat. In truth, Papa was somewhat obsessed with the subject of sexual performance and all of its ramifications, and this obsession was always uppermost in his judgments and in his advice and plans as well. Despite the fact that we were girls, Papa did not restrain himself from bluntness when it came to passing along his erotic wisdom to Petronilla and me just as soon as we entered adolescence—which is to say when the protuberance of breasts drew his attention to our approaching womahoood.

"For your own good—" he would start off many a conversation.

Petronilla and I would listen, fascinated, while he parceled out bits and pieces of sexual folklore—some of it eventually useful, much of it not. For instance, I recall a period when Papa's attention (for what reason I never found out) focused on chastity belts.

"Now, daughters, it will do you no good to protest," he assured us. "If you're properly husbanded, then your spouse will see to the protection of his property. When he goes off to the war, he'll see that you're properly belted and sealed, and you'll accept your lot with the obedience dictated by your gender."

"I will not! I will scream until the device is removed!" Petronilla and I were equally willful, but she always voiced her resentments, whereas I husbanded my energies in order to deal with real rather than theoretical situations. Petronilla had convictions; I was always pragmatic.

"Then you will be gagged as well as pussy-bound!" Papa told her bluntly and dryly.

"It's not fair!" Petronilla was always concerned about fairness, I with personal convenience. "The husband goes off to his war and ravishes every enemy woman in sight whilst the wife remains love-locked at home. Suppose he is killed in battle? What happens to her then?"

"She observes the rusting of the chastity belt," Papa told Petronilla with a face both dour and dire.

"In such an event," I interjected, "I should take a locksmith for a lover."

"There is many a rogue wouldst be a locksmith to a fair lady," Papa cautioned. "Beware the key that jams, Eleanor. Beware the mangled quim."

"What of the lady's bodily functions?" Petronilla phrased the question delicately, in keeping with our upbringing as highborn ladies. "Belted and locked, how may she do her numbers?"

"Before he leaves, the husband appoints a trusted keeper of the key," Papa told us.

"Then the keeper of the key shall be my lover," Petronilla decided.

"Why could Our Lord not have blessed me with sons?" Papa sighed. "The keeper of the key is always a eunuch," he added. "That is seen to before he is made keeper of the key."

"Is there no way to tempt a eunuch?" I was curious.

"Legend tells of not one eunuch so unique," Papa assured me dryly.

"It is a fascinating challenge," I observed.

"Daughters!" Papa moaned.

"You have told us that this is the Age of Chivalry," Petronilla reminded Papa. "Will not some noble knight come along to free a lady from such a predicament? Could he not shatter her pelvic fetters with his knightly lance?"

"Most likely shatter her pelvis with the same blow," Papa told her. "If you are wise, Petronilla, you will not seek such rescue."

Poor Papa! He was, after all, trying to do his best. He

was trying very hard to be both mother and father to Petronilla and me. His advice was meant only to induce a proper womanly attitude of resignation and acceptance in us so that we would not be unhappy with our lot when we married. How could he have known that in both our cases the result would be quite the opposite.

Petronilla in particular determined to live life to the fullest before marriage confined her to such a forcibly chaste state. Although she was the younger, terror of the future Papa painted made her more precocious in seeking the joys of erotic experience than I was. Her precocity found its outlet in a journey we took with Papa to Poitiers to visit our uncle Raymond. It was one of the rare occasions in my life when it might have been said that I was lagging behind in the area of sexual expression.

The sojourn to Poitiers was one of many that we took with Papa throughout the length and breadth of Aquitaine, but it stands out in my mind for titillating reasons that shall surely become obvious. It began with Papa's decision that we should all three ride to Poitiers on horseback rather than by coach. It would save time, and Petronilla and I were both by now as adept in the saddle as Papa himself.

"Still," he worried when we started out, "I do wish you wouldn't ride astride, Eleanor."

"Why do you speak so to me and not to Petronilla?" I retorted, annoyed.

"Because you are the eldest."

"All the more reason not to be concerned about the manner by which I choose to ride."

"I am not concerned for your safety." Papa's jaw jutted out with his customary bluntness. "I am concerned for the evidence of your chastity."

"And not Petronilla's?"

"You are the eldest. Petronilla's virginity is important too, but yours is crucial, Eleanor. You will rule Aquitaine when I am gone. Your chastity may well be all you have to offer in exchange for a strong protector. And Aquitaine must be protected."

"And I," Petronilla hissed in my ear where Papa couldn't hear, "can rut like a rabbit because I will always have my older sister, the Duchess of Aquitaine, to protect me."

I dismissed her remark as a sisterly jest, but I was wrong. Petronilla meant to do quite as she said. And not before long!

It was shortly after this conversation that we encountered a priest on the road. He was young, with a round face, a small potbelly, and soft hands. He recognized Father and was quick to tug the forelock to him. Papa in turn asked for his blessing for our journey.

When the priest bestowed it, his hand managed to slip over Petronilla's bosom. The gesture was repeated when he blessed me. The touch of his nimble fingers was not unpleasant to my rising nipples.

Papa noticed. "Yon priest was too free with his hands!" he grumbled as we continued on our way.

"Indeed, he did coppeth a feel," Petronilla granted.

"Verily, he squeezed the jugs," I agreed.

"Hear me, daughters!" Papa rumbled. "Beware the salvation 'neath the priest's cassock!"

But later Petronilla and I agreed that in some ways a priest might be preferable as a lover to a knight. "All a priest has to do is hoist his cassock," Petronilla said, putting it well. "Whereas a damsel might pass through to menopause waiting for a knight to unhinge all his armor."

"Not to mention the risk of tetanus from armored embraces," I added.

"There are greater risks!" Papa warned, overhearing us.

We looked at him questioningly.

"Lying lovers," he told us. "Remember these words well, daughters. Never believe the man who swears to exit before he spends."

In truth, *mes amis,* not all of my father's advice was first-rate, nor applicable to my own standards of womanhood, but this one piece has always stood me in good stead. No matter the aperture—quim, nether-maw, or mouth—such a promise is always made to be broken. So said Papa. So proved experience!

Other bits of his advice were not so cogent. "Beware the quick hands of magicians and alchemists," he cautioned Petronilla and me, echoing his warning regarding priests. But in truth, I have never found the caresses of magicians and alchemists to be any more sly than those of other men. All men seek by duplicity that which they might freely be granted if they requested it straightforwardly. It suits their egos better to succeed by trickery than by mutual agreement.

Another concern of Papa's was that Petronilla and I be aware of the dangers of adultery. It was not the morality that bothered him—Papa was relatively free of ethics where sex was concerned—it was the threat of reprisal. "Take one too many lovers, daughters, and the next thing you know you and your lover will be faced by a husband with a trowel and mortar foreboding a walled-up future!"

"How terrible!" I exclaimed, shuddering.

"No pricking is worth the bricking!" As usual Papa had a succinct phrase to drive home his point.

Perhaps the reason Papa was obsessed by such concerns on this particular trip to Poitiers was that both Petronilla and myself had just reached the age where we were beginning to flower into womanhood. This development was cause enough for Papa to worry. Our beauty had been commented upon by one and all from the time we were little girls. Neither of us ever had reason to doubt it, nor to counter with false modesty the conceit such knowledge engendered. We knew well the effect of our beauty on others, particularly men, and learned to manipulate our wiles early and expertly. Now puberty supplied more reason for the exercise of those wiles than the mere pleasure of observing the effect of our loveliness on others. We burned inside with appetites we could not define, and the burning but made our beauty glow the more.

If this beauty of ours, Petronilla's and mine, was powerful in tandem, it was nevertheless distinct to each of us. Despite our sisterhood and the ability we shared to inflame men's passions, we were quite different from one another as far as looks were concerned. Close as we were in age, there was never any confusion between us. The flesh of each of us was unique and so too the fairness of visage and seductiveness of personality.

Although I was the elder, with a visage more finely etched and eyes of deeper set, it was Petronilla who earlier displayed the more generous and voluptuous roundnesses of womanhood. This was in keeping with her being always somewhat more earthy than I, or to put it another way, of my possessing a somewhat more aristocratic persona than she. This appearance was misleading to the extent that beneath it I was quite as quick to amorous abandonment as Petronilla and in the long run far more promiscuous. Nevertheless, even when we were girls and not yet quite women, I looked more the lady and Petronilla more the peasant bawd.

Certainly bosoms played a major role in this early impression. Petronilla's chest was adorned with melons whilst her girlhood pubes were still as sparse and wispy as a duckling plucked free of down by the wind. Although I was almost a year older, and although the triangular copper-colored sporran over my mons veneris was already lush and long and silky with approaching womanhood, my own breasts were smaller than Petronilla's, cone-shaped and upthrusting, with long red nipples like little pinky tips dipped in boar blood. Petronilla's plump breasts seemed always to be heaving with her breathing and rippling with their fleshiness and bouncing as if looking for friendly male hands in which to come to rest. Mine were quieter, firm daggers with quivering tips red-hot as coals, pert and poised and waiting rather than inviting.

Our tresses—the dissimilarity in their color and in the way we coiffed them—also contributed to the different impressions we made. My hair was auburn, a distinctive red-brown color with a sheen like polished Etruscan copperplate. I wore it long and kept it neatly arranged— tied in one braid or two as I decided that fashion should decree—and hanging down my back to below my waist. Only in bed, or in bedlike circumstances with company I deemed deserving, did I unloose these tresses and fan them out in all their glory to frame my deep-set, sparkling green eyes and firm-sculpted, nipple-hard breasts. On such occasions, the turning curls at the end of my long hair might tangle with the silk over my pubes. The copper shade would match so exactly that there could be no distinguishing between the curls tumbling from my shoulders to my belly and the ruffled silk curling with the dew of my mound of Venus.

Petronilla's mane was not of so delicate a shade. Nor did she arrange it with such neatness. Her hair was golden blonde like our father William's, thick and copious like his, and usually swirling about her laughing, flirting face in a cloud of unkempt curls. In motion, with her blonde hair rippling and her light blue eyes laughing and her cheeks flushed, she looked like a Viking maiden, pagan and wanton, capable of tearing at raw meat with her strong teeth and of whipping men to the heights of passion with savage lust.

As I have said, I appeared quite aristocratic by comparison. This was deceptive, for I was every bit as uninhibited as Petronilla. I simply looked more the lady.

My face was oval, with high, aristocratic cheekbones and a slight cleft in the chin and hollowed cheeks. My brow was high and testified to an intelligence that was certainly real enough even when I was still a girl. My neck was long and swanlike, my complexion white as alabaster. This visage was in contrast to Petronilla's round features and ready farm girl dimples, quite different from her robust, frequently flushed skin and the generosity of freckles the sun might bring out on her cheeks.

Nor was Petronilla as tall as I. This was not merely due to the discrepancy in our ages. Our forms were simply differently constructed so that even as a girl I was tall and graceful and possibly even imposing whereas Petronilla tended to more fleshiness of hip, thigh, and derriere, having an overall appeal that was both cuter and more cuddly than mine. She conveyed a certain passivity that was much in fashion in regard to the sex objects we medieval women were supposed to be to our men. I, on the other hand, walked tall and with dignity. My sensual appeal was a challenge, where Petronilla's was a surrender.

Yet despite the truth of all of the foregoing, it should be noted that my own derriere—mounted high atop long, slender, shapely legs—was as capable of conveying by its lascivious wiggle a raunchy desire that was anything but ladylike and that was every bit as hot-blooded as my sister's!

Poitiers was to prove it. Our party—Father, myself, my sister, followed by a dozen or so assorted servants on horse- and mule-back—reached the ancient farming region on a warm autumn day just before harvest time. The fields were golden with wheat rippling in the sun-warmed breezes. We made our way through them to a small green forest and then wended our way over a winding path to the foot of a hill. From here we could see the castle of my uncle Raymond, Count of Poitiers, standing guard over his domain from the crest of the hill. After resting our horses briefly, we remounted and proceeded up the trail leading to the castle. As we approached, the drawbridge was lowered. Uncle Raymond crossed it to greet our party in person.

"Welcome kinfolk!" He knelt to Father, for he was his vassal, but he hugged Petronilla and myself just as he had when we were children. Still, Raymond was only eight years older than I, and even with that first hug I could tell that his chest took notice of my blossoming breasts. Indeed, when he hugged my more bosomy younger sister, a look of wonder and appreciation flickered o'er his thin, dark face even as he prolonged the embrace.

Thus from this first moment of reacquaintance, Uncle Raymond betrayed an awareness that his nieces were coming to womanhood. As for us, we too regarded him differently from in the past. He was no longer an adolescent, but a young man full-grown now, not tall, but wiry and intense and quite manly.

He had grown a beard and it gave him the look of a scholar or an ascetic. His hair was black, straight, and long, and this lent his elongated countenance a mournful aura. Withal, his smile was quick and the teeth displayed by it white and even. Raymond was not at all burly like Papa, and truly that was the preferred fashion, but nevertheless he revealed a sensual thigh 'neath his short tunic as he bowed to us, and later, when he preceded us back across the drawbridge, a swirl of wind revealed a linened derriere quite muscular and alive with the promise of spryness.

It was a few days later that I discovered just how spry Uncle Raymond's derriere could really be. That morning Papa had ridden out by himself to gauge the forthcoming harvest so that he might know what to expect of the share due him as Duke of the region. I had gone looking for Petronilla, thinking that we might ride together or perhaps fish in the pond at the bottom of the hill, but I had been unable to find her. Nor was Uncle Raymond about.

Thus, left to my own devices, I wandered out to the stables and climbed up into one of the haymows. I burrowed there, tossing the hay about and frolicking there, albeit in desultory fashion. After a while, I dozed off. I was roused by the sound of voices from the bales of hay on the floor beneath me.

"La! Uncle Raymond! I am too old for you to bounce me on your knee as when we were children." The voice was my sister Petronilla's, and it was both bubbly as the sparkling wine of Burgundy and throaty as a ewe bleating for a ram at mating time.

"Since you are older, it is even better." Uncle Raymond's tone was like spreading syrup.

Unseen, I crawled to the edge of the mow and peeked over so that I could see them. I caught my breath. The hussy! And yet I was both admiring and envious of my sister's abandonment.

Petronilla was sitting astraddle Uncle Raymond's knee and facing him. The serrated hem of her loose blue cotton dress was raised well above her knees so that the leg on which she perched might be gripped between her naked thighs. The lace bodice of the gown had been folded in to widen and deepen the curved V displaying her ample breasts. Her orbs shimmered quite revealingly as Uncle Raymond bounced and dandled her.

"I shall surely swoon from these exertions," Petronilla sighed, although she was truly the most healthy of wenches and had never known a moment's faintness in her entire life. "I can hardly breathe."

"Let me just loosen your buttons so that sufficient air will be admitted to your lungs." Uncle Raymond unbuttoned her bodice further and from my overhead perch I caught a clear glimpse of the naked, wide pink aureole of my sister's heaving left breast.

Now my attention was drawn to Uncle Raymond. His hands had lingered on Petronilla's plump young breasts and this had a noticeable effect on him. He had evidently pushed his tunic out of the way when they first sat down, and now only his drawers separated his manhood from my sister's quivering, flushed flesh. There was a throbbing lump at the juncture of the legs that was putting considerable strain on the linen. It seemed to be trying to break free and uncoil like a snake so that it might travel the distance to my sister's thighs, press under the serrated hem of her gown, and push to that still sparsely blonde-haired spot of forbidden glory.

The sight of these close relatives—my younger sister and my uncle—thus engaged filled me with a randiness that will be best appreciated by those who have similarly found themselves excluded from but witness to such activity. My long nipples hardened and burned against the ribbed mesh bodice of the *bliau* I was wearing. My slender but shapely thighs rubbed together and a honeyed dampness spread beneath my girdle-sheath. The cotton material felt rough against my sensitive, aroused flesh. I ached to change places with Petronilla.

"*Qui*, my dear niece," Uncle Raymond was saying. "You certainly have grown up." He was still bouncing my sister on his knee and at the same time he was stroking the top half-moons of her heaving melon-breasts with his long, aristocratic fingers.

"And you are still growing." Petronilla cast her eyes boldly downward and fluttered her lashes at the throbbing, bulging presence at his groin. Then she lifted her gaze and parted her moist, full, Cupid's-bow lips. Her tongue lolled visibly in open invitation.

I slid my hand inside my bodice as I watched them kiss. I caught my straining nipple between my fingertips and played with it as I imagined their tongues entwining—his thrusting rhythmically, hers luring him deeper and deeper. I watched Uncle Raymond's hands dip deep into my sister's bodice to squeeze her large, naked breasts as the kiss continued. I squeezed my own warm, heaving, naked breast. I stroked its conelike contours. I rubbed my thighs together under my gown and felt my own warm honey spreading over them.

"La, Uncle Raymond!" Petronilla moaned when the kiss was over. She looked down at the bosom he had bared, and observed, fascinated and further aroused, as he continued to caress it.

Uncle Raymond bent and kissed her breasts, first one and then the other. His long tongue extended and licked the deep cleavage between the hard-bouncing mounds. He licked the aureoles, each in turn, tracing their aroused, prickly pinkness with his tongue. He licked the nipples, teasing them with the tip of his tongue. Then he sucked them, at first shallowly, then more deeply, then more deeply still.

Petronilla's fingers tangled in his long, straight dark hair, clutching his head to her bosom, pushing her breast deeper and deeper into his mouth, and she began slapping down with hard abandonment against the thigh that was bouncing her, and her moans turned to excited, demanding, and finally savage groans. "Oh! Uncle Raymond! Oh that feels good! Oh! Harder! Oh! Use your tongue! No! *Oui! Oui!* Whee-ee!"

Trembling with the passion that my sister's passion was inspiring, I opened my bodice to the waist. My firm conical breasts stuck straight out, the nipples so red and stiff and aroused as to appear positively obscene. I squeezed them, panting, burning with lust. And then I raised one and bent my neck until I managed to get the long, quivering nipple tip between my lips. I held it there with my teeth and licked it with my tongue and sucked it as best I could. This, on top of all that had preceded it, filled me with an excitement I had never known before.

Below me, Uncle Raymond stood up and drew Petronilla to her feet as well. His short tunic was twisted to reveal the lance of his lust poking out of his drawers. He removed Petronilla's dress and tossed it aside. She stood before him, covered only from the waist down by her thin cotton camise. Her large, premature breasts swung roundly, nakedly, temptingly. Observing the stiff red definition of my sister's berry-nipples, I sucked at my own nipples more avidly.

"It is time to unveil the other treasures of womanhood," Uncle Raymond told her now.

She stared at him with her large blue eyes and her hungry mouth pursed as he removed the camise. Truly, Petronilla had formed into a woman in every respect save perhaps the sparseness of blonde hair below her belly. Uncle Raymond now paid homage to her new development with his hands.

He traced the abundance of her hips from her tiny waist to the quivering baby fat of her rounded thighs. He stroked the thighs themselves, taking pleasure in their rippling movement and in their parting. He palmed the generous cheeks of her bottom and squeezed them until Petronilla began to writhe and almost to pump under the caress. He separated the jiggling spheres and traced the cleft between them with his fingertips and then probed there until Petronilla was so overcome that she seized his face between her hands and plunged her tongue into his mouth and gave Uncle Raymond a deep, pleading, hungry kiss. When it was over, he sank to his knees in front of her.

When I saw this, I could not contain myself. I wriggled free of my own dress and tossed it behind me in the haymow. I pressed my hand to the silken drawers between my legs and felt how they were sopping with the syrup of my lust. I made a fist and leaned into it with the parted, swollen lips of my pussy and pushed the silk up between them, and I moved my knuckles back and forth as I peered back down at Uncle Raymond and my naked, voluptuous, wanton sister.

The sparseness of blond hair over her quim seemed to fascinate him. He parted what little there was with his fingertips and peered closely at her wet and squirming pussy. He stroked her mound of Venus. He kissed it. He parted the lips. He kissed her pussy deeply. Then, quickly, he stood up and shucked off his drawers and stood there as naked as Petronilla.

"Oh, Uncle!" Petronilla sobbed at the unveiling of his member. Raymond was slender and built quite narrowly, but his aroused penis was fat as a lamb raised for slaughter. Let me hasten to add that there was nothing lamblike nor soft about it in other respects. Indeed, it was as stout and hard as any maiden on the verge of being deflowered might have wished. "Uncle! Uncle! *Oui!*" Petronilla cried, "Uncle!" And then, following his example but as if in a daze, she slipped to her knees and paid homage to Uncle Raymond's pulsing pike with her lips and tongue.

"Enough!" He stopped her after a few moments. "I've no wish to spend prematurely." He stroked his dark beard.

"Lie down on your back on the bale of hay, Petronilla," he told her.

She did as he wanted.

"Now stretch your legs straight up in the air."

A film of perspiration was visible on her naked, panting breasts as she strained to comply with this instruction.

"Now open your legs as wide as you can. That's it. Part your thighs."

She pushed with her hands to widen the space between the baby fat.

"Now take your fingers and hold open the lips of your quim."

Uncle Raymond and I both stared as Petronilla revealed the passion-slicked, pulsing pink meat of the inside of her pussy.

"Beautiful!" he murmured as he mounted her. "Beautiful!"

Petronilla cried out sharply as he entered her, piercing her maidenhead, but a moment later her sturdy legs locked around Uncle Raymond's slim hips and she began to rise and fall ecstatically with each new thrust of his prick. "Marvelous!" she bleated. "Wonderful! *Magnifique!*" And she dug her nails into the cheeks of his pumping behind, drawing blood in her eagerness to draw him deeper and still deeper inside her.

It took all my willpower to keep from breaching my own maidenhead as I watched them and frigged myself. I identified completely with all that my younger sister was experiencing. Not just my greedy quim, but my mind as well was on fire to devour that big, thick cock pumping in and out of her clutching young quim. Indeed, my fist pumped with that prick, and my cunt prepared to spend with the heaving cunt of my squealing, hard-fucking sister.

And then, with a burst of hysterical laughter, Petronilla seized Uncle Raymond around the neck, heaved upward with her belly and her wildly bobbling breasts, and began a series of powerful spendings that tore at the very roots of the pumping cock buried inside her. Raymond clutched at her ample bottom and pulled her down so that her climaxing cunt spread over him. Then his own fulcrum jerked upward and he started to discharged the hot cream of his lust deep inside Petronilla's quim. She screamed with the sheer joy of the sensation, and one geyser of man-cream followed another until it began spilling out between her legs and over both their still-writhing bellies and thighs.

The sight of this carried me over the edge. I pushed my panties down around my ankles and clutched my own squirming quim with both hands as I started to come. My hands clawed at my climaxing pussy. I echoed Petronilla's scream without willing it. And I thrashed about so fiercely with the finale to my orgasm that I became tangled in the silken drawers down around my ankles and tumbled from the haymow to the soft bales of hay below!

I landed atop poor Uncle Raymond just as he was rolling off my deflowered sister. For a moment there was a mix-up of arms and legs involving all three of us. It was straightened out after some confused thrashing about, and I found myself with my head nestled just under Uncle Raymond's balls and his limp but still formidable penis curled over my cheek.

"What the devil!" He was the first to speak.

"Eleanor!" My sister immediately realized the circumstances. "You were spying on us!"

"By accident." I tried to excuse myself.

"You lost all of your clothes by accident?" Uncle Raymond was dubious.

"I still have my bloomers," I said, making pathetic protest.

"How modest that you conceal your ankles with them." Petronilla's sweetness had bite. "Would that your no-no was similarly covered."

"You're a fine one to speak of modesty, Sister," I reminded Petronilla. "You, who have just surrendered your chastity with such eagerness!"

"And don't you just wish that you could rid yourself of yours in like fashion?" she shot back.

I could not stop the blush that swept over my cheeks in confirmation of her words.

"Is that true, Eleanor?" Uncle Raymond's voice was interested; his prick stirred against my cheek.

Sprawled naked with risen nipples and honeyed thighs, how could I deny it? I could only nod silently and lower my hungry green eyes behind their long lashes.

"She wants you to take her maidenhead just as you did mine," Petronilla assured him.

"Is that what you want, Eleanor?" Uncle Raymond's hand fell casually across my bosom and he toyed with the firm flesh-cones of my breasts.

"Oui!" I murmured softly, my heart beating wildly. Indeed, at that moment it was what I wanted more than anything else in the world.

"But surely you realize that I cannot serve you so, sweet Eleanor." The fingers of his other hand tangled in the moist copper curls tufting my lower belly.

"You deflowered Petronilla!" I pouted.

"Jealous wench!" Petronilla snorted.

"It is not the same thing." Uncle Raymond stroked the swollen lips of my naked, throbbing pussy. "Petronilla will not someday be Duchess of Aquitaine as you will." The shaft of his prick stiffened noticeably; the velvet tip grazed the side of my nose. "The welfare of the state does not hinge on her chastity."

"A good thing!" I snapped. "Since she no longer has any, thanks to you, dear Uncle!"

"I am still your uncle, Eleanor!" Uncle Raymond cautioned. "Mind your tongue!"

"I will mind my tongue!" I stuck it out full-length and licked the shaft of his prick. "That is how I will mind it! Now, sir, I wouldst have you drop this hypocritical pretense of statesmanship and do unto me as you have done unto Petronilla." So saying, I straightened to a kneeling position, took his thick erection in hand, and moved to possess it with the moist and hungry mouth between my legs.

"Nay, wench!" The flat of his hand on my soft belly kept me from achieving my objective. "Thy father is my liege and I am his vassal. Enough strain has been put on the fealty owed him for one morning. I will not be the instrument of deflowering his eldest. Your chastity is too important to the future of Aquitaine!"

Petronilla laughed, which did not make things any better.

"Do me as thou hast done my sister!" I demanded, flinging myself astride Uncle Raymond's thighs and attempting to impale myself on his upstanding prick.

"I will do thee as thee deserves!" He caught me by the hips with both hands and raised me and twisted my naked body and then lowered me in a way that forced me to sprawl out facedown across his lap. Holding me this way firmly with one hand, Uncle Raymond proceeded to spank my naked bottom with the other.

My sister did not bother to hide her pleasure at this turn of events. She chortled gleefully. She clapped her hands in time with the hand striking the reddening cheeks of my writhing derriere.

She was, however, too hasty in taking satisfaction at my punishment. As the spanking progressed, my squeals of surprise at the sharpness of the first blows began to turn to drawn-out moans of pleasure as my ardor was raised by such intimate discipline. My squirmings over Uncle's naked thighs were no longer random now. Indeed, I contrived to rub my flaming pussy up and down the rigid shaft between his legs as the punitive slaps continued. True, he would not allow his instrument to enter me, but this lewd friction spurred by the fire he had kindled in my buttocks and loins was surely the next best thing. "*Oui*, Uncle!" I gasped. "I am very naughty! I deserve to be spanked! Strike! Strike my bottom cherry-red! Punish me until—! Until—!"

"Really, Eleanor!" Petronilla recognized the onrush of the orgasm that had me in its grip. "Really!"

"Really!" I echoed, squeezing Uncle Raymond's cream-filled prick between the straining muscles of my naked inner thighs. "Really!"

"Really!" Uncle Raymond joined the chorus. An instant later his lust erupted and his silvery nectar sprayed over my heaving belly and thighs.

"Thank you, Uncle," I sighed when it was over for both of us.

"Let us depart this place." Uncle Raymond pulled on his clothes and signaled to Petronilla to do the same.

23

"Well, Eleanor," she told me as they were leaving, "at least I am a woman now. But you, dear Sister, are still a virgin. So there!"

On that note, they were gone and I was left lying naked and alone on a bale of hay in the stable.

I was not, however, alone for long. A lad wearing a sheepskin over leather breeches and footwear contrived of straw wrapping tied with cloth entered the stable and stopped short as he saw me lying there nude. "Wha—? Wha—? Wha—?" was the best he could manage by way of acknowledging my presence. He stood rooted to the spot, loutish and marred.

Oui, marred. An angry red birthmark ran down one side of his face like a thumbs-down judgment from Heaven. It was jagged and fiery and lent to his otherwise square-cut and stolid visage an evil cast. His physique was short and wide, although in no way fat and seemed solid in the manner of a poised bull or a rooted old oak tree.

"Wha—? Wha—? Wha—?" he repeated and sprouted an erection to stretch the coarse fustian covering his groin.

"My name is Eleanor," I told this bumpkin, my passion rekindled. "What's yours?" I wriggled seductively that he might better appreciate the expanse of bare flesh spread out before his eyes.

"Geoffrey." He stared and took on tumescence.

"Come here, Geoffrey." I sat up and reached out for him with both arms. The red nipples hardened at the tips of my pear-shaped breasts and beckoned him.

He moved toward me as if bewitched.

I stretched and grasped his hard-on through his homespun, using this grip to pull him toward me. "Have you ever made love to a woman, Geoffrey?" I asked the lout.

He shook his head dumbly, his birthmark flaming, his dull eyes taking on fire as they darted from my breasts to my pussy.

"Then it will be the first time for both of us," I told him. I would show them, all of them, my father, my sister, my uncle, all of Aquitaine! They needed a virgin because they needed a pawn in the game of power politics. Well, I would not be their pawn! And I would not be their virgin! I pulled the bumpkin's aroused prick from his pants and tugged him to his knees between my wide-flung legs. "Fuck me!" I told him. "Fuck me, Geoffrey!"

The oaf was nothing loathe. Indeed, the flaring of his blemish signaled that if anything, he was too eager. Within less than a minute I knew that this was indeed the case.

Geoffrey mounted me. I slung my thighs over his shoulders to give him easy access. He pushed his hairy and rather craggy cock between the lips of my waiting cunt. His plump, hirsute behind shuddered mightily. He slammed into me with all the finesse of a peasant's hoe breaking winter ground. I felt a sharp, intense pain, and then something gave way and the whiteness of my thighs was stained with blood. Almost immediately the pain was vanquished by the thrill of his stout cock abrading my aroused clitoris as he pumped deep inside my quim. Unfortunately, with equal immediacy Geoffrey clutched my bottom, pushed me upward, and proceeded to come.

I enjoyed the spending while it lasted, but in truth it did not last very long. I was still holding feverishly to his cock with my pussy as his pike softened. I was still trying to coax out a memorable climax from my newly deflowered quim. Alas! I had still not succeeded when Geoffrey withdrew altogether and sheathed his instrument.

"Have to go," he announced.

"Your chores," I guessed, still wriggling with frustration.

"No." He sucked noisily at the cheek with the angry birthmark. "I'm not from here. I'm traveling through with my pa and he got taken with the runs and we stopped for him to use the privy."

"Really?" I had never encountered a peasant with the sensibilities Geoffrey ascribed to his father. The usual thing would have been to go behind a tree.

"Really," the oafish boy assured me. "Must be through by now. Be coming after me soon. Best go."

"Oui," I agreed. In truth I was glad to be rid of the lout. "You had better leave before he finds us here like this."

After he left I climbed back up into the haymow and retrieved my clothes. I was indeed disappointed. If this was all there was to being deflowered, then why was there so much fuss surrounding it?

Nevertheless, despite the somewhat less than adequate collaborator I had chosen, and despite the lack of fullfillment I had gained at his hands, I felt a certain satisfaction regarding my deflowering. I myself had decided upon it and no one else. Without care for Crown or politics, I had selected my course and followed it. I had taken charge of my own destiny. It was the first time in my life that I had acted so.

It would not be the last!

Chapter Two

If I thought that by deciding upon the conditions of my deflowerment I was establishing a permanent control over my destiny, I was sadly mistaken. I was of royal Aquitainian birth, but I was also a woman, and these were after all the Middle Ages. I could manipulate circumstances (indeed, I learned to do so very well!) but always according to winds of fate beyond my control. I was soon to be tossed, a helpless feather, into the hurricane of those winds.

There was no forecast of that hurricane on the evening of the day that Petronilla and I lost our chastity. We ate dinner with Papa and Uncle Raymond as usual. It was served in the great hall by Uncle Raymond's palace staff, and the succession of courses, with their abundance of delicacies, had us concealing yawns behind our hands before the nightly banquet was half over. I believe it was between the trout in *sauce relevée* and the venison *fines herbes* that Papa began (for reasons that elude my memory) a rambling discourse on the wicked city of Paris to the north of us in France.

"A chill place of cold intellect and sparse neighborliness," he assured us, "and yet there is that in the climate which makes the blood run very hot indeed."

"I have heard that the city is quite wicked." Uncle Raymond clucked his tongue disapprovingly.

I made a rude sound at his hypocrisy, and Petronilla kicked me under the heavy oaken table.

"Indeed, that is so." Papa sucked thirstily at a beaker of pale golden wine. "I myself can attest to the wickedness of Paris. I visited there when I was scarce a man and—" He cut himself short, glancing from me to Petronilla and then conspiratorially at Uncle Raymond. His wink was a case of male sharing—lewd and excluding of us.

"I hate it when you do that, Papa!" Petronilla told him bluntly.

"Such matters are not for the ears of young ladies." Intoxication made Papa hypocritical. Out of earshot of others, he never hesitated to discuss the most lewd subjects with us.

"Then why did you bring Paris up in the first place?" I sided with Petronilla.

"You have molded daughters of strong character, my liege," Uncle Raymond said, amused.

"Of strong will, you mean," Papa grumbled. "Their character has yet to be established."

"Perhaps Eleanor and I should go to Paris to test its mettle," Petronilla suggested sarcastically.

"It is the last place I would wish my daughters to visit." The thought seemed to sober Papa. "The very air of

Paris turns the gold of maidenly virtue to the dross of wanton lust.''

"Really?" I could not keep the interest out of my voice. "But surely you exaggerate, Papa."

"I do not. Hear me, daughters. Heed your father! The purity of spirit, of soul and body, to which you have been reared in Aquitaine will not stand up against the fleshly temptations of that northern Sodom, Paris! I shall not live forever," he sighed. "I shall not always be here to restrain your impetuous natures, Eleanor and Petronilla. When I am gone, you must stand guard over yourselves, over your own virtue. When that time comes, my daughters, I warn you to shun Paris as you would the plague."

"When that time comes," I could not resist saying, "we will have Uncle Raymond to advise us as to our virtue. Won't we, Petronilla?" This time I anticipated her kick under the banquet table and avoided it.

"Just stay clear of Paris," Papa repeated, grumbling ominously and quaffing another full beaker of wine. "Remain in Aquitaine and never go to Paris!"

It was autumn in Poitiers when Papa spake so. It was the following spring in Chinon when, as if in fulfillment of the dire premonition to which he had given voice, he quite simply and unexpectedly dropped dead. In the interim, he and I and Petronilla had completed a circuit of Aquitaine, his realm.

This journey was something more than the trip to Poitiers had been. We had traveled in force with all of Papa's knights and their squires. The household staff of our castle had accompanied us, and so too had an assortment of priests and minstrels and other entertainers. The purpose of the sojourn was to hold fast the fealty of all of Papa's Aquitainian subjects, nobles and peasants alike.

Toward this end, we stopped at one castle after another so that local lords might bend the knee to Papa, kneeling before him and swearing once more to remain loyal to him. Thus was subjugation commanded of lesser men. Papa's shrewd eye gauged the earnestness of each tugged forelock of each serf, and he was quick to spy insolence and to punish it, and just as quick to praise devotion and reward it. Papa was always a scrupulously fair man, stern but just.

The empty wagons of our caravan filled with produce and dairy products, sides of beef and venison, and casks of the *vin rouge* of Aquitaine. These were the tribute paid Papa, as were the livestock herded in our wake. Millers provided us with sacks of flour, and in the towns we gorged ourselves on gifts of hot, fresh-baked bread and the local currant jellies. Our knights collected the tolls from the keepers of the bridges, and often Papa himself collected the taxes from the Lords of the manors. Soon our wagons were as weighted down with gold coin as they were with the opulent produce of Aquitaine.

At night we would be the welcome guests of one such Lord or another. A feast would be prepared for us in his castle, and we would be entertained by minstrels and jesters, jugglers and fools. There might be music—fiddles, lyres, even Spanish castanets—and dancing. Mostly Petronilla and I would move through some sedate, albeit rustic round, but sometimes the heat would escape our bodies in a daring fandango.

They say that travel is broadening, and indeed it is true. We crossed paths with many foreigners during this journey—

with dark-eyed young Spaniard men with bold fingers, with rakish Gascons with feathers in their comical caps and bold gleams in their darting eyes, with quick-tempered Frenchmen whose hands seemed always to be on their phallic sword hilts, with pious Italians who stroked their beards as if they were made of female flesh, and even with an occasional Englishman, blonde and brawny with lust. We met rich merchants clothed in velvet and poor pilgrims in drab sackcloth. We genuflected to Bishops and tossed coins to pathetic beggars stretched out limbless by the side of the road. And—most interesting to Petronilla and me—we met highborn ladies in transit from all the major cities of Europe and dressed in the latest fashions offered by those metropolises.

"How low the bodices are in Paris!" Petronilla exclaimed to me in a whisper as we watched the entertainment at one castle. "No wonder Papa fears our going there!"

"Hush!" I replied, for she was distracting me from watching a well-formed young acrobat in *chausses* most immodestly tight.

Petronilla quieted and joined me in ogling the nimble tumbler. Papa did not notice the groinward direction of our gazes. He was too busy gorging himself with his fifth helping of suckling pig stuffed with rum-soaked apple bread. Papa never grew obese like King Louis VI of France, better known as Louis the Fat. Papa was always a brawny man, athletic and thick with muscle. Still, he did love to eat and to drink strong brew, and he never denied himself.

Now he polished off the last of the pig and turned his attention to a haunch of venison. He washed it down with mead, a thick, sweet, powerfully alcoholic drink made of fermented honey. Then he finished off the meal with mulled wine and sugared pastries from Bordeaux. An hour later, after retiring, he was stricken.

He did not die immediately. Papa was strong, and at only thirty-eight years of age, he had a powerful desire to live. Nevertheless, he recognized that will alone would not be enough to get him through the hammer blows of the seizure that had him in its grasp. Noble man that he was, Duke William X of Aquitaine to the end, he summoned me to his bedside to deliver his parting words of advice.

"Alas! I have no son to rule Aquitaine in my place, Eleanor," he told me. (He was also a chauvinist to the end, my beloved father.) "You are my eldest daughter, and you will be Duchess of Aquitaine, so heed me well. You are a woman and therefore will be looked on as weak. There will be immediate threats to you. Lesser knights will move to seize your person as a means to establishing claim to Aquitaine. Beware rebellious vassals. Beware ambitious Dukes whose lands border upon ours. You must be shrewd indeed if you are to survive the turbulence that will follow my death. And if you don't—" He paused and drew a deep breath and hugged his chest as if it had been struck another painful, powerful blow.

"Papa!" I held his free hand to my breast and fought back the tears.

"If I don't survive, Eleanor—" He forced himself to speak, each word carved from the stone pressing down on his chest and crushing the life from him. "You and Petronilla must separate. You must send her away immediately so that if something happens to you, she will still be alive to take over. If your enemies know that, Eleanor, they will not be so quick to act against you."

"Where shall she be sent, Papa?" I patted the perspiration from his poor fevered brow with my silken kerchief.

"Send her to your uncle Raymond at Poitiers. He is one vassal you may be sure can be trusted."

Does Death, I wondered, always ride the steed of Irony?

"But Uncle Raymond has just recently married," I blurted out.

"What difference?" Papa clenched his teeth against another agonizing hammer blow to his chest. "Do not vex me with irrelevancies, Eleanor. There is no time."

"It shall be as you wish, Papa," I soothed him. "Petronilla shall be sent to Uncle Raymond at Poitiers." The sorrow welling up in my breast was too great to permit further argument. Nevertheless, knowing my sister, I had a fleeting moment of sympathy for Uncle Raymond's new bride.

"As soon as he hears that you are fatherless and helpless, the Count of Burgundy will move," Papa continued, warning me. Burgundy was our neighbor to the northeast with whom we shared the French border. The Count of Burgundy was a vassal of Louis the Fat, like Papa, but Burgundy was the weak ruler of a weak land compared to the Duke of Aquitaine. Still, the Count was known to be ambitious. "You are marriageable, and he will come to woo you directly he hears of my death."

"I will spurn him," I assured Papa. "He is not worthy of Aquitaine."

"Then he will come to woo, and stay to fight. What he cannot claim by ardor, he will take by force. Be sure of it, Eleanor."

"I will surround the castle with knights. I will raise the drawbridge. I will see him dead ere I take him to husband."

"Spoken like the true Duchess of Aquitaine thou shalt be, daughter!" Papa managed a painful smile. "But our neighbor the Count of Burgundy is not the only one you have to fear. The Lord of Gascony hungers for independence from the rule of Aquitaine and, rebellious subject that he is, will doubtless try to claim thy person, Eleanor, as the means to rule that which has heretofore ruled him."

"I will have him hanged if he bends not the knee to Aquitaine!" I assured Papa.

"And if he bends the knee in quest of wife?"

"I will bestow a serving maid on him. He has not the rank for Aquitaine. Nor does the Count of Burgundy. None save a Prince shall be my husband and rule Aquitaine with me."

"You swear it?"

"I swear it by all that is most holy, Papa!"

"Then I shall die content."

Less than an hour later, Papa did just that. Gold coins were placed atop the eyelids of William X, Duke of Aquitaine, incense was lit, and a Bishop spattered the deathbed with holy water whilst a dozen priests chanted poor Papa on his journey from this world to the next. I dried my eyes and kissed my dead father's still-warm cheek and left the room.

Immediately, and against the grain of my grief, I issued the orders necessary to the circumstances. Couriers, the speediest horsemen available, were dispatched to Paris to bring the news of my father's death to his sovereign and mine, King Louis VI of France. Tradition dictated this haste. In the wake of a Duke's death, there were always small rebellions and moves to seize power. It was the duty of the King, as well as in his self-interest, to restore order and reestablish his own rule as supreme over whoever should succeed the deceased Duke. And it was my duty as the heiress to Aquitaine to immediately inform the King of events and—not so incidentally—of my continuing loyalty to him.

All of this was complicated by my particular status at the time of Papa's death. I was still very young, and unmarried. The King had the right to deem me unfit to rule and to appoint a regent to rule for me. He could, if he wanted, break up Aquitaine among the Lords who had sworn fealty to my father but not to me. He could marry me off to any one of them, or to some foreigner if he chose. It was his right as King to give me in marriage to any man of noble birth—young, old, rich, poor, healthy, sick, handsome, ugly—and it was my feudal duty to accept the French King's marital decision unquestioningly.

Obviously it was important that Louis the Fat be enlisted to act on my behalf quickly! And so I enclosed a postcript to the letter, informing him of my father's death. In it I pointed out the political realities this circumstance imposed on both Aquitaine and France. I begged his protection as my monarch and assured him that my father's fealty to him should continue unbroken from me. I called to his attention my youth and my unmarried state. Subtly, I reminded him of my beauty and of my eligibility to become a bride. My father's dying wish had been that I should wed a Prince, I told him, altering the circumstances slightly to suit the case I was pleading. After all, I had been told that the King's son was most handsome. . . . Aquitaine and France would be united, I argued. What a domain that should be for a King and Queen! Thus would I solve the problem of my protection and of the integrity of Aquitaine's borders and her wealth. I begged the King's pardon for putting matters so boldly, ascribing it to grief, and to my fear that unless he moved quickly in my interest—and in the interests of France—Aquitaine and her bereaved Duchess might fall to some scoundrel who was quick but less than worthy. Even in mourning, I remembered to send my love to his unmarried son, the heir to his throne, also named Louis, whom I had never met. Then I quickly sealed the letter and sped the courier on his way.

This done, I summoned the majordomo of our household staff and made arrangements for the funeral. It would be held with all of the pomp and the pageantry dictated by Papa's position. But it would be delayed a few days because I wanted to give the couriers ample opportunity to reach the French border before letting the Count of Burgundy and the Lord of Gascony and other ambitious and ruthless warrior-knights know that the powerful Duke of Aquitaine was dead, leaving his vulnerable realm to an eldest daughter who was quite young and slim and beautiful, but also unmarried, unprotected, and ripe for the plucking.

Petronilla and I wept together, sisterly at last in our grief. I told her of Papa's wish that she go to Uncle Raymond in Poitiers so that we two might be separated as a safeguard to the succession of our family's reign over Aquitaine. Petronilla's breasts rose and her blue eyes sparkled at the prospect of seeing her deflowerer again. I knew her too well to bother cautioning her against adultery with so recent a bridegroom. If there was a way to be found to Uncle Raymond's bed, Petronilla would be sure to find it.

"Where will you go, Eleanor?" she asked me.

"Bordeaux. Our castle there is the best fortified. It can withstand a siege if that is necessary. I must play for time, Petronilla. I must hold off ambitious suitors, ambitious conquerors, until France can act in my behalf."

"Bordeaux," Petronilla sighed. "And I will be in Poitiers. All of Aquitaine will lie between us, Eleanor."

"The distance is deliberate. Papa decreed it so. It is for our own protection."

"But we have never been separated before, and now to be separated by an entire kingdom—"

"It will only be until I can arrange to return stability to Aquitaine." I hugged Petronilla. "Then we shall be together again."

Papa was buried three days later. Directly following the lavish ceremony, Petronilla and her entourage set out for Poitiers. Surrounded by Father's small army of knights and servants—mine now—I embarked on the journey to the fortress castle at Bordeaux.

It was, of course, impossible to keep the movement of so large a force a secret. Likewise, it was not possible to still the tongues of so many men. Word of Papa's death was whispered to those whose lands we passed through, and in the eternal manner of bad news was soon well in advance of our line of march. Thus, I am sure, did it reach the quivering ears of Gascony.

Even as we marched ponderously south, a force of armed knights headed by the Lord of Gascony was fording the Garonne River and moving west by north from Gascony through Aquitaine to intercept us. We were still far from the haven of our destination when the first contact was made between our two groups. It was dusk when the banner of Gascony appeared in a cloud of dust atop the crest of a hill lying directly in our line of march. Seeing it, I immediately called a halt and ordered the commanders of my knights to deploy them in a defensive position.

About an hour later a messenger rode into our encampment under a truce flag. His master, the Lord of Gascony, craved an audience with Eleanor, the new Duchess of Aquitaine. "Tell your master that I shall be happy to grant him an audience for the purpose of receiving his vows of allegiance," was the reply I sent back.

The Lord of Gascony was too wily to make an issue of the condition I set. When he came into our encampment and approached the throne that had been set up for me in front of the roaring bonfire, he did his best to make a series of sweeping bows of homage, and then to kneel in acknowledgment that I was indeed his Duchess. He was somewhat hindered by the heavy armor in which his crusty old soldier's body was encased.

"I am a plainspoken man," he told me, "a simple warrior who says right out that which is on his mind. I hope you will allow me such frankness, Duchess."

"Speak," I agreed. "Straight talk will be welcome."

"You are very young, Eleanor," he began.

"True. . . . Duchess Eleanor," I reminded him. "Continue."

"You are a woman alone—"

"I have my loyal knights." I indicated the guards standing about us who had been instructed to keep their swords half drawn.

"You are in need of protection from a strong man, an older man, a soldier."

"Such as yourself?" I smiled sweetly, innocently, and fluttered my long lashes.

"Who better, my Duchess? I have the experience, strength, and wisdom that can only come from living. I have lived."

"True. I have noted the discrepancy in our ages," I told the Lord of Gascony.

"I am old enough to be your father," he granted, "but that is all to the good."

"You are old enough to be my grandfather."

"Perhaps . . . perhaps. . . ." He looked at me shrewdly. "You are very young. You need an older man to provide for you, my Duchess."

"Provide what?"

He reached inside his armor and withdrew a velvet box with a red ribbon around it. "Chocolates from far-off Switzerland." He presented them to me with a flourish. "A token of my affection."

"I hoped, rather, a real tribute to your new Duchess," I retorted pointedly, accepting the box of candy.

"And this too is for you, my Duchess." He produced a swirl of multicolored silken hose and waved it before my eyes as if by doing so he might secure my enchantment.

"Just what is it that you are proposing?" I wondered as I accepted the Dutch-style stockings. "Marriage? Or concubinage?"

"I have been a soldier too long." He hung his gnarled old head. "I know not how to treat with ladies of high station, having spent too much time, I fear, in the company of lowborn wenches."

"Next you will be gifting me with silken drawers."

"I have some here." He fumbled inside his armor.

"And offering to help me on with them."

"A husband's prerogative."

"Ah. Then it is marriage that you are proposing."

"It is indeed my humble desire to be your husbandly protector."

"And if I should spurn such protection?" I inquired.

"I beg you, do not do so, my Duchess. You will be prey to forces far too strong for you to control."

"And if I do not marry you, will yours be such a force?" I asked him pointedly.

The Lord of Gascony lowered his rheumy old eyes. His meaning, however, was obvious.

"Then it is against yourself and your own forces you propose to protect me, is that it?"

"I have also brought you butter from a Gascon farm." He avoided the question and indicated a tub borne by one of his lackeys.

"The alternative to your proposal sounds suspiciously like a threat of treason," I softly told the Lord of Gascony.

"My knights surround your camp, Duchess." His tone was also low so that only the two of us might hear. "They are battle trained and used to my command. You are inexperienced, and so I will offer you this advice. Many knights do not respond to orders from a woman. Do not depend on your warriors to defend you in this situation."

"Oh, I most certainly shall not," I agreed, my green eyes wide and childlike.

"Then shall we plight our troth for all to know?"

"I think not."

"But then, what shall you do, Duchess?"

"Come closer, and I will whisper it in your ear for you alone to hear."

The Lord of Gascony did as I bade him. When his face was close to mine and his scrawny chicken neck rising unprotected from his armor, I reached into the flowing sleeve of the brocaded Persian-style jacket I was wearing and took out a small, thin stiletto with a very sharp point. I pressed this point against his throat. "This," I told him, "is what I shall do. This is the alternative."

"But I am here under a flag of truce!" He tried to hold very still, but nevertheless he quivered against the threatening blade tip.

"You are here as a loyal subject of Aquitaine, and I am your Duchess," I told him. "Fealty demands that you obey my orders. And my orders are that you shall ride with us to Bordeaux!"

"A flag of truce!" he repeated indignantly.

"Obedience to your Duchess!" I pricked his neck with the point of the stiletto and drew a drop of blood.

Thus was the Lord of Gascony persuaded to lend his protection to us as we continued on our journey to Bordeaux. Instead of attacking us, his surrounding troops acted as our guard. For he was right, you see, *mes amis*: I was but a very young and very weak woman in need of protection. And because I was young and weak, and most of all because I was a woman, I did not bind myself to manly ethics, but rather devised a morality of my own more in keeping with my vulnerable gender. And this ethic, the ethic of the womanly dagger held to the male throat, did indeed serve me well throughout all of the difficulties of my female life.

In a nutshell, the ethic is this: *Pensez à numéro un!* which means, Look out for number one!

"What you did was not honorable," the Lord of Gascony grumbled when at last we parted before the moat of my castle in Bordeaux.

"Perhaps not." I patted his gnarled cheek, a Duchess' liberty. "But it was effective."

Although I had reached the safety of my Bordeaux castle, my troubles were not yet over. Only a few days later, there appeared on the horizon an army under the command of the Count of Burgundy. Before the main body of this force reached the castle, a knight who served under the Count but owed favor to my dead father defected and brought us news of his master's intentions.

"Abduction" was the word he quoted. "The Count means to snatch the Duchess so that Aquitaine is left leaderless, and then to step in and fill the breach."

"And what does he mean to do with me?"

"To secrete you in a dungeon in Burgundy until such time as your freedom may suit his purposes."

"Then this Count from neighboring Burgundy does not wish to marry me," I mused.

"He is mulling it over. There are certain obstacles—"

"Obstacles?"

"He has a wife."

"Ah."

"And she has powerful kinsmen whom he hesitates to cross."

"I see."

"Nevertheless, the Count of Burgundy matches your youth and beauty against his wife, who grows long in the tooth, and would shorten your time in the dungeon by ridding himself of her and marrying you."

"Divorce?" I inquired. "I must deal with Holy Mother Church in Aquitaine. I don't think that I could marry a divorced man."

42

"Do not fear. Divorce is not what the Count of Burgundy is considering. He intends a cleaner solution."

"He means to kill his wife to marry me," I realized.

"Not immediately. But eventually, *oui*. And to make it seem an accident if he can."

"And he would do all this for love of me whose beauty is but rumored to him, me, upon whom his eye hath never fallen. Nay! I think not. For lust of Aquitaine perhaps, but not for love of Eleanor!"

"Then you must take measures quickly to forestall the intended abduction, Duchess."

My informant was right as to that. Guards were posted in hiding and lay in wait for those Burgundy knights charged with seizing me. When all had swum the moat and infiltrated our stronghold, we sprung the trap on them. In all, eight Burgundy knights were captured, and at dawn the next morning their severed heads were raised on pikes from the castle parapets for the edification of the Count of Burgundy.

The display angered him. The Count was famous for his bile, his throbbing temples, his red-faced rage. He laid waste to the countryside, slaughtered the serfs working the farmland that provided our food, and then laid siege to the castle itself. The siege effectively cut us off from the outside world.

We had to send out raiding parties at night to insure our food supply. Occasionally these were intercepted by the enemy and did not return. When this happened, I would find myself greeting a dawn of horror wherein the heads of some of my most loyal knights would be impaled atop a row of stakes on the far side of the moat. In the vortex of such happenings and such pressures, innocence and girl-hood vanished and a regal womanhood was forged.

The siege grew worse, and yet still worse. Food had to be rationed among the servants, and only the knights were allowed to drink wine. Then the Count discovered the source of the underwater stream that fed the wells in the castle courtyard and dammed it up, forcing us to ration water as well. Our situation was growing truly desperate!

This was the deteriorating situation when the Count of Burgundy sent me a message under a flag of truce. In it he offered to lift the siege if I would consent to accompany him back to Burgundy as his honored guest. He asked no more of me than that.

And what of Aquitaine? I didn't have to ask. Once I was gone, his troops would plunder it freely. And the Count would already have his army in position to claim it as his own. Even my own knights would have no choice with me gone. They would either have to bend the knee to the Count or flee the country.

The message I sent back thanked the Count for his offer of hospitality but pleaded a previous engagement. I had a date to rule Aquitaine, I told him. It would probably keep me from visiting Burgundy for the next twenty or thirty years.

His response was to storm the castle the next morning. We beat them off, but at great cost. Many lives were lost on both sides, but our limited force within the castle walls could not bear this loss so well as their larger army. And we could ill spare the boiling oil we used to drive their ladders from our walls; it was cooking oil, and the last such in our dwindling food supply.

I met with my commanders that night. They were blunt,

as I had ordered them to be. We could not withstand another such attack by the Burgundy forces. They proposed that I allow them to spirit me from the castle that night in preparation for the inevitable defeat.

After due consideration, I rejected that idea. For me to flee my castle and go into hiding would be tantamount to surrendering Aquitaine to anarchy. And it would only be a matter of time before the Count of Burgundy or some equally ambitious feudal Lord caught up with me and either forced me to marriage or killed me. Better to stand firm here at Bordeaux and fight to the end with my troops as befit the Duchess of Aquitaine, Eleanor, daughter of the beloved and mighty Duke William X.

Morning dawned to the ominous sound of thundering hooves as the Burgundy forces assembled to attack. I toured the castle walls, speaking encouragement to my loyal soldiers although I knew that they could not help but be overrun once the attack was launched. The sun climbing the sky signaled that the moment was coming closer. I was thankful that I had dispatched Petronilla to Poitiers, no matter what extramarital mischief she might have spurred there, for it was beginning to seem quite possible that she might indeed be called upon to rule Aquitaine one day soon. Surely the sounding of the enemy clarion would signal the end of the short reign of Eleanor as Duchess of Aquitaine.

But then, like an echo, there was an answering clarion from the hills beyond. Suddenly there was a rescrambling of the Burgundy army. Instead of massing for attack, they were milling about in an effort to hastily pull up the stakes of their encampment and depart. I spied the Count of Burgundy himself in the vanguard of this unseemly and unexpected retreat. He was putting the spurs to his mount and riding off with his lieutenants in great haste whilst elements of his force were still assembling themselves for this whirlwind leave-taking.

The dust of their departure had scarce settled when the reason for it appeared. A massive caravan appeared, complete with five hundred knights in armor, thrice that number of foot soldiers, yet again as many servants, countless mule-drawn carts, the materials for erecting tents and pavilions, as well as provisions and utensils for this large group. Six wagons covered with homespun, I would learn later, contained only gifts for me.

It was not the size of this caravan that drove off the Count of Burgundy and inspired our cheers of greeting for its arrival. In truth, the fighting force from Burgundy was far larger. No, it was the banner borne so proudly at the head of the train. This was the flag of France, a flag to which both Burgundy and Aquitaine pledged loyalty. The Count had fled because he dared not risk the all-out war with his King, the King of France, Louis the Fat, which his confronting the French would surely have provoked.

I had been rescued. My prayers had been answered. Louis the Fat had sent me his son. Prince Louis had come. My Prince had come!

Prince Louis did not deign to camp in the mess left by the Count of Burgundy. For this reason his pavilions and brightly colored tents were set up at some distance from the castle. The site chosen was a flat green meadow separated from the castle by a high, unnamed river. Immediately his servants were put to work making a raft to carry him across the river for our first meeting.

Ah, *mes amis*, what can I say about my impressions of

Louis at this, our first meeting? He was tall, as close to boyhood as I was myself to girlhood, and so perhaps a bit gangly. I noted immediately that he was not graceful, and this awkwardness did not improve with age. He appeared anything but the warrior-knight I was in need of to maintain my reign over Aquitaine. And if he seemed more priestlike than soldierly, nevertheless, he had the blond ringlets of a Cupid and eyes so blue that one might be tempted to wade in their depths. And if his smile was thin, it nevertheless seemed genuine.

"My father has sent you a letter." He handed it to me.

I opened it and started to read.

Prince Louis' blue eyes widened in surprise. "You can read!" he exclaimed.

"Since I was going to be a Duchess, my father insisted that I learn," I told him. "Can you read?" I asked him as an afterthought. Very few people could, even among the nobility, even among royalty. The letter from King Louis, for instance, had not been written by him personally, but had been written for him with the anticipation that it would be read to me by a scribe maintained at my court for that purpose.

"Oui." Prince Louis surprised me as I had him. "I studied to be a priest," he explained. "If my older brother hadn't died so that I was next in line for the throne, I would have been ordained by now."

I read the letter and then looked up at him again. "Your father wishes us to marry," I told him.

"I know."

"He asks me to consent."

"I know that too."

"He is my King. I consent." I knelt before Prince

Louis. "Is this marriage your wish too?" I asked him, looking up.

"My wish was to have been à priest." His expression was woebegone, his voice filled with reluctant truth.

"I see." N. exactly every young girl's dream proposal. I got to my feet. "Then why did you come?" I asked Prince Louis.

"I am an obedient son. And Father is my King as well as my sire. He wished me to come. He wishes us to marry. I will do as he wishes."

"Oh, joy! Oh, rapture!"

Prince Louis' thin smile appeared. "You have a quick tongue," he observed. "When I make marriage vows with you, I will keep them," he added, quite serious now. "I will be a dutiful husband to you, Eleanor. And I will look to your Aquitaine with as much concern as to France. Their joining will make a mighty kingdom for us to rule over together."

Words to stir a maiden's heart! Still, it was what I wanted. A *fille* has to take care of herself, after all. I certainly had never lost sight of the politics of my marital prospects. Indeed, I had contrived this very situation. And so—

"I will be a good wife to you, Louis." I kissed him on the lips to stress the sincerity of my pledge. His answering kiss was—well, *mes amis*—it was priestly.

Three days later another missive arrived by courier from Louis the Fat. He was ill, very ill, possibly dying. It was his wish to see his son married and France and Aquitaine safely joined before he died. He asked that the traditional betrothal waiting period be waived and that Prince Louis and I be married immediately.

48

So it was that the following Sunday Prince Louis, heir apparent to the throne of France, and I, the Duchess of Aquitaine, led a lavish wedding procession through the cobblestoned streets of Bordeaux. The din of the church bells from the surrounding countryside was all but deafening. The blare of the clarions heralding our nuptials was swallowed up by it. Townspeople and peasants thronged the streets, all dressed in their best clothes in honor of the occasion. Colored flags and ribbons and banners lined and crisscrossed our path. Tugged forelocks greeted us at every turn and deep curtsies pointed us like arrows to the steps of the Church of St. Andrew.

It was an old church with a musty, dark interior. The incense was so thick during the ceremony that it was difficult to breathe. Despite the lit candles, I could barely see Prince Louis' face as we exchanged our marriage vows. In truth, I took more satisfaction in the small ceremony that followed these nuptials and formalized our position as Duke and Duchess of Aquitaine.

A sumptuous wedding feast followed the ceremony. It was during this celebration that I began to get a glimmering of just what sort of man I had married. Young as he was, Prince Louis proved prissy and judgmental. He called a halt to the singing of love songs because he thought them in poor taste. He refused to take part in the dancing, which his training as a Church novitiate had taught him was an evil practice. And when I accepted the invitation to dance with one of my knights, my new husband's thin-lipped disapproval was plain for all to see.

Ever headstrong, although never as impulsive as Petronilla, I would not let myself be so disapproved of publicly. My first dance had been with an old friend of my father's, and truly it was a most stately round. But now I sought the most energetic of my young Aquitaine knights and lured him into a fandango that had most of the Frenchmen echoing their Prince's disapproval and all of the Aquitainians cheering their Duchess' spirit. It was not, I suppose, a tactful thing to do, and surely not an auspicious way for me to start our marriage.

Once the fandango was over, I did indeed feel contrite. I tried to make amends to Prince Louis for my brazenness. He, in turn, made an effort with his thin-lipped smile to put the incident behind us. In this spirit we left our guests to their lobster and oysters and mullet and sole, their roasts of fowl and boar and venison, their sweetcakes and fruit and the barrels of wine and champagne provided to celebrate our union and made our way to the ducal chambers whence our marriage was to be sealed.

Here Prince Louis and I briefly separated once again. The ladies of my household were waiting for me in an antechamber so that they might prepare me for my wedding night. Having drunk much wine, they were quite tiddly and excited and vivacious with vicarious anticipation of what they assumed would be my deflowerment.

They stripped the wedding gown from my body with warm and clinging hands. My undergarments likewise were removed, and in a trice I stood before them nude. There was much admiration and clucking over my young, firm body, many compliments directed to the high, sculpted breasts with their blood-red dagger nipples, naughty nudges regarding the utilitarian aspects of my pert, saucy derriere and boldly tilted mons veneris with its silky sporran of shining copper hair. Soft hands vied with one another to bathe me—lovingly, lingeringly, tracing the sensual alabaster line of my flesh from my long neck to my narrow waist and sleek hips. There were whispers and giggles regarding the litheness and suppleness of my long, tapered legs, and suggestions as to how they might be arranged around the body of my new husband as he made love to me. Indeed, so much did my ladies take vicarious titillation in such talk and such caressings that I was forced finally to scold them for dallying and keeping me too long from my waiting bridegroom.

This had the desired result of hurrying the preparations. Now they were more serious, more conscientious as they brushed out my long auburn hair and tied it loosely with a velvet ribbon. They disciplined their hands to linger less as they anointed my naked bride's body with perfumed ointments. They even overcame their reluctance to cover my nudity with the pale lavender chemise I would wear to my wedding bed. They oohed and ahhed over the way this ankle-length garment clung to my ripe young flesh and accentuated its delicate ivory tones, but finally, sensing my impatience, they knelt to pay homage to me as Duchess, kissed my hand, and bowed themselves out. Then, alone, I joined my bridegroom in the boudoir.

Prince Louis was already in our marriage bed, covered by the silken sheets. I was a little disappointed. I knew that he would sleep in the nude as did all noblemen who prided themselves on being virile warriors, and I had looked forward to my first view of my new husband in this natural state. Now, in the glare of the many candles that had been arranged around the bed, he could judge the sensuality of my form in the thin, revealing chemise, but I could not see his. Indeed, the covers were pulled up to his chin.

"You will have to tell me what is expected of me, Sire," I told him, managing to tremble with modesty and to dissemble as women have doubtless dissembled since Eve led husband Adam down that first garden path of his own imagining. "I have no experience in this matter and must depend on your wisdom and guidance." The bobble of my breasts under my camise was pear-shaped, but my naiveté was strictly a bite out of the old apple.

Prince Louis' answer, however, took me greatly by surprise. "Alas, Eleanor," he told me, "I fear my inexperience is as great as your own."

"I beg your pardon?" I sat down on the edge of the bed.

"I have been trained to the priesthood, not to husbandhood. I was meant to be a monk, not a benedict. I was trained to celibacy, and if not for the death of my brother thrusting me into succession to the throne, I would have been content my whole life long to live chastely. I freely confess, Eleanor, I have not the vaguest idea of how to treat with a woman, let alone a wife."

"Are you a virgin, then?" I stared at him.

"As unplucked as yourself."

"Umm." I decided to let that pass unchallenged. "Well—" I took matters into my own hands and pulled back the sheets. "There is a first time for everything." I let my green eyes wander boldly over my new husband's naked body.

It was a thin, long body, still more adolescent than manly. It was sparse of hair and perhaps more bony than muscular. Still, that was preferable to fat or flab or the sag of too great maturity. Despite his gangliness, Prince Louis' chest was hard and his legs quite sturdy. His belly was flat and the tuck of his bottom not unpromising. And as to his Parisian pickle—

"What a shy fellow." I picked it up delicately between two fingers. If not its girth, its length at least was promising. But it was as yet too soft a gherkin and quite lacking in both the brawn and brine of tumescence. "But we shall be warm friends and this shyness shall be overcome," I promised, stroking the length of the shaft.

"There is a problem," Prince Louis commented after a moment.

"I can see that." Despite its flaccidity, the warmth of the instrument in my palm was exciting to me, and my always long nipples were hardening visibly against the lavender material of my chemise.

"The problem," he continued, "is that what you are doing is sinful."

"I beg your pardon?"

"Fondling me thus is sinful."

I considered it. "Do you really think so?" I did not stop stroking his penis.

"What you are doing will surely lead us to commit the original sin."

"I certainly hope so." I tangled my fingers in the sparse blonde curls in which his tight balls were nested.

"You are arousing my lust." His penis stirred. "That is sinful."

"We are man and wife." I bent and kissed him on the lips. I deliberately rubbed my warm breasts over his naked chest.

Prince Louis gasped as he felt the nipples digging in through the silk of the camise. "Still, I cannot shake the feeling that this is sinful." He squirmed but did not attempt to remove his hand when I carried it to my heaving breast.

"One day you will be King of France and I will be Queen." Slowly, kneeling, I pulled the camise above my knees and then my thighs. "We will have to provide an heir for the throne." I lay back and stretched one naked leg up in the air and turned it this way and that so that my new husband might admire its litheness and shape. "There is only one way to do that." I straddled him and pressed his hardening penis against my silken belly. "We will have to make love." Lust moistened my pussy and parted its lips as I felt the increasing hardness.

"But it is a sin!" he moaned.

"Perhaps." I pushed down the bodice of the lavender camise and bared my quivering cone-shaped breasts. "But if so, it is a sin that patriotism to La Belle France demands." I arranged his hands around the eager mounds of flesh. I bent and kissed his thin, reluctant lips. I parted them with my tongue. I pushed my own tongue deep into his mouth. I felt his cock—the one part of him that had somehow escaped his conscience—bucking and throbbing against my mons veneris.

When the kiss was over, I rose up and removed my camise. I tossed the silken sheets away from us. I straddled Prince Louis and mounted him. I did not have to hold up his penis. It stood up by itself, long and thin. I slid down its length wantonly and covered his lips with my fingers to silence him when he once again began to murmur protests against the lust he could no more stop than could I. I squeezed his balls and Prince Louis' bottom began to rise and fall, pushing me up toward the beamed ceiling and then dropping me to the hard, spreading impalement that felt so marvelous. I began to laugh excitedly and to urge him on to greater exertions.

I was on the brink of spending, but had not yet spent when he grabbed my writhing derriere with both hands and pulled me down against him hard, belly to belly, and fired the lotion of his lust deep inside my hot, wet, grinding quim. *"Oui!"* I screamed. *"Oui!"* I laughed. "Harder! More! Don't stop! Don't stop!"

But Prince Louis did stop, and most abruptly too. Not only that, but he withdrew whilst I was still not satisfied. He scrambled from the bed, long, limp prick gleaming with the mingling of my honey and his jism, and flung himself into a corner of the room on his knees.

"What are you doing?" I lay there panting, pussy throbbing, frustrated, unfulfilled.

"Praying for forgiveness." He faced the wall and bowed his head.

"But what about—?" My fingers squeezed the moist, quivering fruit of my pussy.

"I did not know how powerful the temptation would be! I fear for my ability to withstand it again!"

"Don't withstand it!" I begged him. I parted the lips of my empty pussy and raised it to him, an offering.

"You don't understand, Eleanor! I fear for my soul!" He started to pray.

Observing him, the circumstances provoked in me a bitterly anti-Church reaction. If clerical training had so deprived me of wifely satisfaction, then better to be a pagan! Look at what had happened, after all! My husband had spent with a satisfaction he could not hide, and then had rushed to absolution without regard for my needs! Woe! the lot of woman! Better to be a pagan wench than the Queen of a Christian zealot! And with this thought, this bitter thought, I closed my eyes and conjured up a woodland orgy by which to frig myself in order to finish that which my husband had not deigned to complete.

Here was Pan apiping, his erect prick shimmering golden amid the foliage of the forest. There was a centaur, horse-cock blood filled as he mounted a woodland nymph with a bottom like twin pink pillows. And here was yet another, a suckling nymph with a sister's heaving breast stretching wide her mouth. In all there were twenty fantasy creatures, obscene, not human, entwining in the most sinful patterns and with the most complete abandonment.

Into their midst, in my fantasy, I strode naked and laughing. They surrounded me and caressed me. They kissed my mouth with long, lascivious, licking tongues. They sucked my sensitive breasts until the nipples threatened to burst. They squeezed my buttocks and rubbed between them and probed until my head was spinning with sensual hunger. I flung myself to the grassy ground and raised my arms and opened my legs wide and bade them all to come to me, to take me as best they could, and to propel me over the edge of that cliff whence my bride-groom had left me hovering.

A nymph garlanded with flowers spread a wide, pink pussy over my mouth for me to lick. Pan slid under me and claimed my bottom and breached it in the most immoral manner and reamed it painfully and thrillingly. A centaur prick slid up and down in the cleft between my pear-shaped breasts. And finally a unicorn inserted his horn in my pussy, forcing it all the way up, fucking me with it so hard that all I could do was wrap my legs around his neck as I began to spend and shriek with my release. . . .

"Eleanor? Are you all right?" My new husband had finished praying and was on his feet beside the bed, looking down at me with some concern.

"I'm all right," I panted, squeezing my burning thighs together with the last of my orgasm. "I'm better than all right!"

For six days and nights following my wedding night, there were parties and feasts in celebration of the marriage. On the seventh day, however, a messenger arrived from France with news that brought an abrupt end to the festivities. Louis the Fat was dead!

Corpulence as much as any other cause led to the demise of King Louis VI. This obesity had given him time to anticipate his end. Foreseeing it, he had provided for France well in arranging for his son to marry me and for his nation thus to be joined under one rule with opulent Aquitaine. Having accomplished this, Louis the Fat was free to expire, and that is what he did.

Thus did my husband, Prince Louis, become King Louis VII of France and Aquitaine. Thus did I become Queen Eleanor. And thus did duty force us to leave Aquitaine to take up our residence where the seat of the government over which we presided was located—Paris.

Oui, mes amis! King Louis VII and I, Queen Eleanor, left immediately for Paris. "Shun Paris as you would the plague!" Papa had said, but circumstance would not allow the shunning. "Never go to Paris!" he had cautioned, but now I was on my queenly way there.

Would Paris be as immoral and dissolute as Papa said?

I wondered.

I hoped!

Chapter Three

Wisdom is not innate, but acquired. Frequently it is passed on by parents. In the absence of parents, however, what better source for a young bride than her mother-in-law? I do not jest, *mes amis*. The lessons I learned from my mother-in-law—although they may not have been quite the ones she intended—stay with me to this very day.

Her name was Adelaide—Queen Adelaide. She was, of course, the mother of my husband, King Louis VII. And until his death she had been wife to Louis the Fat.

This role had left its mark. Fat though he may have been, Louis the father, unlike his son, was reputed to have been quite lusty. His weight had borne down Adelaide at will, and his will had been frequent. Nor had his constant strayings with other women lessened his demands on her. A roll with a wench had but whetted his appetite for his wife. And it was for poor Adelaide, as one may imagine, a very heavy scene.

Indeed, it had left her strangely shaped. She was, by the time I met her, an oddly flat woman. There is no other way to describe her. Where other women had curves, she had planes. Where other women swelled, Adelaide leveled off. She had breasts like those hoecakes cooked in a pan (pancakes, they are called by the peasants, I believe), and a derriere as concave and waffled as a lady's fan. Even her thighs were more like flat-cut timber than the rounded trunks of trees, and she was spread wide from hip to hip by the weight that had so oft pressed down upon her.

I felt sorry for her, and from this emotion I learned the first lesson from my mother-in-law. Heed me, *jeunes filles*! No matter how piteous your mother-in-law may seem to be, do not fall into the trap of sympathy. Always you will find that it has been set to catch you in a disadvantage.

"All men are beasts," she whined to me.

"I understand why you feel that way," I said, patting her hand.

"Except my son, Louis."

"That is true," I agreed with a sigh. "Louis is not a beast."

"Unlike most men, my son Louis does not take advantage of helpless women and vent his lust on them!"

"Perhaps that is because he is a tad shy of lust to vent," I suggested. "Perhaps Louis could be just a wee bit more aggressive."

That very night my mother-in-law told her son that he had better watch his wife very carefully; she had marked adulterous impulses!

On another occasion she brought me to her dressmaker. "You are a provincial from Aquitaine," she reminded me, "and this is Paris. It is here that fashion is decided. The French are used to a Queen conversant with the latest styles."

She meant herself, of course. I thought she looked dowdy, but I didn't say so.

"You are fortunate to have the benefit of my advice. The Queen will have a gown of this red brocade," she told the dressmaker. "Drape it, please."

The dressmaker arranged the material to fall over my camise. "Like so?" she asked Queen Adelaide.

"The bodice must be cut much deeper. We must see more bosom."

"Surely that is too revealing!" I protested when Queen Adelaide pushed the dressmaker aside and adjusted the combination of exposed breast flesh and brocade to suit herself.

"Nonsense, Eleanor! Just because you are a provincial is no reason to attire yourself like one. You are a Queen of France now. Some might say that you have not enough to flaunt in the bosom department, but be that as it may, you most certainly must use what you have to best advantage."

And so the dress was cut to her specifications. I wore it to one of the first balls given in my honor as Queen. I felt as if every eye was on my exposed bosom. After the ball, my husband confirmed that at least his eye had been so directed.

"Brazen!" he told me. "Shocking! This is Paris, Eleanor, not a farm in Aquitaine! Mammaries are covered here! Really, my dear, you have displayed yourself quite shamelessly!"

"But your mother—" I tried to tell him.

"It was Mama that called to my attention just how

revealing your costume was. She said that she had tried to tell you tactfully to conceal more of your bosom, but that evidently her message was too subtle to get through to you. However, Eleanor, from now on if there is any doubt in your mind as to what is proper, I would strongly suggest that you consult with Mama.''

And do the opposite! I promised myself silently. But I didn't say that aloud. I had just learned another lesson from my mother-in-law, but it wasn't the lesson of not criticizing her to her son. That I knew without her telling me.

One evening after I had retired, she sent word by messenger, requesting me to join her in one of the palace sitting rooms. I put on a robe over my camise and went there. When I arrived, Queen Adelaide was not there.

In her place was a handsome young chevalier in her employ. He poured two glasses of wine and then positioned himself close beside me on the couch. Before I knew what he was about, his arms were around me in the most intimate of embraces. Startled, my green eyes darted over his shoulder just in time to gaze upon my mother-in-law arriving in the company of my husband, King Louis!

I shall pass over the ensuing scene, the explanations, the denials, the protests, the disbelief. The chevalier was sent away, ostensibly in a state of abject disgrace, but in my heart I was sure that his patroness, my mother-in-law, would see to it that he was well provided for in his banishment from Paris. It had all been planned! Of that I was sure! And just as surely, I would never convince my husband that such was the case.

In one sense, I suppose I was fortunate. Louis' attitude toward the incident was more sorrowful than punitive. The flesh is weak. That much he had learned training for the priesthood. And woman's flesh is the weakest of all. So went the chauvinist corollary. In other words, he had gotten what he expected. Given his mother and his religious training, what else could he expect? Women were treacherous, and never more so than when one took them to wife. Naturally I would betray him.

And that, *mes amis,* was a self-fulfilling prophecy if ever there was one!

Before it was fulfilled, however, Queen Adelaide impugned my morality from another direction. The problem, she assured her son, was in the blood. And to prove her point, she cited the example of my sister, Petronilla, word of whose scandalous affairs had traveled all the way from Poitiers to Paris.

The carnal relationship between Petronilla and Uncle Raymond had become so intense and so flagrant that his wife had left him. That the sister of the Queen should behave in such a manner, that she should cause such a scandal, was an embarrassment to the throne. So said my mother-in-law; so believed my husband.

"You must send her a strong letter immediately, Eleanor." That was Queen Adelaide's suggestion. "And insist that she stop this incestuous affair with a married man!"

"Of course," I acquiesced meekly. I knew that such a letter was but an exercise in futility. I might be Queen of France, but my influence over Petronilla in a matter of this nature would be nil. Nevertheless, I sent it. Why not? I never argued or fought unless there was something to gain from the argument or fight.

Petronilla quite ignored the letter, just as I had known she would.

This constant stress on morality by my husband, the King, and by my mother-in-law and by others as well, was quite at odds with what Papa's warnings had led me to expect of Paris. Anticipating Sodom-on-the-Seine, I found myself instead in an environment far more strict and narrow and intolerant of sensuality than that of Aquitaine. I was a southern noblewoman and my blood was warm. The royal Paris into which I had been thrust seemed frosted over with northern cold and totally lacking in the temptations to which Papa had feared I would succumb. In future, love would change that, but for now I was oblivious to the seductions of Paris and saw only the impersonal facade she offered to the eye of any new arrival.

I had a sweeping view of the city from the ramparts of the Cité Palace, the massive fortress castle built by the Franks in ancient times. The home of the royal family in Paris, the Cité Palace, loomed up on the Ile de la Cité, the island in the Seine between the Left and Right Bank suburbs of the city. It could only be reached via a heavily fortified bridge, and then only by the opening of the constantly guarded tower gate. Outside the castle proper, but within the compound of the fortress, were a series of buildings housing all that was necessary to the comfort and well-being of the royal family. These included the stables, the kitchens, various granaries and livestock pens, a blacksmith forge, and even a private chapel. Beyond, toward the tip of the island, was an arbor of fruit trees and an arrangement of sculptured gardens where it was often my pleasure to stroll on warm days.

The main impression when looking out over the city

from the tower was of frenetic activity and confusion filling narrow streets between close-packed wooden houses with overhanging eaves intended to shut out the heat of the sun, but which also deprived the cobbled byways of light as well. At different times of day, these crowds would shift from one street to another. The reason for this shift was that each street specialized in the merchanting of a specific product or activity.

There was a Bakers' Street. There was a Winesellers' Street. There was the Street of the Drapers. Most popular after classes at the University let out was the Street of the Jews, where students went to exchange foreign currency or to secure short-term loans from the moneylenders. Barred by law from owning property and from participating in most other businesses, the Jews had made themselves indispensable to the Parisian economy by rendering such services.

The thing I found hardest to get used to in Paris after the serenity of Aquitaine was the noise. The echo of wooden wheels rolling over cobblestones and of horses' hooves clopping was constant in one's ear. The loud clang of bells from Paris' many churches and cathedrals was constant. And the merged shouts and babble of the populace were a never-ending murmur, wafting across the Seine to Ile de la Cité.

This babble became more understandable from the vantage point of my garden wall. From here I could watch and listen to the students and teachers who congregated on the bridge that led to the Left Bank where the University was. Some of the teachers had actually constructed makeshift wooden houses on the bridge, and when the weather was good they would lecture to groups of students from the front stoops of these jerry-built structures. And as was the custom, the students would dispute with them the fine points of religion and philosophy and—most of all—the esthetics of art and prose and poetry.

Thus observing one balmy afternoon, my attention was caught by a particularly heated discussion. A teacher had drawn a crowd with a fervently romantic disquisition on the metaphysics of the famous love affair between the student Abélard and the beautiful daughter of aristocrats, Héloïse. It had occurred only twenty years before, but already the romantics were shrouding the facts in legend. "Theirs was a pure love," the lecturer was intoning, "a love transcending the merely physical."

"Hold on!" A sarcastic young voice brought the speaker up short. "Are you trying to tell us that Abélard and Héloïse did not fuck?"

"If that is a question, young man, could you phrase it less coarsely?"

"Do you mean that they didn't screw?" The sceptic stood. The rakish tilt of his scarlet cockade identified him as a Gascon. He was broad-shouldered and clean-shaven, his face too craggy to be aristocratic, the features too expressive and mobile to be merely handsome.

"What is your discipline, boy?" the lecturer demanded witheringly.

"I am a poet."

"Of verses scrawled on walls beside latrine ditches, I'll warrant!" the teacher gibed, drawing a laugh from the crowd.

"I am a Gascon poet. We believe in mixing realism with romance."

"A Gascon! Ah! That explains all."

The crowd guffawed again.

The poet took the laugh at his expense good-humoredly. "All except the matter of Abélard and Héloïse," he persisted. "There still seems to be a question as to whether they got it on or not."

"They what?" The teacher looked truly bewildered.

"Made it. Balled. Fucked."

"If you mean was their love carnal, then in my opinion it was not. It is my contention that they were above that. And by being above it, their love became both transcendent and transplendent."

"But you are altering the facts to suit your theory," the Gascon poet persisted. "The facts are that Abélard busted Héloïse's cherry and this so angered her kinsmen that they had his nuts cut off!"

"It is true that he was castrated," the teacher granted in a lofty tone. "But it was a mistake. Their love was pure. It was not physical."

"Then he lost his balls for nothing?"

"If spiritual love is nothing, then I fear so."

"*Merde!*" the turbulent Gascon poet exclaimed with disgust. Elbowing his broad-shouldered way through the crowd of students, he departed. "*Merde!*"

His image remained in my mind. I had seen more handsome men, and certainly men who appeared to more noble advantage. Indeed, this poet was perhaps even a bit ridiculous to behold. And yet he was brimming over with life, rude with it, brazen, fearless of the scorn of the crowd, shimmering with a kind of crude sensuality. More than once in the turbulent days and weeks that followed, I pondered his sensual lips forming those barnyard words which had proven so offensive to the romanticizers of poor

castrated Abélard and his passionate Héloïse, who fore-
swore love for piety, and with her lover's loss swore vows
of chastity and became the Abbess of the Convent of the
Paraclete, a post in which she served to this very day.
Silently, I agreed with the Gascon poet's earthier interpreta-
tion of the already legendary love affair.

This agreement made me perhaps more tolerant of my
sister Petronilla's situation. As time went on, her liaison
was growing more difficult for her and creating pressures
on me as well. The wife of Petronilla's lover, Raymond of
Poitiers, had powerful friends at court, and she was demanding that the King step in and end the situation. Of
course, Queen Adelaide also wanted her son to act. Finally
Louis did indeed write to Raymond. Uncle's reply was that
he would sooner die than be forced to live once again with
his shrew of a wife.

King Louis, my husband, pondered the situation. Finally he struck upon a course of action which he considered a suitable compromise. Naturally, what it really did
was to displease all involved.

The seeds of this compromise had been sown during the
First Crusade. At that time the holy army had conquered
Antioch, the Turkish city which had once been the capital
of ancient Syria. The city had been fortified and ruled by a
Christian Prince appointed by the Pope ever since. Re-
cently the Prince of Antioch had died.

Now Louis, through clerical intermediaries, prevailed
upon the Pope to appoint Raymond of Poitiers as the new
Prince of Antioch. This was a great honor for Uncle
Raymond, of course. There was only one catch. It was
made clear to him that he was forbidden to bring Petronilla
to Antioch with him.

Uncle Raymond was a practical man. A ripe young mistress was certainly to be treasured, but the opportunity to reign as an Oriental Prince came but once in a lifetime. And so he bid my furious sister farewell. Nor was her ire in any way lessened with the knowledge that her lover's wife was also not among those accompanying him to Antioch.

"The art of statesmanship," King Louis confided to me in our marriage bed, "is not so difficult, Eleanor, as it is made out to be." Saying which, he rolled over and, a moment later, began to snore contentedly.

But Louis' self-congratulations were premature. Rejected by Raymond, Petronilla immediately embarked on another love affair. In the end, this one was to prove far more disastrous for the Crown than her fling with Uncle Raymond.

Again the object of her affections was an older man— one old enough to be her father, in point of fact. His name was Sir Raoul of Vermandois. Like his predecessor in my sister's affections, he too was married. His wife was the niece of Theobald, Count of Champagne, an extremely influential and powerful nobleman. The Count was a stiff-necked and prickly aristocrat who set great store by his family's name and reputation. His vendettas against any who sullied them could go on for many years. One of the worst mistakes I ever made led me to be the object of one such vendetta.

The Count's nephew-in-law, Raoul, was completely enchanted by Petronilla. The pair petitioned the King to use his influence with Church Bishops to secure an annulment of Raoul's marriage to Theobald's niece. Petronilla also wrote to me, begging me to persuade the King to help them.

She was my sister. One love had already been denied her because of my husband's intervention. Knowing Petronilla, I foresaw nothing but a series of such confrontations ahead if she was again denied. "Let the Bishops grant the annulment," I advised Louis. "In the long run it will avoid trouble for the Crown."

I could not have been more mistaken!

The Bishops acceded to the request of their King and granted the annulment. Immediately, Petronilla and Raoul were married. And the fury of Theobald, Count of Champagne, at this insult to his family was unleashed.

He went directly to the Pope. The Pope in turn issued firm instructions to Yves of Saint-Laurent, the papal legate in France. My sister, her bridegroom, and the Bishops who had arranged for the annulment of his first marriage were all excommunicated!

This, however, was not enough to satisfy the Count of Champagne. He assembled his knights and marched on the castle shared by the newlyweds to punish them himself. Terrified for my sister, I prevailed upon Louis to send troops to protect her.

The result was a standoff. Interference by the King infuriated the Count of Champagne even more. Once again he complained to the Pope. This time the King himself, Louis VII of France, was excommunicated!

Quite literally, this was a fate worse than death to Louis. Married or not, King or not, at heart he was still convinced that the way of the pious monastic was the only true way and that the fate of his soul was far more important than anything that might befall him here on earth. In truth, this excommunication drove him to the very brink of his sanity.

The first evidence of this came in Poitiers. Uncle Raymond's departure had left a vacuum. Various knights sought to fill it, and warfare broke out among them. "I will teach these rebellious Aquitainian rebels of yours a lesson, Eleanor," Louis announced. But the words echoed hollowly and his blue eyes were haunted with the fact of his having been renounced by his Church.

He led an army to Poitiers himself. He put down the rebellion quickly and brutally. He held public whippings and hangings of all those who were even suspected of participating in it. He personally wielded the sword that hacked off the hands of the noblemen who led the rival factions.

When he returned to Paris, the first thing that I noticed about Louis was that his blue eyes were no longer mild. He had not—alas!—become passionate, but neither was he the passive, priestly introvert I had married. There was madness in his gaze now. His muscles twitched; his very flesh seemed primed to confirm the devil within that had caused his excommunication.

"France is not safe while Champagne simmers with rebellion!" he told me grimly, although in truth neither the region nor its Count had taken further action against the King since the aborted attempt to punish Petronilla and Raoul.

Louis could not sit still. It was as if the choice for him was between killing and contemplating his own damnation. He chose killing. At the head of a large army, he marched on Champagne.

The army failed to make contact with the enemy forces under the command of the Count of Champagne. Frustrated, Louis attacked the virtually undefended village of Vitry.

While the citizenry fled, his soldiers torched the thatched huts and wooden buildings that housed the shops of the town. Starting from the outskirts and proceeding toward the center, the flames consumed all there was of Vitry.

This included the cathedral where some thirteen hundred townspeople sought sanctuary. Most of these were helpless women and children. They were cooked to ashes in the oven King Louis ordered his soldiers to ignite. The collapsing roof of the cathedral and its blackened walls entombed the ashes.

The dreadful deed left its mark on Louis. He returned to Paris a haunted man. "The Pope was right to excommunicate me, Eleanor," he told me in a quivering voice. "I am indeed possessed by the Devil. How else could I commit such a horrible act against helpless people?"

The Devil? How convenient, I thought. Thus even a King can shuck responsibility! But I did not speak my thoughts aloud.

Consider, *mes amis,* how soon in every age mass murder is forgotten. *Oui!* How quickly, in every age, the focus shifts from horror to the difficulties of repentance and absolution. And after all, Louis was but a King. At Vitry, one might say, he was only doing his job.

Bear this in mind, *mes amis,* and forgive me when I report that poor King Louis was truly a pitiful figure under the weight of his excommunication. He was in pain, true pain, and what does it matter—what does it truly matter?—if his repentance was more a matter of fear of consequences, terror of burning in Hell through all eternity, rather than regret over those turned to crackling by his royal order. After all, Heaven is all-forgiving, is it not? Redemption is a path for all. Salvation is available to peasant and to King alike. And whose is the fault if the King is perhaps in a somewhat better position to afford it?

In Louis' case this meant affording the Abbot Bernard. Still young, with eyes like coals and the tongue of a prophet, the Abbot Bernard was the foremost churchman in all France. Already in his own lifetime, his religious zealotry and pious ferver labeled him a candidate for sainthood. Pale, with hair so sparse as to seem burned into his skull, and the inward-turned demeanor of the true ascetic, the Abbot Bernard was in fact what Louis had once aspired to be. Men and women alike trembled when the thunder of his voice defined their sinfulness for them. Nor did he flinch from any caste in inflicting such definitions. All were equally sinful in his eyes, Duke and peasant alike.

Accepting this, King Louis VII of France went to the Abbot Bernard, prostrated himself before him, and begged for guidance and help in the lifting of the excommunication that had been passed upon him. What must he do to atone for his sins? How best might he avoid the eternity of Hell?

Prayer, abstinence, and flagellation! Such was the Abbot Bernard's prescription for the salvation of Louis' soul.

"Forswear the flesh of the temptress!" Such was the Abbot Bernard's answer to the unasked question on my mind. To wit: Can this marriage be saved?

Saving the royal marriage was not his concern. Saving the soul of his King was. The Abbot Bernard made no bones about the fact that he viewed me as a pulchritudinous roadblock on the road to salvation. "Penance!" he prescribed for poor Louis. "Abstain from lust! Pray to God! Do not indulge the flesh, but mortify it!"

In plain talk, this meant separate bedrooms. As a husband, King Louis had never raised the average incidence of coital frequency in Paris, but at least he had deigned to relieve the monotony once a week or so. Now, thanks to the Abbot Bernard, he denied himself this indulgence. And where before my marriage bed had left me merely frustrated, now it left me completely desolate. Thus it was that whilst my husband laid bare his body to the lashings of husky, whip-wielding young priests laying on the mortification under the direction of Abbot Bernard, I became extremely restless.

At first I dealt with this in the manner of wives since time immemorial. I squandered my husband's wealth—surely the world's oldest and most successful attention-getting device. Always the alternative to adultery has been a new wardrobe, or redecorating. Frequently, although intended as alternatives, such steps are merely preludes to the adultery that, after all, always was inevitable. *Oui*, inevitable, for in this wicked world a woman must in the end look out for herself, her own needs. She must look out for number one.

I set about redecorating the castle. This met with howls of protest from Queen Adelaide, who was responsible for the present decor. I asserted my rank—I was Queen of France now, not she!—and drew heavily on the royal treasury for the purchase of expensive, brightly colored tapestries from both Brussels and Persia, for Oriental carpets, for new fireplaces and picture windows. I imported furniture and hired carpenters and masons and changed not only the interior of the castle, but its structure as well. And then the bills began pouring in to the Royal Exchequer.

Louis summoned me. "You will bankrupt the treasury if you continue!" he lectured me.

"A man's castle is his home," I reminded him. "I'm just trying to make it nice for you."

"Make it any nicer and it will belong to the banks instead of to the Crown," he remonstrated. "These are hard times, Eleanor. We must all pull in our cinches. We must all bite the shaft of the arrow."

"You certainly have a way with words, Louis," I granted.

"The people are hungry. They are grumbling. They blame the Crown. Your extravagances are not helping our image, Eleanor."

"Give them a war," I suggested. "It will take their minds off their troubles. My father used to say there was nothing like a good war for solving shortages. It thins out the ranks of the consumers, he used to say."

"I just gave them a war." Louis shuddered. "And now I am whipped nightly by husky young priests as penance. I made God angry with my war."

"Then make a holy war," I advised. "That will please God. Make a Crusade."

"Strangely enough, that is the advice of the Abbot Bernard. He thinks that if I can find a reason to lead a Crusade, it will influence the Holy Father to lift my excommunication."

"It will also provide opportunity for plunder to our grumbling peasants." As ever, I viewed things practically. "They will be able to rape and kill with free consciences, for the victims will not be Christians. It will take their minds off royal expenditures."

"I will think on it," Louis promised. "As yet I have no good reason to mount a Crusade, but if one should arise—

Meanwhile, Eleanor, the rabble's mind remains very much on royal expenditures, so kindly watch your household budget.''

"You have my word," I told him. I kept it too. I drew no more on the royal treasury for renovations. I halted all redecorations of the castle. Instead, I spent the King's gold—the taxes and tolls and levies imposed on his subjects—on the most lavish new wardrobe that Paris could provide. The only things a *fille* can really be sure of, *mes amis,* are the clothes on her back!

"The trappings of a hussy, a harlot, a wanton, and a spendthrift to boot!" was the not-unexpected judgment of my mother-in-law.

I ignored it. But I could not ignore the disapproval of the Abbot Bernard. His influence over my husband, the King, was too pervasive. And despite the fact that I was his Queen, he minced no words in his disapproval of me.

"Lilith incarnate! The soft flesh of the serpent encased in the trappings of Jezebel!" His eyes burned with loathing. His voice thundered with condemnation. "Such women in such trappings lure the flesh of men to burn in Hell for all eternity! Beware!"

"I don't think Abbot Bernard likes me," I suggested to Louis.

"He is shy of all women. He fears the trap 'twixt their thighs. 'Twas fashioned by the Devil, he says."

"And you agree?"

"No more expensive clothes and jewels, Eleanor," Louis ordered, avoiding the question. "We can't afford it. Spend no more."

Spend no more! He meant gold, my royal husband, but so long as he followed his misogynist Abbot, it was another sort of spending he denied me. But I was Eleanor, daughter of William of Aquitaine, granddaughter of the Troubadour, descendant of Charlemagne himself. They were all lusty men, and though I was a woman, I was of their blood. Spend no more, indeed! Enough of monastic husbands and priestly judges! My thighs were not formed to circle empty air, my pussy to encapsulate no other lover save Merry Hand! If my husband would live with me as brother, then needs be I must quickly find another to serve me as husband! Hear me, *mes amis! Vous faites ce que vous avez à faire!* You do what you have to do.

Decision creates its own opportunity. A few days after my conversation with Louis, on a balmy summer afternoon I strolled in my garden until I came to the wall from which I could observe the activities of the teachers and students who congregated on the bridge leading to the Left Bank. Immediately my attention was attracted by a loud altercation which was taking place. The disputants were the same two that had attracted my interest once before. As on the first occasion, they were debating the nature of the affair between Héloïse and Abélard.

"Spiritual!" the teacher insisted. "Not of the flesh!"

"Hot and sticky and filled with lust!" the Gascon poet countered. "Their fucking tilted the world!"

Tilted the world?

I summoned a servant. "That young man." I indicated the argumentative Gascon. "Fetch him here to me."

Tilted the world!

"What do you mean?" I asked the question of the poet as he prostrated himself before me on the leafy floor of the garden, the position dictated by his humble station and my exalted queenliness.

"Majesty?" He cocked his head and snared his scarlet cockade in a low-lying branch.

"Leave us." I dismissed the servant. "Abélard and Héloïse," I told the Gascon. "You said they tilted the world with their lovemaking."

"No, Majesty. I said they tilted the world with their fucking." His cinnamon eyes twinkled up at me.

"You are impudent!" I stared him down. "Very well, then." I deigned to laugh. "Their fucking." The word tripped strangely from my tongue—strangely and titillatingly. "What did you mean by that?"

"I meant that it was pure hot, wet, raunchy lust. That silly lecturer would have us believe that it was nonphysical, ethereal. His silliness would romanticize all the juice out of it."

"But you won't convince him, nor he you. Why do you bother going on with the argument? From my observation, it is in its third or fourth week with no change of position on either side."

"Third or fourth month, to be accurate, Majesty."

"Then what profit in pursuing it?"

"I'm a Gascon!" He had perfect white teeth and now he flashed me the smile of a buccaneer. "I believe in lust. I am constitutionally unable to stand idly by while it is bad-mouthed."

"What is your name?" I asked him.

"Bernard de Ventadour, Highness."

"You may rise, Bernard de Ventadour, before the extreme subjection of your posture renders you a crookback."

"I would wear my disability as a badge of pride attesting my obeisance to my Queen."

"Spoken like a true poet." I was amused.

"I am a poet, Majesty."

"I know. And doubtless that is why you speak in metaphor. Love that tilts the world, indeed!" I fluttered my fan and surveyed him over the top of it with inquisitive green eyes.

For a poet, he was sturdy, neatly built, not at all frail. He turned a fine leg, stood straight, and was muscular of thigh. His chest bespoke sinews and was in keeping with the wideness of his shoulders. His bottom cheeks were the sort that Petronilla and I used to giggle over not so many years before and squeeze our hands in hunger for and describe in whispers as "cute" and "virile" and having "more bounce to the ounce." Had we not been girls then, we surely would have gone on to wonder if the flesh between his legs lived up to the proclamation of his buttocks. I wondered now.

As to the face of this poet, this Gascon, this Bernard de Ventadour, it also was at odds with his literary image. It was leathery with outdoor living, creased with sunlight although still young, and hewn more like virile crag than cerebral visage. On the other hand, it was a road map of emotions. The constant flickering of its expressions made love to me from the moment he stood erect, made love to me as openly and clearly as if he had laid hands on my royal person.

"Love that tilts the world!" Bernard de Ventadour repeated now, his voice confirming the bold expressions. "That is what Abélard and Héloïse had. But that ass on the bridge would end such love forever by giving theirs the lie."

"And you?" My voice quavered. My breasts were heaving and pushing up from their bodice toward his insolent appraisal.

"I am a true poet. I am a Gascon. Such love is the only thing that makes life worthwhile." His hot stare seared the clothes from my body.

"And it tilts the world. But you can't know that for a fact."

"It would take two to know it," he admitted. "Two in love like Abélard and Héloïse. And they could not be sure until after the world tilted. Still—" He took a bold step toward me. "How shall two people know if they do not put it to the test?"

"And if they are mistaken?" I was trembling. I sat down abruptly on a low tree branch.

"Then what will they have lost, save time?" The poet stood directly in front of me now with his arms spread wide as if in explanation of the obvious or in supplication or in demand.

"I am a married woman," I heard myself saying weakly.

"Héloïse had problems too. They did not dissuade Abélard."

"I am the Queen. My husband is the King of France."

"Then he should have me killed for what I am about to do. And that would be a kinder fate than the castration inflicted on Abélard." So saying, the poet enfolded me in strong arms and brought his mouth to mine.

How shall I describe what followed? My experience had been limited to my deflowering by a too-quick lout in a stable, and my marriage bed, even when active, was overshadowed by the inhibitions of my guilt-ridden husband. Bernard was different. Did we, like Héloïse and Abélard, tilt the world? Judge for yourself, *mes amis*!

The full demand of his belief was behind Bernard's kiss. Even as his thrilling tongue stiffened and probed my warm, sucking mouth, one of his hands fell to my lap where I sat on the tree branch and urged my thighs to part under the silk of my summer gown. Slim-hipped, he stepped between my knees and remained intimately wedged there whilst the kiss was brought to a conclusion that included the caressing of my heaving breasts both through the material of my gown and inside my bodice. My green eyes were smoldering, I knew, when I opened them at the end of the kiss.

Without a word, the Gascon led me into the concealment of a grove of trees. Here he lifted my breasts from the bodice of my gown and surveyed them. "Beautiful!" he pronounced. "Lovely."

My breasts had grown in marriage. They were larger than in girlhood, but still pear-shaped, still tipping skyward with nipples that were long and red and hard. Bernard bent his head and licked one of these nipples now with the tip of his tongue. The sensation tickled and laughter bubbled to my lips. Then he licked the nipple with the length of his tongue. It felt like velvet. A thrill ran down from my breast to my belly and my pussy. A spurt of honey disgraced the tight crotch of the drawers under my camise.

"Kiss it," I sighed. I clasped my hands over the back of his strong neck.

He kissed it. Then, softly, he sucked it. Then he sucked the nipple more demandingly. Finally he opened his mouth wide and engulfed my white, heaving breast.

"*Oui!*" I was beside myself. "Ahh! That feels marvelous! Suck harder! Harder!" My nails raked his back and dug into his chunky, muscular derriere. Impatiently, I pushed his tunic out of the way and tore at the material of his drawers.

Still sucking and biting my naked breast, Bernard reached down with both hands and found the hem of my gown and raised it. He tucked it into the girdle at my waist. My camise was similarly disposed of. Then he pulled down my drawers.

"Oh, love!" I moaned as his hand caressed my naked belly. *"Chéri!"* I pushed it down farther with my own hand and felt his fingers tangle in the moist silk triangle of copper curls. "Darling!" My pussy rose and the lips opened to meet his questing hand.

I was standing against a tree, my heaving breasts hanging nakedly out of the bodice of my gown, my lower garments raised and tucked to lay bare my shapely, quivering thighs, my squirming belly, my honeyed cunt. I was leaning hard on my back against the trunk and my legs, wide-spread in front of me, were bent at the knee with the feet dug in to give me leverage. My pussy, the fulcrum of my body, was tilted upward. Because of Louis' program of atonement under the supervision of the Abbot Bernard, I had been long without a man. I was frankly open and sticky with desire.

Bernard felt it. His hand squeezed my soft hairy pussy as he would a ripe plum. He continued squeezing it as he kissed me again. His finger slid up its tight, syrupy surface in rhythm with his tongue invading my mouth. I sucked his tongue with eager lips. I clutched his finger with eager lips.

"I want you!" I moaned when the kiss was over. "I want you now!"

"Yes, Majesty!" The poet stepped back and quickly

removed his tunic and his drawers. His cock sprang free—naked, red, stiff, and quite cruel looking.

"Oh!" I gasped. I reached for it with both trembling hands.

He stepped into me, tight between my legs. His prick wedged between my thighs, the shaft hot and hard against the lips of my pussy but without penetrating it. The Gascon reached behind me and caressed the burning cheeks of my plump, pert, bouncing derriere. He reached under the cheeks and pulled his prick through between my legs so that the head stuck out the other side, under the cheeks of my ass. I craned my head about and looked at it over my shoulders. Holding the bright red, wedge-shaped head of his cock, Bernard sawed back and forth against my pussy until I was awash with the thrilling sensations this provided.

"Awash" is exactly the right word, *mes amis*. This erotic maneuver had pumped honey from my pussy and bathed the shaft of Bernard's cock in it until it glowed. And it pushed my desire to fever pitch.

"Do it!" I begged him. "Fuck me! Put it in me! Fuck me now! Now! NOW!"

Eyes glittering, mighty cock throbbing, the Gascon placed his hands under my burning bottom and raised me. I clutched him around the hips with my knees. I locked my hands around the back of his neck. I pushed forward, kissing him, devouring him with my tongue, digging my burning nipples into his hard chest, forcing my tight pussy onto the impalement of that brutal cock.

"Fuck, Eleanor!" No "Majesty" now! He slammed me back against the tree and rammed his cock into me so hard that I felt as if I should be split in two. And then the fear was gone and what I felt was filled—filled with hot, fucking, hard man-shaft. "Fuck, Eleanor! Fuck! FUCK!"

I fucked. . . .

My legs were at right angles to my hips, so eagerly did I fuck. And the more I fucked, the more eagerly I fucked. Until—

"I SPEND!" I heard myself shrieking. I slapped my open cunt fiercely and wetly against his groin. "I SPEND!" The green, leafy branches spun overhead and my whole being boiled down to the sweet, pulsing orgasm which had seized my cunt, the orgasm which was wrenching my lover's hard cock in every direction even as he continued to fuck me with deep, hard, intense strokes. And then after an ecstatic eternity, it was over. . . .

Only it wasn't. Bernard de Ventadour was still hard. He had refrained from coming with me. Now he proceeded to show me what fucking could be like when two people are not in a hurry.

He bore me to the ground and let me feel his full weight as he penetrated me with a circular, screwing motion that was unlike anything I had ever felt before. His cock seemed to stroke my clitoris in this position. The tip continually probed a spot just behind it that was so sensitive that I spent again before I even knew that I was going to do so.

Still Bernard did not stop. He turned me over. He mounted me as the stallion does the mare. He reached under me and played with the lips of my pussy as he fucked me so. He even worked his finger inside me and played with my clitty. Thus, with his hot balls bouncing against the wide-spread cleft of my derriere, I came yet again.

And it was not over even then. He lay on his back and

84

lowered my poor, sore pussy over the magnificent tower of his hard-on. He fucked me more deeply than ever then, and I screamed that it hurt and begged him not to stop, never to stop. The perspiration poured off us. I sank my teeth into his shoulder and spread my cunt over his belly and, rocking, started to come again. This time Bernard seized me by the bottom and held me to him. His prick rose like a volcano erupting. A geyser of scalding man-cream filled my clutching, climaxing cunt. I screamed with the sheer joy of it and squeezed to claim as much of this bounty as I could. He came for a long time, and I came with him. We fucked until we were dry.

And did the world tilt?

You bet your ass it did, *mes amis*!

I was in love. Bernard de Ventadour, poet of Gascony, had proved his point beyond any doubt as far as I was concerned. Love was physical! Love was lust! And I loved him for it! Indeed, while he would not be my only lover, he would always be the love of my life, my one true love!

Feeling this way as our affair progressed, I tended to be somewhat foggy of mind in his absence. Thus it took me a moment to absorb the full import of Louis' news a few weeks later when he imparted it to me. "What's that, dear?" was my first reaction. I made the effort and focused on him. "What did you say?"

"The Pope has pardoned me!" Louis was happier than I'd ever seen him. "The excommunication has been lifted. My soul has been saved."

"Oh, good." I patted his cheek. "How nice for you, dear. However did you persuade His Holiness?" I remembered to ask as an afterthought.

"I didn't. The Abbot Bernard did. He convinced His Holiness that I would be just the man to lead a Second Crusade if I were restored to the Church."

"A Second Crusade? But what reason do you have for a Second Crusade, Louis?"

"None, Eleanor. To be honest, none. But the arrangement with the Pope is that I must find a reason. And once I've found it, the Second Crusade will be launched with me in command."

And that, *mes amis*, is how history was made!

Chapter Four

Of all the tragedies that may befall woman, Love is the greatest. Plagues pass and earthquakes settle, but Love's dull ache is a lifelong affliction. Cupid's arrow is unremovable. Its piercing leaves a wound that festers to the grave. So it was with me and my love for my troubadour, my poet, my Eros, my wild and crazy, jealous Gascon, Bernard de Ventadour.

As they say, *mes amis*, I had it bad and that ain't good.

From the first overpowering joining of our flesh, we were lost, the two of us. True love is a welding of physical ecstasy to emotion, of tactile lust to a sensuality that for lack of definition can only be characterized as spiritual. It is rare, it is binding, and it contains within it the inevitability of its own destruction.

True love is a treasure and a treasure must be guarded. The sentinels of carnal emotions are the twin demons of possessiveness and jealousy. They are cannibals, these demons. They devour the very relationship they have been assigned to protect.

Did Bernard's cinnamon eyes wander ever so casually over the bosom of another? My long, sharp fingernails poised instantly to pluck them from their sockets! And if the act should extinguish the light of love in their depths, then better a blind lover than a faithless one! Indeed, better no lover at all in this welter of emotions called Love, this Gordian tangle the ages have ne'er been able to free of their snarl, this knot which, rather than share, we would perforce destroy with the sword we call Pride.

Hear me, women! If your lover has eyes for another, pluck them out!

And Bernard? Did his poet's sensibilities lend more perspective to his love? Alas, no. He was every bit as wild, as irrational, as violent in his possessiveness and jealousy as I was in mine.

"You flirted!" he would shout, pinning me to the bed, piercing me, snarling his anger as he pounced his lust.

"I only smiled at the man!" I would try in vain to cool his fury with a long, clutching, loving roll of my groin under his angry weight.

"You batted your eyes at him!"

" 'Twas but a mote beneath the lid." With affection and understanding, I would try to temper the furious sword imbedded in my scabbard.

"You gestured in such manner as to offer him clear sight of the naked upper half of your left breast whence it parted from your bodice!"

"An accident!" Warm and wet and clutching, my pussy would do its loving utmost to reassure him. "Such movement was never by design. The fellow appeals to me not at all.''

''You are devious, Eleanor! Hot of blood! Faithless!'' And Bernard would explode deep inside me, rage and jealousy but adding greater force to the release of his love—and of mine.

Thus were we both caught in the trap of our passion. The more ecstatic our trysts, the more unbridled our lovemaking, the more we each of us regarded the other as out of control and possessed of indiscriminate lust. We each saw the other as possessed by an experimental erotic spirit, one that would seek new partners as surely as we explored each other with new and varied means of titillation.

Indeed, such uninhibited experimentation created its own problems. Jealousy construed it as evidence of infidelity. For example, there was the night that I suggested to my lover that he hold me by the thighs with my ankles on his shoulders whilst I supported myself on my hands and was propelled about the room by the force of his prick entering and leaving my pussy in this upside-down position.

''Who taught you this?'' he demanded as he readily acceded, his angrily thrusting cock providing new thrills to my uptilted pussy in this unaccustomed position.

''Nobody taught me!'' I gasped, walking on my hands as I fucked. ''I conceived it myself.''

But he didn't believe me. ''Your husband, I'll wager!'' His heavy, hairy balls bounced furiously against my buttocks.

''My husband, the King, still atones for the slaughter he wreaked,'' I reminded Bernard. My cock-filled bottom was vibrating with a sensual hum, and the blood was rushing to my head. "We live together as brother and sister."

"With incest rampant among royalty, that is small reassurance!" He brought me up against a wall, bent me fully double, and holding my hips, proceeded with some urgency to the finale of the scene.

"Mon Dieu!" I panted, squirming. "If I wanted my husband, I would have him! I reject him for you! Is that not obvious?"

"No. Not obvious." He pounded away at my wide-stretched, welcoming quim. "Just last night you kissed him in front of me."

"I kissed him?" The blood rushing to the tingling nipples of my upside-down breasts, my onrushing orgasm rising to meet his down-pumping prick—the situation made it difficult to concentrate on our conversation. Then I remembered. "On the cheek. I kissed Louis on the cheek."

"Your lips were parted." The ridge of jism gathering along his imbedded shaft was palpable.

"Nonsense!" I bayed, starting to come. "The whole court was present. I was but greeting my husband, the King, with a kiss on the cheek. How can you be jealous of that?"

"You are wanton!" He exploded deep inside of me and kept pumping hotly, savagely. "You kissed your husband in front of me! You insulted me!" And geysers of wondrous man-cream filled my delirious quim.

Well, *mes amis*, I do not say that it made any sense at all. I only say that this is the way it was. My lover, whom I adored, was constantly insecure, insufferably possessive, and unreasonably jealous. Love ne'er was different, nor will it ever be.

Bernard too had it bad, and that wasn't good.

Meanwhile, my husband, to whom I gave very little thought and who more than matched his neglect regarding me, had been provided with a most unlikely excuse for the Crusade he wished to launch. It is important here that I pause to make distinction between the excuse for a Crusade and the reasons for it. The reasons for a Crusade never vary. They are as follows:

1) Loot. It is both immoral and illegal to steal from one's neighbors, one's fellow Christians, but it is ethical and licit, as well as highly profitable, to invade a far-off heathen land and pillage the pagans.

2) Sex. Rape, adultery, and orgies are considered destabilizing to the home community and upsetting to family structure, but as outlets for soldiers bringing Christ to the infidel, such activities are looked upon as merely the high-spirited and inevitable outlets for pressures imposed on men serving their country and their God far from home.

3) Conquest. Territory is the measure of a monarch's greatness; colonies are the jewels in his crown; the occupation of non-Christian lands and the exploitation of their peoples makes for a better standard of living at home and thus a more secure crown.

4) Killing. Men lust to kill. It is a release from their daily misery, yet the killing of one Christian by another is a sin, and so it is necessary to vent the appetite upon those who have not accepted Christ.

5) Escape. The nagging wife, the demanding employer, the bill collector, the whining offspring, the cock's crow ushering in ennui—all these comprise responsibility of one sort or another, while war, a Crusade, offers freedom from

decision-making, the opportunity to travel, a general sense of release.

Such are the reasons for war, for colonization of pagan lands, for the Holy Crusades. But they will not do for an excuse. No, no! History will not honor such justification. My husband, King Louis, needed—as past, present, and future leaders always need and often provide for themselves—an incident. In Louis' case, one was provided for him.

Forty years earlier, the First Crusade had ended with Christian occupation of large chunks of Turkey, Syria, and the Holy Land itself. This Christian occupation had also fallen heavily on Christians, for when this area was not Allah's, which is to say part of Islamic territory, it was Byzantine, which is to say Greek Orthodox. Nevertheless, the Pope installed Christian rulers from France and Germany and Spain and even far-off England to reign over these captured provinces in the name of Holy Mother Church of Rome. These satraps maintained their own troops, paid for by levies upon the territories they occupied, in order to enforce their authority. Thus was a pattern established which will doubtless stretch out over the future into eternity.

Over these forty years, the peoples of the occupied territories had frequently rebelled against the colonizers. Home rule and the restoration of their own religion to a position of primacy in their own lands were constant rallying cries. Usually these local uprisings fizzled out after one or two brutal encounters with the occupying troops. The rebellions were hardly cause for so much as a raised eyebrow back in the capitals of Europe.

Recently, however, there had been a rebellion of a more

serious dimension. The Muslims had launched a *Jihad*—a holy war—to drive out the demon Christians. First they laid siege to the city of Damascus. Then they marched through Syria to Edessa, capital of the First Crusader State, and captured it.

The fall of Edessa presented two serious threats to Christian dominance over the region—one immediate, one ultimate. The ultimate threat was that the Muslims would overrun Jerusalem and reclaim their own Holy Land from the Christians. The immediate threat was to Antioch, which lay between Edessa and Jerusalem.

Not just the Holy Land itself, but the entire lush and profitable region conquered by the warriors of the First Crusade was in danger of falling back into the hands of the native Muslims if Antioch should fall. It was the most strategically positioned city in the region, possibly one of the most strategically positioned cities in the entire world. From Roman times it had been known as "the Gateway to the East," and it was military gospel that he who controlled Antioch controlled all Araby.

The city sprawled on the left bank of the Orontes River in southeast Turkey. From this point the river runs down a valley some sixteen miles to the Mediterranean. This valley is guarded by Mount Pieria and Mount Cassius. Between them. the only entrance to the region in a twenty-mile range of impassable mountains is the Bailan Pass. It is this crucial pass which geography has placed under Antioch's control. From here there is easy access via Cilicia and Asia Minor to the west. Likewise, there are commercial and military routes to the east. To the south are the lush vineyards and grain-producing plains of the Coele-Syrian area the natives call "Lebanon." To the northeast are the valleys of the upper Euphrates and the plateaus of Armenia. But these trade routes, these roads for marching armies, all lead in and out of Antioch. There is no way of bypassing the city if one is going from one direction to another. Thus Antioch is the key to the treasure chest, whether it be the one raided by Crusaders eastward bound, or Muslims sacking Europe.

But enough of geography. Let us speak of irony. Antioch was threatened. This was the excuse Louis needed to launch his Crusade, the Second Crusade. He would raise troops and march to its rescue and reap much plunder as he once again brought the cross of Jesus to the infidel. And in rescuing Antioch, he would also be rescuing my Uncle Raymond, whom he himself had banished there! Indeed, the very first rallying cry of the Second Crusade would be "Save Christian Prince Raymond of Antioch!"—my uncle, my sister's seducer, the scandalous adulterer of Poitiers.

"But I don't give a *merde* about Raymond of Antioch," Bernard de Ventadour protested when I first broached the subject of the Crusade to him.

"Don't you want to serve God?" *Oui!* I fear I had been carried away by the nonstop rhetoric of the recruitment campaign being carried on by Church and Crown.

"I don't want to serve him up my body all porcupined with infidel arrows!"

"You owe fealty to your King."

"I'm sleeping with his wife, for God's sake. Fealty would be the height of hypocrisy."

"To your country, then. You are an able-bodied man. The time has come for you to ask what you can do for your country."

"I know what I can do for my country. I can lie low. I

can stay out of the way. Believe me, Eleanor, I would make a terrible soldier. I don't take to hardship well at all. I whine a lot. I get seasick crossing the Seine. I dislike exclusively male company. I'm not one of the boys. I throw up if I drink too much. I'm squeamish about mass rape. I get very frightened at the prospect of being hurt or killed.''

"Are you a coward, Bernard?" I demanded.

"I'm a poet. I stand in opposition to my entire society. What could be braver?"

"I mean in terms of battle. Physically. Are you a physical coward?"

"Oui." He looked me in the eye. "I am."

"I love you!" I burst out laughing and threw my arms around him. "I really love you!"

"Then let your husband go off to lead his Crusade and cease trying to influence me to join him. Actually, this is a heaven-sent opportunity for us to be together in his absence."

"You don't understand," I told him. "I have to go with Louis on the Crusade."

My beloved poet stared at me. "In God's name, why?" he asked finally.

"I have to set an example for the other ladies so that they too will accompany their lords."

"But why should they?"

"Louis wants this to be a moral Crusade. He has only recently had his excommunication lifted and become eligible for salvation. He wants this Crusade to be an exercise in Christian virtue. He wants wives, not camp followers, connubial bliss, not rape and orgy."

"Under that crown lies the reasoning mechanism of a madman!" Bernard dared speak the treason. "Knights go on Crusades just so that they can get away from their wives and rape enemy women and indulge in orgies. Even if he makes them bring their wives along, they will find a way to indulge their lusts. And what about the common soldier? Is he to bring his wife as well? Impose this on him, and you'll not have many recruits.''

"The King does not concern himself with the souls of common soldiers. They will have their camp followers. They will be free to defile the pagan women as they will.''

"A true Christian, your husband, the King. Not egalitarian perhaps, but then he is King, and I suppose that would be asking too much.''

"What I am trying to say to you, Bernard, is that like it or not, I am Queen and I am involved in this Crusade. I am also in love with you. I don't want us to be parted. I want you to come on the Crusade too.''

"Poets don't belong on Crusades. We're bleeders, one and all.''

"Seriously, Bernard.''

"Seriously—'' He sighed. "Poets are romantics. They die for love. Who else is that crazy? All right, I'll go.''

When he made this decision, my lover could rest secure that it would be a long time before he was called upon to implement it. Popes may decree Crusades. Kings may lead them. Queens may lend support. But it is the common man who must fight them, and the first battle, the first campaign is to recruit large numbers of such commoners to the cause.

"Holy war! Holy war!'' The King's heralds rode up and down the countryside proclaiming the Crusade. "Join the holy war and save your soul! Join the holy war and share the infidel booty!''

"A Crusade, it seems, must be sold like the latest elixir preventing impotence," Bernard said cynically.

"The people are simple folk. The approach to them must be simple. It must appeal to them on an emotional rather than an intellectual level."

"What you mean is it must appeal to their fear of Hell and their greed for gold."

Bernard de Ventadour was right, of course. Nowhere was this more apparent than at the rally held to raise support for the Crusade at the hilltop above the small town of Vezelay. Here the Abbot Bernard worked over the assembled crowd with an evangelical fervor that seemed to rebound like thunder from the surrounding hillsides. Thin but tall, the holy man hovered over them, his tunic blazoned with the scarlet cross of the crusader.

"Unite for Christ!" It seemed a miracle in itself that such booming tones could emerge from such a frail body. "Renounce the pettiness that turns you one against the other. Join hands in Christ! Link arms in holy war!

"Take the cross!" he continued. "God will forgive you your sins! Take the cross! You will have your everlasting reward! Take the cross! Heaven shall be yours! Take the cross! Take the cross!"

King Louis himself was first to succumb to the emotional fervor. He flung himself at the feet of the Abbot, his royal face awash with tears. He took the cross.

By prearrangement, I pledged next. I knelt before the Abbot (who detested me and openly considered me to be the very embodiment of an Aquitainian Jezebel) and swore to die for Jesus if need be. Most important, I pledged both the wealth and manpower of Aquitaine to the cause.

Our example soon had the desired effect. "Give us

crosses!" The throng pressed in on the Abbot, borne on a tide of emotion to enlist in this holiest of Holy Crusades. "Give us crosses!" First the local aristocracy and their ladies, and then the peasants claimed their heavenly right to die for Jesus. The Abbot ran out of wooden crosses to give to those who committed themselves and took off his cloak and cut it up to provide cloth crosses to the unending crowd.

It was impressive. A faucet had been turned and would not be turned off. With God's blessing, the blood ran hot for battle.

The sun started to set, and Louis muttered to me that we should have started earlier. Now those who had not yet joined would disperse. By tomorrow they would have had time to think, and their passion for the Crusade would have cooled. It would probably not be possible to revive it.

I had a sudden inspiration. I slipped away from the rally and gathered my ladies about me. I commanded a captain of the guard to round up white horses for us to ride. Then we all of us donned crusader tunics with blazing scarlet crosses on the front of them. We put on high, amazon-style gilt boots and helmets with plumes. Then we unsheathed our swords, mounted our horses, and rode back to the crowd, which was already beginning to disperse.

Waving our blades and screaming, "Death to the infidel! Glory to God!" we soon had the crowd's enthusiasm refired. Indeed, whenever some possible recruit would try to slip away, one of my amazons would ride him down and herd him back toward the Abbot. Thus we were both an inspiration and a threat in the service of recruiting warriors for the Crusade.

That was the first time my amazons rode. Their appearance caused widespread comment. The Abbot Bernard denounced us as "sirens on horseback, servants of Satan!" But in truth, we served Christ well that day.

It would not be the only time we amazons rode. The next time we might more justly deserve the Abbot's censure. Certainly we would be more brazen than that dusk at Vezelay. But then we would also be a lot more deadly!

"You and the Abbot are an effective combination," Bernard de Ventadour told me. "He terrifies them with Hell and you arouse them by bouncing around on horseback like the Furies. You could sell them the alchemists' formula for turning dross to gold, let alone a cause as holy as a Crusade."

"Strange, is it not?" I didn't disagree with his estimation. "And yet the Abbot truly loathes me."

"Why?"

"My womanhood, I think. It threatens him in some way I don't quite understand. He looks at me and feels a stirring. He believes that feeling to be the work of the Devil. And so he would burn me at the cross to save his own soul." I shuddered. "I'll be glad to get away from him."

"Away from him?" Bernard regarded me quizzically.

"*Oui*. I am to go to Aquitaine to raise arms and men and money for the Crusade. The Abbot will go to Germany to rally the Hun. Louis will stay here in France. And you—"

"And me?"

"Will come with me, darling. You will, won't you? It's truly a heaven-sent opportunity. I can show you Aquitaine, which is paradise on earth. We can be alone, far from my husband. We can make love. . . ."

99

"I don't know." Bernard frowned a mock frown. "I have heard that Aquitainians eat Gascons for breakfast."

"Only Aquitainian Queens," I assured him. "And you'll like that. Truly you will."

I was right. He did.

Our sojourn in Aquitaine, however, was more than merely a lovers' idyll. Given my assignment and pressures of time to assemble the Crusade, I was kept quite busy in Aquitaine. I put in many a long day in the service of the cause.

My purpose was twofold. I recruited manpower to join the Crusade and to fight it. And I raised money to finance the holy war.

I was fortunate. My father had been very popular among his vassal knights in Aquitaine. They shifted their loyalty to me unquestioningly and took pride in deeming themselves vassals of their young female Duchess, as well as being her protectors. When I made it clear that I would be going on the Crusade, my knights were quick to rally around the cause. "For God and Eleanor!" they chanted. And if privately their eyes had glittered at my promises that they should have liberal shares of the Arabian loot, I nevertheless did not doubt the sincerity of their fealty to me.

They had it in their power, these feudal knights of Aquitaine, to press their serfs into military service merely by their authority as landholders. A peasant who balked at being so impressed might be whipped or put in the stocks for some indeterminate period until he changed his mind. Or he might merely be put off the knight's estate, free to wander but without means of securing food or a roof over his head, since he would have no satisfactory explanation to offer a prospective master for why his previous master had expelled him from his property. Thus the support of a knight was tantamount to the enlistment of the men under his command into the Crusader army.

Nevertheless, I wanted more than fatalistic and possibly surly compliance with the feudal caste system. I wanted an enthusiastic rank and file to guarantee Aquitainian primacy in this mixed European army. Toward this end, I took an egalitarian approach and campaigned among the peasantry themselves for support for the holy cause.

"God needs you!" I told them, my green eyes shining, my auburn curls tossing in the breeze. "I, your Duchess, need you! I will fight for God beside my husband, King Louis of France. Will I have the loyal Aquitainian salt of the earth to protect my flanks in the heat of battle?"

"You will!" they would roar. "For Christ and Eleanor!" they would roar. And then, among themselves, not so very different after all from their masters, the great unwashed of Aquitaine would whisper of plunder and of how Arabian houris wore silken trousers that were slit at the crotch.

With Aquitainian fervor thus stirred up, the task of raising Aquitainian gold for the cause was made easier. Under my sponsorship, fairs were held outside towns and cities all across Aquitaine. Baked goods were sold, as were hand-sewn garments and blankets and shawls. Games were played. Minstrels sang and traveling troupes put on pantomime shows and short Greek plays. There were jugglers and fire-eaters, clowns, and acrobats. And the proceeds from all of these activities went into the growing coffers financing the Crusade.

I also organized tournaments in which knights vied with each other at a variety of manly arts—some of them deadly. Indeed, I shudder to remember how many young men lost life and limb competing in these contests with lance and battle ax, mace and sword. The dusted floors of the makeshift arenas would be slippery with spilled blood and the defecation of terrified and dying horses. Years later, I would hear romantic ballads about the gallantry of knights tilting in gentlemanly jousts, and I would remember with some cynicism a truth that was as brutal and bloody as the fiercest battles to come in the Holy Land.

Yet it must be said that these tournaments raised far more money for the Second Crusade than the fairs or any other activities. The populace thronged to pay admission to watch the nobles maim and kill one another. There was, I suspect, a message there, if one had but the wit to fathom it.

Some of the money I raised came from Aquitainian institutions. Emulating my father, I added a "crusader surtax" to the tax on the yield customarily paid to me by the estates of Aquitaine. I imposed a levy on wine sellers, overcoming their objections with pointed references to patriotism. I also granted special privileges related to the raising of funds through fairs and other celebrations to the churches and monasteries of Aquitaine in return for outright donations to the war chest of the Crusade. The Bishops of the abbeys could scarce refuse to make such a contribution to such a holy cause, particularly when I granted them in exchange the means to recoup the gold donated.

The net results of all my efforts were more than satisfactory. Aquitaine became virtually the leader of the Second Crusade. We supplied more manpower than any other area in Europe. And we financed more of the cost of the venture than any of the other participants, as well. (Of course, what this meant, under the terms of the Crusade, was that Aquitaine would have a greater share in the treasure we brought back from the East.)

By the end of my tour of Aquitaine, our success was both obvious and gratifying. It inspired us all the more to make the most of our opportunity before we departed Aquitaine for France. In this spirit I made a side trip to call on a rather recent vassal knight of mine, one Geoffrey of Rancon.

This Geoffrey's father had but recently died, and he had just succeeded to the ownership and rule of his domains. I had no recollection of either father or son. Still, I was his Duchess and it was only politic to make his acquaintance and to also make the attempt to enlist him in the Crusade. Toward this end my entourage, headed by myself and my lover, Bernard de Ventadour, proceeded to the castle of Rancon.

The young knight who greeted us looked very familiar to me, but I could not think why he should. He was garbed in the usual finery of noblemen, which is to say dead-animal skins and a fashionably short tunic of purple velvet and a long-sleeved gambeson of quilted leather. These ultra-manly accouterments stressed the solidity of his physique, which was close to the ground and wide with muscle without being fat. A faded, dull-red birthmark ran jaggedly down one of his red, rural cheeks. He greeted us with a sparsity of words, but then I had noticed before that these country lords were not given to either sophisticated greeting or conversation.

I was surprised when after I had retired to my chambers, a servant came with a note from my host, asking an immediate audience with me. It was late for such a visit. Geoffrey of Rancon had not seemed the sort of knight to behave with any degree of impetuosity regarding his Queen. Curious, I sent back word that I would receive him. Then I put on a robe over my camise and awaited him.

Shortly, he arrived. "My Queen." His lips lingered as he knelt to kiss the back of my hand.

"Sir Geoffrey." I indicated that he might be seated. "The hour is late," I pointed out. "If we might get directly to the reason for your visit—?"

"To rut."

"Well!" I gasped. "That is certainly direct enough. But what makes you think, good sir, that—?"

"Highness!" His voice was chiding and he had no hesitation in interrupting me. His attitude conveyed that he had some right—

"You!" I gasped. Suddenly memory had come flooding back in on me. That ugly jagged birthmark on his cheek! "That Geoffrey! You're that Geoffrey!"

"Of course, Highness. You cannot have forgotten one who played so crucial a role in your life."

"You deflowered me!" I gave utterance to the memory.

"With your willing compliance, Highness. So willing, indeed, that some might have termed the event a seduction of the male."

"But you were a stable boy!" I was bewildered.

"No, Highness. A bedraggled traveler, but not a stable boy."

"You dressed like a peasant and behaved like an oaf!"

"It was my father's conceit that we should tour the countryside in such fashion, in order that we should comprehend the peasantry in their actions in absence of their masters. He felt, my father, that this would lend us wisdom in ruling over them.''

"You acted the part very well," I told him dryly. "You looked a lowborn lout, spoke like one, and even took my chastity with the lack of finesse one would expect of an unfeeling peasant.''

"I was very young, Highness. I was quick to lust and had no control. But I am older now, and more experienced, and believe that a debt is owed to both of us by Eros, the debt of a second chance.''

"Why should I believe your boast of amorous improvement?" I wondered.

"But put it to the test and see if it be idle.''

Ah, sisters, *jeunes filles*, surely you will appreciate my feelings in this matter. On the one hand, I had a lover whom I truly loved and to whom I had no reason to be unfaithful. On the other hand, how many times are we granted the opportunity to rewrite the catastrophe of our loss of chastity? The first time is never the best time— never!—but the seamstress Fate who sewed the biology of woman has made it the most important. That importance remains after the event and demands that further adventures blur the disappointment. And what better tool for the blurring than the tool of the original deflowerer?

In this spirit I opened my arms to Geoffrey of Rancon. He came into them. He parted my robe. He pushed down the top of my camise. He kissed my nipples. He removed my clothing and then his own. Then, both of us naked, he took my hand and placed it between his legs. He was hard. He pressed my fingers into the throbbing shaft. He reached for my mound of Venus.

No! I could not go through with it! This Geoffrey of

Rancon, built too close to the ground like a pawing bull, this Geoffrey with his ugly birthmark aflame on his cheek now with his lust, this Geoffrey with the mantle of a nobleman and the touch still of a stable boy—he was not for me! My loins did not want him! First though he may have been, another joining would change nothing. It was Bernard de Ventadour I loved, the poet I wanted, the Gascon for whom my body lusted, for whom my pussy softened with syrup. No! I would stop right now!

"Faithless slut!"

It was too late! Bernard de Ventadour stood in the open doorway to my room, the erection which had preceded him through it already dying with his betrayal. His craggy features were harsh with hurt and rage. The snarl on his face was angrier and uglier than Geoffrey of Rancon's birthmark.

"No!" I moaned. "Wait! I wasn't going to—!"

"This is a rape I am witnessing, I suppose?" His deep poet's voice was heavy with sarcasm.

"What is the meaning of this?" Geoffrey took notice. "How dares this minstrel intrude on his betters in this fashion?"

"He's a poet, not a minstrel," I said dully. "Please, Bernard—" I made one last attempt to save my love before it flew away altogether. "I was going to stop him. I wasn't going to go through with it."

"By your leave, Majesty." He drew himself up, quivering.

"What are you doing here, poet?" Geoffrey demanded. "In the Queen's boudoir?"

"I have had a message from Gascony. An illness in the family. It demands my immediate return home. I have come to beg permission to leave at once."

It was a lie, of course. I recognized that immediately. One does not come to one's Queen to request such permission with a full-fledged erection. Bernard had come to make love to me. "Don't go, Bernard," I pleaded. "Don't be jealous. I love you."

"Duty demands that I go at once!" Bernard insisted, his voice harsh.

"Then begone," Geoffrey snarled. "Interrupt us no further."

"With your permission, Majesty." Bernard bowed and started to back out of the room, closing the door as he went.

"My love!" I sobbed. "Good-bye, my love!"

And then he was gone. My one true love was gone— gone out of my life!

"Let us continue." Geoffrey lifted my camise and parted my thighs.

What difference does it make? I thought to myself dully. I had lost my love and what I did or didn't do with my body was of little importance. Indeed, perhaps Geoffrey's erotic stirrings might relieve the dull ache which filled me.

In the event, such was not the case. He flung my legs up and mounted me much as he had the first time. His prick plunged in and out of my pussy and then, just as I was beginning to feel the stirrings of some sensual response, he briefly spurted his lust into me and removed his épée from my scabbard.

It was just like the first time. That brief spurt, and then it was over. Geoffrey had learned nothing over the intervening years. And as for blurring the disappointment of that first sexual encounter which had deprived me of my chastity, well, the attempt proved no more successful than any other attempt to correct the errors of history.

Perhaps the main accomplishment of the interlude was that Geoffrey of Rancon enlisted in the Crusade. He rode at the head of his troops with us when we started back for Paris. And from then on the jagged red birthmark which marked his cheek was never very far out of my sight.

The day after our caravan crossed the border into France en route to Paris, we crossed paths with the party of the Abbot Bernard returning from Germany. They were proceeding by a rather circuitous route in order that the Abbot might squeeze some donations for the Crusade from various monasteries under his jurisdiction in the west of France. Such was my lovelorn state that I looked on the Abbot—whom I knew detested me and whom I had good reason to be wary of—with more favor than usual for the simple and silly reason that his name, like that of my departed lover, was Bernard.

Since by reason of his Church status, he was the closest to me in rank of anyone in either of our parties, protocol demanded that we take our meals together. Thus it was at dinner that he commented upon my obviously distraught state. "The soul of Your Highness is not at peace," was the way he put it as a servant removed my dish with the food virtually untouched.

"That is true," I sighed.

"Peace may be found only with God," he intoned with his zealot voice. "You must make your peace with Him."

"I know not how."

"You must confess your sins and heartily beg His forgiveness."

"In due time," I sighed.

"Now, Majesty!" The coals of his eyes burned into mine. "I will hear your confession."

"I can't confess to you," I protested. "You detest me. I know that. You think that I am an evil and libertine woman, a Jezebel."

"That is immaterial. I am God's instrument. That is why I see through you to all your wanton appetites, all your lewd practices, all your foul woman's wiles that you use to entrap men—your husband, my King, included—in sin! And that is also why I can grant you absolution from the torture your soul knows because you have not renounced your vile thoughts and desires and practices. I will hear your confession, Eleanor, Duchess of Aquitaine, Queen of France!" he thundered, his thin body quivering like a stiletto that has struck to the heart. "And I will hear it now!"

I was intimidated; I was shaken. I was afraid of the Abbot Bernard, and his contempt for me made me acutely uncomfortable. At the same time, I had been raised in the Church. I believed that ultimately one must seek absolution. I was heartsick and confused at this time. I did not want to spend eternity in Hell, and at least for this moment, in his overwhelming charismatic presence, I truly believed he had the power to consign me to such a fate if I did not do as he wanted.

"Very well." I sank to my knees in front of him. "Forgive me, Father, for I have sinned." I clasped my hands. I bowed my head. I began to recite the litany of my immoral acts.

Standing over me like a stern judge, the Abbot Bernard would from time to time interrupt as if to stress the awfulness of something I had done. "You played with your naked breasts and stroked the nipples so that they would get hard so that you might experience wanton lust?"

"*Oui*. But I was all alone," I added defensively.

"Alone with your God!" His fervor was tangible. "Flaunting your woman's sex before Our Lord!" Under his priestly robes his thin body shook with indignation. "Continue!" he commanded finally in a tone of utter loathing.

I continued. I confessed how I had fantasized to bring myself to orgasm on my wedding night. Again the Abbot interrupted.

"You visualized yourself being sodomized by a beast!" A film of perspiration coated his thin, bony, ascetic forehead.

"*Oui*."

"With your bridegroom beside you in the bed?"

"*Oui!*"

"Oh, perfidious woman!" He pointed a quivering finger down at me. "Continue!" he commanded before I could respond.

I resumed speaking, and soon was describing my first adulterous encounter with Bernard de Ventadour.

"You seduced him on the ground, in the garden?" The Abbot looked feverish.

"On the grass. *Oui*."

"And you enjoyed it. Describe that enjoyment."

"His member filled my woman-place. It excited me beyond belief. My nipples stretched to touch the sun. My pleasure-hole clutched and writhed and vibrated to his lovemaking. I wanted it never to end."

"And that was only the first time?"

"*Oui*. There were many times after that, all equally satisfying. Our love was ripe, complete."

"YOUR LOVE WAS SATAN'S HANDIWORK!" The Abbot was beside himself. "Describe what else you did on these occasions," he demanded, not shouting anymore but his voice nevertheless still vibrating with emotion.

"We experimented with many different positions."

"Such as?"

"He would lie on his back and I would mount him and ride him. In this fashion his organ would penetrate me to the fullest and I would be in control of my orgasm and be able to prolong it deliciously." I squirmed, suddenly wet between my thighs with the memory.

"You must have been possessed by the Devil!" The Abbot Bernard muttered. And yet it was obvious that he too was squirming somewhere deep inside his voluminous robes. "What else did you do?"

"I would position myself on my hands and knees, and he would mount me in the fashion of the beasts in the field."

"Bestiality! Surely proof of Satan's presence!"

"It was a hellish pleasure," I could not help but agree, although my breasts were heaving with the memory.

"And was there sodomy in this position?"

"Sometimes my lover did indeed switch targets. The unexpected thrill was indescribable. Even now I tremble with the memory."

"You are a shameless hussy!" Abbot Bernard shook me by the shoulders. His long, thin fingers stretched to touch the naked half-moons of my breasts above the bodice of my gown.

"Sometimes I sat on his lap, facing him and put it in me myself." I was becoming hysterical with fear of Hell and the need to confess and the arousal of erotic memory. "And sometimes I would take it out and kiss it and lick it and put it in my mouth and suck it. And sometimes—"

"Enough!" His robe was poking out at just about the

level of my nose. "You are possessed, Queen Eleanor! Possessed! We must exorcise this demon in your flesh, this fiend of Hell who resides in your bosom. Stand up!" He drew me to my feet. "I know you are there, Devil!" he thundered. His narrow priest's hands closed over my bodice and squeezed.

I gasped. My pear-shaped breasts rose. The nipples grew hard and hot through the material against his quivering palms.

"I can feel the heat of the hellfire in your breasts," the Abbot Bernard told me. He loosened my bodice and withdrew my breasts so that they rested nakedly on top of my gown. "Instruments of the Devil!" His fingertips accused, poking the firm flesh, then settling against the burning nipples. "We must remove their fire," he told me. And he palmed both long, hard, burning, naked nipples in his hands.

"Ohh!" I moaned. My loins tensed. Deep between my legs my clitoris strained. "Ooh-ooh!"

"I will suck the sinful flame of the incubus from your witch's nipples!" Abbot Bernard announced. And so saying he bent his head and opened his thin-lipped mouth wide and took my poor, gasping breast deep into it.

I felt his tongue lick the hard, quivering nipple, and then trace the sensitive, pink aureole around it. I could not hold back my moans as his mouth worked over the vulnerable white flesh of my breast. Indeed, these moans grew louder as he switched his attentions from one of my breasts to the other.

"I will exorcise the evil spirits! I will cool their heat!" He sucked and licked, licked and sucked.

Without my willing it, my hand dropped to the base of

my belly. This exorcism had me beside myself. I pushed the material of my gown between my legs. I made a pocket for my fist there. I leaned in hard against this fist with my wide-spread, honeyed cunt. I rubbed against it and my moans grew louder.

"O wily Satan, Beast of Hell!" Abbot Bernard realized what I was doing and left off sucking my breasts. "The Fiend has left the lure of your woman's bosom," he explained, "and retreated to the most forbidden place. He knows that by pursuing, I endanger my very soul. But I am unafraid!" And so saying, he sank to his knees in front of me, pried my fist from between my legs and wedged his perspiring, feverish, fervid face there in its place. "I am unafraid!" his voice, muffled now, proclaimed once again. "I will do battle with Satan! I will save your soul, Eleanor!"

"Oui!" I panted, clutching his head to my writhing belly. "Save my soul!" And I savored the hot breath on the silky sporran over my mons veneris as it penetrated my clothing. "Save my soul!"

"The Devil must be driven out!" The Abbot Bernard lifted the hem of my gown all the way to the girdle at my waist and tucked it in there. He tucked up my camise in similar fashion. Then I felt his hot, clutching, perspiring hands on the flesh of my thighs through the drawers I was wearing.

"Pull them down!" I sobbed. "Drive the Devil out!"

"Begone, Satan!" He ripped them off in tatters. His hands seized the hot, squirming cheeks of my bottom and held them firm. His head narrowed the space between my trembling thighs.

And then I felt it! His tongue was on the swollen lips of

my pussy. I opened wide to it and began to laugh hysterically, uncontrollably. My pussy slapped wetly against his questing mouth.

"Laugh, Satan! I have you now!" He buried his mouth in the sensitive pink inner meat of my quim. His tongue slid up my tight, twisting cunt. He sucked deeply of my honey, licking it as he sucked.

"Lick it!" I seized his bony skull. "Suck it!" I crouched to spread my cunt more fully over his mouth. "Eat me! Eat the Devil in me! Devour him!"

I began to jerk so violently that I toppled the Abbot Bernard from his crouching position. I didn't care. I sat on top of his upturned face, pulling the lips of my pussy wide with my fingers so that I might savor the licking and sucking to the fullest. And in this position, screaming, "Begone, Devil! Begone, Devil!" I began to spend over his mouth with long drawn-out, almost painful movements that were so intense that in all truth my savior was in danger of being suffocated.

After a long time, my orgasm ended. I removed my naked, honey-slicked bottom from its perch atop the Abbot's fevered face. He was slow in getting his breath and focusing his eyes.

"Is the Devil exorcised?" he asked finally.

"*Oui*," I assured him. "He is gone."

"He is a strong adversary."

"*Oui*."

"But a worthy one."

"*Oui*."

"I am glad for your sake, Queen Eleanor, that I have banished him."

"*Oui. Merci*, Abbot Bernard." Had he too spent deep

inside those robes of his, I wondered? But I never found out.

Two days later we were in Paris. A month after that, we embarked—King Louis, myself, the Abbot Bernard, Sir Geoffrey of Rancon, and various other luminaries—upon our Crusade. We left with a great deal of fervid piety and religious zealotry. The infidel was the Devil, and we were bringing the purifying sword of God.

I could not help reflecting that more than any other one person, the Abbot Bernard personified this anti-Satan spirit of the Second Crusade!

Chapter Five

From the very beginning, *mes amis*, the Second Crusade was a travesty. As in all military campaigns, its efficacy was determined by the quality of its leadership. Thus, the primary purpose of the blood shed by the rank and file was to wash away the stupid mistakes of these leaders. But they were such bunglers, their errors of judgment so beyond excuse, that the oceans of scarlet shed in the name of Christ were not deep enough to conceal the ineptitude of the Crusader Generals from history.

At the head of all the invading Christian armies was King Louis, my husband, although as a practical matter only the French and Aquitainian forces were under his direct command. Louis considered strategy-planning sessions to be unnecessary because God was on his side by virtue of his having sworn to remain chaste—even to refrain from intercourse with his wife!—until the Crusade was successfully concluded. He was firmly under the influence of that half-crazed religious zealot, the Abbot Bernard, who believed that all infidels must die by burning for the sake of their souls and that therefore it was not necessary to devise tactics to fight this Holy Crusade with lance and sword. King Louis was also swayed by my opinions, but these were worth as little as the Abbot's. I confess that at this point in my life I was but a love-starved and heartsick woman, mourning the foolish loss of the Gascon poet more dear to me than any other could ever hope to be. I was trying to compensate for the empty feelings this loss engendered with a variety of frivolous activities which—to put the most generous face on it—frequently interfered with the process of the Crusade.

Finally, there was the Emperor Conrad of Hohenstaufen. The Abbot Bernard had persuaded Conrad and his Huns to join the Crusade. Supposedly, he and they were under Louis' command, in keeping with the edict of the Pope. But in actuality, Conrad marched separately and commanded his own German army. Indeed, they set out in advance of us, giving rise to the first of our many difficulties.

The attack against the infidel was to be launched from Constantinople, the richest and largest city in eastern Europe and the capital of the Byzantine Empire. The French and German armies were to gather there, along with smaller armies of mercenaries from other Christian countries. The first march of the Crusade, therefore, led through Germany, Hungary, and Bulgaria to the city on the Bosporus which was the gateway to the treasure-filled East.

Emperor Conrad wanted first chance at that treasure. He had joined the Crusade because he foresaw that opportunity and not for any of the pious reasons subscribed to by Louis and the Abbot Bernard. In that spirit, he deliberately made it difficult for Louis to catch up with his army and had alone marched out of Constantinople to lay siege to the coffers of Islam.

Our army left Paris on May 12, 1147, anticipating a sojourn of two, or at most three months before reaching Constantinople. In actuality, we did not arrive until October 4, almost a full five months later. One major reason for the delay was the Emperor Conrad.

By preceding us, Conrad and his troops had picked the countryside clean of provisions. Being Germans, they had something in common with the gentry and the peasantry through whose lands they passed. Thus, they were housed and fed, wined and even provided with women at prices that were not unreasonable. And when a certain amount of squeezing was attempted in these matters by the Hungarians and Bulgarians, Conrad had no hesitation in reverting to the time-honored practice of turning his men loose to pillage and plunder and rape over the countryside.

This was a holy cause, and Louis had taken a pledge that no Christian should come to harm or loss from any man under his command. He took quite literally all of the strictures laid down by the Pope through the Abbot Bernard. In no way was he as adaptable as his Crusading partner, the Hun Conrad.

King Louis had never learned that most important lesson: *Pensez à numero un.* Look out for number one!

Because of his naiveté, our French army was truly a chicken ripe for plucking when it entered Germany. The German tradesmen had honed their bartering skills on their countrymen, and now they applied them without mercy on us. They considered a hundred percent surcharge basic in dealing with scurrilous Frenchmen. As we moved deeper into Germany, the doubled prices became tripled prices and the gouging forced Louis to repeatedly send one or another of his Barons back to the treasury in Paris for more funds to finance the Crusade.

In vain his knights pointed out to him that they were being taken advantage of shamelessly. In vain did they plead with him to let them commandeer those provisions that they were rapidly becoming too poor to purchase. Louis enforced strict orders against looting. As things got worse, there were daily hangings of soldiers who had stolen food. These were done publicly as an example to keep the practice from spreading.

As we moved into Hungary and Bulgaria, the situation worsened. These were Christian nations, our allies, and had even contributed small forces to the Crusade. Nevertheless, the Hun had ravaged these lands on the march to Constantinople, and it was assumed that we would do the same. Now the merchants did not increase the prices to sell their goods to us. On the contrary, they claimed to have no goods to sell. And if we found that they were lying, it still added up to the fact that food and horses, wine and women, were not for sale to the hated Crusader warriors.

Their bellies growling, more and more common soldiers rebelled against Louis' edicts and detached themselves in small bands from our main force to terrorize and loot the countryside. There were more and more public whippings and hangings, more and more public chopping off of hands and offending penises in an attempt to reimpose the strict Christian discipline of the Crusade. But these measures had little effect. By the time we reached the Bosporus, parts of our army were in open mutiny and all of it was in sad disarray.

I must confess here that in addition to the foregoing, I too bore some responsibility for dragging out our miserable journey from Paris. At its start, the Abbot Bernard had specifically banned certain elements from marching with the Crusade. These included acrobats and jugglers, minstrels and poets, storytellers and puppeteers, jesters and all other manner of entertainers who had always been welcome at court since I had replaced Adelaide as Queen. While lower-class camp followers and upper-class wives were allowed, the Abbot had also prohibited unmarried noblewomen from coming along on the Crusade, and he had limited the number of woman servants I was to be allowed to bring as well.

Truly, *mes amis*, I was appalled. Was I to be deprived of servants, entertainment, and companions? Was I expected to live as a common soldier on this Crusade? I was, after all, the Queen of France! And I was a woman who knew how to take care of herself!

I did what any Queen—any woman—would do in such circumstances. I went to the king, my husband, and I wept. I sobbed, I wailed, I howled for his kingly reprieve from such harsh strictures. "There has even been a limit put on the number of gowns and the amount of underclothing I may bring!" I protested, outraged. "And I have been told that I may not bring my jewelry!"

"Every additional wagon slows us down more," Louis tried to explain. "Every noncombatant is a burden. The Abbot is correct, Eleanor. I will not go against him."

Very well, then! I had no choice! I went to the Abbot himself!

"I will bring jugglers," I told him. "I will bring minstrels. I will bring serving women. My ladies will accompany me. Nor will I be deprived of the accouterments of a Queen. I care not how many wagons are needed! My jewels, my finery, my furs, my lingerie, my gowns—all will join this Holy Crusade!"

"You shall not defy the will of God!" the Abbot roared. "You will abide by the restrictions!"

"I will tell my husband what has passed between us," I told him sweetly. "I will tell everyone at court. I will write to the Pope. All shall know how you abused your position as confessor, as Abbot!"

"None will believe you!"

"They will! I am Duchess of Aquitaine! I am Queen of France!"

"And I am God's chosen instrument on earth! They will believe me!"

"Perhaps," I granted. "But there will be ample doubt left over to bring you down, Abbot. Perhaps there will even be so much as to have you recalled to Rome before we embark on this Crusade. The word of a Queen may not be believed, but in such a matter as the sinning of an Abbot it will not be taken lightly."

"Begone!" he roared. "Witch! Spawn of the Devil!"

"And my caravan shall be as I wish it?"

"*Oui! Oui!* Now begone, temptress, before I forget myself and cut the Devil from your body with my sword!"

And that, my dears, is how it came about that the number of my wagons on the Second Crusade was almost as great as the number of wagons carrying weapons and tents and equipment for the army. *Vous faites ce que vous avez á faire.* You do what you have to do!

One wagon alone, heavily guarded, contained nothing but my jewelry. It took five others to transport my wardrobe and another five to carry the garments of my ladies-in-waiting. I insisted, of course, that Louis and I have our own personal kitchen, and that required another three wagons—one for cooking equipment and dishes, one for produce, and one for small live game which could be freshly slaughtered for each night's meal. And of course there was another wagon that was the ambulatory equivalent of our Paris wine cellar.

My lady's stable—the white horses, the grooms, the saddles and bridles and coats of arms, the feed—was the equivalent of a full cavalry troop. Our servants equaled in number a regiment of foot soldiers, and our entertainers half again that number. All of these people had to be fed, of course, compounding the problem of provisions for the long march.

The chroniclers of the Second Crusade would see to it that history would never forgive me for these excesses. But what do chroniclers know of treating a broken heart? What does history care about my constant need for diversion and luxury lest I fall ill with pining for my lost poet-love, Bernard de Ventadour? *Oui, mes amis!* How else should a Queen medicate such a deep and ever-festering wound of love if not by divertissement and the balm of luxury?

Still, something more was needed, something definitely not being provided by my chaste-sworn husband—something more concretely fleshy and suitably oblong. It took the five long months of the march before I found it. It took Constantinople to provide for number one.

Constantinople!

It was said that two-thirds of the riches of the civilized world were contained within the walls of the Byzantine metropolis. Its people, lowborn and highborn alike, considered themselves to be by blood the heirs to an ancient Greek culture far superior to anything that followed it, and certainly high above any of the philosophies or arts or sciences devised by the Celtic barbarians (which is how they lumped together French, German, and Aquitainian). Even their religion, handed down to them from the first Christian Emperor for whom their city had been named, was considered far superior to that followed by the masses of Europe beyond Greece. And if the common man of Constantinople was no better off than the common man of Paris, he nevertheless was surrounded by evidences of visible wealth which could not but convince him that his was the superior state.

Certainly I had never before seen anything like this dazzling city. Our caravan approached it from the landward side, and thus my first view was of the inland ramparts near where they join the walls overlooking the Sea of Marmara. As we came closer, I could see the famous Golden Gate to one side of where the two bulwarks met. It was a magnificent arch crafted of pure hammered gold and guarded by square towers of purplish-white marble. In the October sun, this first Byzantine vision was like something out of ancient legend.

The city itself was mounted strategically on a triangular promontory about four and a half miles long. It was built, like Rome, upon seven hills, and was completely surrounded by walls. The landward wall, extending the full four and a half miles, was made up of a double line of ramparts separated by a deep moat. The inner wall was 15 feet thick and 40 feet high. Both walls were guarded by 60-foot-high towers positioned every 180 feet along its length. The seawalls—one running along the Sea of Marmara, the other along the Bosporus Strait which links the Sea of Marmara with the Black Sea—while consisting only of single ramparts, were likewise heavily fortified.

There was good reason for these precautions. No city in Christendom was as wealthy as Constantinople, and no city in Christian history had been attacked as frequently. The Persians, the Arabs, the Bulgarians, the Russians, and the Pechenegs had all laid siege to Constantinople over the past five hundred years. Not one of these sieges had been successful.

The temptations that had led to these sieges were visible everywhere as soon as we passed through the Golden Gate and entered the city proper. Opulent Byzantine palaces towered over geometrically planned streets terraced to suit the hillsides and neatly lined with olive and citrus trees. The lowliest citizen prided himself on his garden, and a riot of floral colors dotted front yards and tumbled over walls from boxes on the high, narrow windows.

Such beauty, however, was only the setting for the riches that were everywhere. All over the city there were pedestals supporting priceless marble sculptures. Some of these monuments to Byzantine warriors and Christian Emperors and heroes out of ancient legends were one and two stories high. They were in turn surrounded by minarets, some of them steepled in pure gold or silver, others encrusted with priceless jewels. These striking pillars and porticoes and domes overlooked the largest, most strategically positioned and best-guarded harbor in the world.

Mosaic pavements dating back to the fourth and fifth

centuries provided intricately worked entryways and court-
yards to the palaces of the wealthy. Many other works of
art distinguished these palaces one from the other. Here
was a Delphic serpent crafted of gold and dating back to
479 B.C. There was the obelisk of Constantine VII glittering with bronze plaques that were still shiny, although they
had been exposed to the elements for more than a hundred
years.

At the tip of the peninsula stood the Acropolis. Next to
it was the Great Palace of the Emperors, a massive collection of interconnected buildings. These included the Tri-
clinium of the Nineteen Beds, where coronations took
place, the Hall of Gold—a storehouse with walls and
ceilings of gold where only golden treasure was stored—
the palace of Justinian, the palace of the Chalce, and many
others.

The current Emperor, Manuel Commenus, and his wife,
Bertha, did not choose to live in the Great Palace. Instead,
they resided in the Palace of Blacharnae in the northern
section of the city. They were somewhat shielded here
from the damp sea air, and had access to purer drinking
water from the newer reservoirs and aqueducts which crisscrossed Constantinople in imitation of certain Roman cities.
"The wealth in the storerooms of the Blacharnae Palace
alone," my husband, Louis, confided to me, "is said to be
enough to feed the populace of Paris for a decade. And
that is but a drop in the Byzantine bucket of Manuel
Commenus."

"You could feed all France with the gold of the rooftops,"
I replied, truly dazzled by the glittering steeples and domes.
"But then, that is not the purpose of royal treasure," I

remembered. "The purpose of royal treasure is to provide for royalty royally."

We stopped talking as the emissaries Emperor Manuel had sent to greet us showed us into the courtyard of the Blacharnae. It was paved with marble, and its imposing pillars were decorated with intricate gold and silver leaf. Passing through it, we were shown through a series of hallways decorated with rainbowed mosaics depicting the feats of valor and the military victories of the Emperor Manuel and certain of his forebears. Finally we were led into the presence of the waiting Emperor himself.

Manuel Commenus was seated on a mammoth throne carved out of pure gold. The sparkle of priceless jewels which decorated it was truly blinding. It was positioned on a high platform in the great hall of the palace, and the dramatic effect was to make all who approached this throne feel quite insignificant, regardless of their rank. Certainly it worked in the case of Louis and myself. King and Queen of France though we were, we could not help but feel humble when looked down at from such an impressive seat of treasure positioned at so great a height above us.

"Welcome." The Emperor greeted us in a voice that was surprisingly soft and cultivated and well-modulated. "Welcome to Byzantium."

"We bring you greetings from His Holiness, the Pope," Louis replied, his French accent echoing hollowly in the vastness of the great hall.

"I am truly honored that His Holiness should remember me." A certain indolence, perhaps even a hint of boredom, crept into his voice as Manuel went through the necessary formalities. "And I am grateful to His Holiness for the magnificence of Christian royalty he has dispatched to help shield my humble realm against the infidel. And for the boon of such a beauteous Christian Queen,'' he added, nodding down at me.

From under lowered lids, I returned his gaze with some interest whilst he and Louis continued exchanging these ceremonial mouthings. A Byzantine Emperor was an exotic and romantic figure to me, and I was quite curious about him. He certainly did look the part!

He was covered from neck to foot in an ermine-trimmed robe of royal purple. Although it was balmy October in southernmost Europe, the granite walls and vast area of the great hall rendered it quite cool and drafty, and it seemed fitting that this garment should be crafted of heavy velvet. It was set off to some effect by the golden crown decorated with sapphires and rubies and emeralds which sat atop his head.

The Emperor's features were quite Mediterranean, golden olive in cast, sensual in a way that bespoke both moisture and heat. Shiny black curls tumbled free of his crown— indeed, it was the curliest hair I had ever seen on a man, King or commoner. His cheeks were smooth and round and gleamed vivaciously, the bones pronounced. The forehead above them was high, broad, intelligent. The only hair on his face was at the tip of his chin, a sort of short, curly beard in the old-fashioned Egyptian style. His nose was pronounced, strong, hawklike. His mouth, the area around the full lips quite clean-shaven, was very expressive, perhaps almost lewdly so. Indeed, the total impression of his visage was one of a traditional Greek epicure.

''I don't trust him!'' Louis announced later when we were alone together in the luxurious quarters assigned to us.

He was not, I knew, referring to the lacy, dark eyes which had dipped down from the throne above to appraise the contents of his wife's bodice. Louis was not concerned that Manuel might have designs on me. Indeed, it never even occurred to him. He was speaking strictly in terms of the Second Crusade.

"Why not?" I responded to Louis' comment.

"I sense that he is more concerned with maintaining the balance of Byzantine power in this region than in spreading the word of Christ, or protecting the Holy Land from the infidel, or joining us on our pilgrimage to Jerusalem. I would not put it past him to be playing politics with the Turks. If it was to Byzantine advantage, he would not hesitate to conspire with them to sell out the Crusade to the Arabs. Did you notice, Eleanor, that he made no mention of either the plight of Antioch or the whereabouts of the other half of our army under the Emperor Conrad? No. I don't trust this Byzantine," Louis concluded with ultimate logic. "He is too Byzantine."

That night, at the banquet given in our honor, Louis brought up one of the questions on his mind.

"Our intelligence is that Antioch is in no immediate danger," Manuel told him, removing paper-thin slices of broiled lamb from a skewer, eating them, and then dipping his well-manicured hands into a finger bowl fragrant with lemon.

"And the source of your intelligence?" Louis inquired.

"Turkish merchants whose caravans and ships travel regularly between here and Antioch."

"But can these Turks be trusted?"

"They are neutral. They are interested only in conducting their business."

"But they are not Christian."

"That is true." Manuel selected a candied fig and licked the honey from it with a tongue that was long and dark and intriguing beyond the act. "Nevertheless, they do not take sides."

"And not taking sides, they would lie for a price." Louis appealed to their common allegiance, his and Manuel's. "They would not be bound by loyalty to God as you and I would."

"Probably not." Delicately, quickly, Manuel stifled a yawn. "In this part of the world, men frequently do not behave with the loyalty to God displayed by Europeans. Indeed," he added, "your fellow monarch, Conrad of Germany, was so strongly in the grip of that loyalty that he could not wait to leave Constantinople to bring the revealed word to the heathen."

"Conrad has left!" Louis could not keep the agitation from his voice. "How long ago?"

"A fortnight." Manuel took in a shiny, oily olive with his pursed, full lips. "Straight to the east he sailed. He begged arrangements of me to ferry all his troops to the mainland of the Orient. Ah! What a pilgrim light was in his eyes as he turned toward the Holy Land!"

"Toward the Holy Land!" Louis clenched his teeth. He knew that Conrad was not after salvation but booty, and that the sparrow first on the scene is not only first served, but also feasts on the fattest worms. "He had strict orders to wait here so that his army might merge with mine under my command! The orders were from the Pope!"

"Indeed?" Manuel sipped from a tall golden beaker of sweet fig brandy. "Perhaps he had a visitation from Heaven.

Perhaps an angel told him to proceed. That would be a higher authority, would it not?''

Louis stared at him, at a loss as to how to respond. There had been no sarcasm in the Emperor Manuel's voice, and yet— ''I must consult with my religious adviser, the Abbot Bernard,'' he said abruptly. ''Excuse me.'' King though he was, Louis bowed his way out of the banquet hall.

''Your husband seems upset.'' The speaker was the Empress Bertha, the German wife of Emperor Manuel Commenus. ''He left before my strudel was served.''

''She makes it herself,'' Manuel informed me with no inflection whatsoever.

''From my own recipe,'' Empress Bertha added proudly.

She was a plump, pie-faced woman with hair like straw and cheeks like an alpine sunrise. Her voice was high, screechy as a piglet's, discordant as the sounds of losing battle. Flesh surrounded her frame as well does the body of a sheep. It was not so much that she was fat as that she was so very, very abundant. Neck, elbow, and knee all had sausage rolls. Her breasts were as heavy as the udder of a cow before milking. The clothes she wore billowed about her haunches and belly, unable to accommodate the alternating mounds and creases of the roundnesses of flesh. She would (one knew without seeing) have thighs like oak logs and upper arms constantly perspiring with the weight of excess flesh.

Bertha and Manuel had been married when they were both children. It was a marriage of state, although the reasons for union between Byzantium and Germany had long since been lost in the fogs of history. Manuel made no pretense of fidelity to her. This was widely known, as was the fact that he no longer slept with her. Nevertheless, she served the ceremonial function of his wife, and he was courteous and even complimentary regarding her strudel.

"I would like to try some of your strudel," I told Bertha politely.

"I will have a piece too, Bertha," the Emperor told her.

To my surprise, she dismissed the servants and served it herself. It was thick with apples. It had a thin, flaky crust. An aroma fragrant with cinnamon wafted from it. When I tasted it, the strudel virtually melted in my mouth. "Delicious!" I pronounced with absolute honesty. I wolfed down one piece and started on another. "Absolutely delicious."

Manuel, nibbling on his own slice, was watching me closely. His eyes were glittering strangely.

"You must give my pastry chef the recipe," I enthused.

"It is a closely guarded Byzantine secret," Manuel said quickly before Bertha could respond to me.

"Byzantine?" My laughter was unexpectedly breathless and my face felt suddenly flushed. Why? "But surely strudel is a Middle European delicacy."

"One must be adaptable," Bertha explained.

"What are those delicious little seeds that keep getting stuck in my teeth?" I wondered.

"The secret ingredient," Manuel told me.

"Take a hit from this side of the pan," Bertha advised. "I picked it cleaner."

"What secret ingredient?" I was beginning to feel pleasantly dizzy.

"The seeds go down more easily with a little fig wine," Manuel advised.

"Some strudel!" I heard myself giggling from a long way away.

"It's all in the ethnic." Bertha winked.

"The ethnic?" My laughter trilled. "In Aquitaine we call it Mary Jane."

"The barbarians use *kif*?" Manuel was surprised.

"We are not barbarians!" I was indignant. "And if *kif* is what I think it is, you can get a five-franc bag on any street corner in Paris."

"A five-franc bag?" Manuel placated me by holding another slice of strudel to my lips.

"Or loose joints." I ate the strudel and licked the crumbs from his beautifully manicured fingertips.

"I must go and clean the strudel pans." Bertha had been trained to diplomacy. "Perhaps you might show Eleanor the water pipe," she suggested to her husband. "I'll wager that is one innovation not to be found on Parisian street corners."

"I'd be very interested," I told Manuel. "I've heard about the Turkish water pipes, but I've never tried one."

"It will be my pleasure." He offered me his arm.

I was escorted by Manuel from the dining hall to a small chamber furnished in Oriental style. There were low divans and many multicolored cushions of various sizes strewn about the intricately tiled floor. The draperies were of lush silk, and gold leaf seemed to scamper across the ceiling and the walls. One wall seemed to be a sort of louvered closet, but the doors to it were closed. A large hookah stood off to one side.

"If you've never smoked a water pipe before," Manuel told me, "you're in for an experience. I have some really fine *merde* for us.'' He crumbled some hashish leaves and fumbled with the apparatus.

"Really good *merde* is hard to fine,'' I remarked.

"This was smuggled into Constantinople by camel caravan.''

"Where did it come from?'' I inquired.

"Acapulco.''

"Acapulco?'' I looked at Manuel blankly. "Where's that?''

"Somewhere south of the Holy Land, I think. I'm not sure.'' Manuel drew on the water pipe, held his breath for a long moment, then exhaled with a sweet smile of satisfaction.

"Oh.'' I watched him.

"Come try this, good Queen Eleanor,'' he invited.

"All right.'' I crossed over to the hookah.

He showed me how to purse my lips. "Inviting,'' he pronounced when I had it right. "Most inviting.'' But rather than pursue the judgment, Manuel showed me how to insert the mouthpiece and how to suck on it.

"Oui!" A light-blue cloud swirled between us as I exhaled. "That is truly good *merde*!''

"Take a second hit.''

I did as he suggested. The scene before me softened. The colors didn't exactly blur, but their vibrancy mellowed and the shapes of things gave up their angles and corners and became pillowy. "What's in the closet?'' I wondered aloud.

Like a suckling baby at the nipple, Manuel's dark eyes were sleepy with delight as his full lips surrounded the mouthpiece. He gave it up reluctantly to respond to my question. "I'll show you,'' he said.

An intricate Persian carpet floated by under the soles of my feet without seeming to touch them as we crossed to the closet. Manuel opened the door and stood back so that I might appreciate the contents. His olive face was gleaming, his short Egyptian beard tilted impudently.

One-half of the closet was filled with female garments of a style I had never seen before. The other half seemed to be a hodgepodge of male weaponry and armor. I looked at him questioningly, my eyes misty green with the effects of the hookah.

"A guest room," he explained. "The last inhabitant was a Turkish Sultan. Not a Christian. These"—he indicated the female apparel with a sweep of his hand—"are the costumes of his houris."

"But they are so flimsy, so transparent, so very scant."

"Of course." Manuel gestured toward the other side of the closet. "The armor and weapons are Byzantine," he told me. "They were gifts from me to the Sultan in appreciation for certain services rendered."

"But he left them here?" I inquired.

"He was dispatched rather hurriedly."

"Dispatched?"

"It seems that I was not the only one to whom the Sultan was rendering services. He was also conspiring with certain Syrians regarding the triumph of Islam over Greek Christianity. My disappointment in his character when I learned of this was marked."

"And so you had him . . . dispatched." I shuddered.

"Hurriedly dispatched." Manuel made a broad gesture indicating the contents of the closet. "So hurriedly that he had no time to make disposition of either his houris' garments, nor his Byzantine souvenirs."

Reflecting on the transience of existence, I strolled back to the hookah and took a deep, satisfying pull from the mouthpiece of the water pipe. Smoke curled into my lungs and purred there before I let it make its escape. I offered the device to Manuel, who had followed me from the closet.

"Fascinating," I remarked, meaning the clothing, the armor, and the weapons. "And is that suit of armor really the sort of thing that Byzantine knights wear into battle?"

"Byzantine Emperors. The suit of armor used to be mine," Manuel told me.

"It doesn't seem possible that you could get into it. Let alone out of it. When you had to," I added meaningfully.

"It isn't easy, but it can be done."

"Show me!" I suggested, my green eyes dancing to the hookah's rhythm.

"Do you mean, Queen Eleanor, that you want me to put on the armor for you?" His own deep eyes smoldered lazily. "I had rather hoped that we might progress to the shucking of garments, rather than the donning of mail."

"Oh?" I stood to my full tall, slender height and looked down my aquiline nose at him with my most regal gaze. "And what gave you cause for such brazen ambition?" Unfortunately a sudden *kif*-induced hiccup ruined the effect.

"It is said that your husband, the King, has vowed a chaste marriage bed until the Crusade is over. That seems a most cruel verdict upon a woman of so passionate a nature as yours."

"And what makes you think I have a passionate nature?" Surely it was the *kif* that was making me perspire and not his insolent stare piercing the clothes covering my body.

"My faith in God. No deity could be so cruel as to

endow a Queen with such beauty and leave her bereft of passion.''

''You certainly do have a Byzantine tongue in your head!'' I was amused and dizzy and—*oui!*—intrigued. ''But I want to see you in your armor.'' Some perverse demon of the water pipe made me decide to tease him. ''Don it and then we'll discuss this shocking idea you seem to have that I might be tempted into infidelity.''

''All right.'' He took a deep drag from the hookah. His head bobbed a little. The *kif* had affected him as it had me. ''I'll put on the armor if you'll put on one of the houri costumes.''

''Why not?'' I was suddenly reckless. ''I have always wondered how those creatures felt when they dressed themselves for their Sultan. It is so different from Aquitaine.''

Manuel arranged the doors so that they were a screen between us as we changed. I finished first and flitted back to the low divan. I took a quick suck of the hookah and then arranged myself on the cushions.

Due to my intoxicated state, there was a feeling of standing outside myself and observing—even appraising— the effect of the houri costume I had chosen and the pose I had struck. The garment was peach colored, a delicate cross between pink and orange, and was quite gauzy. The material had a sort of shimmering transparency which afforded glimpses of my high-arched, cylindrical breasts and of the white sweep of my long, curved thighs.

The costume was cut low over my breasts and hugged them tightly. The outline of long, stiff nipples was visible, and when I looked down at myself, I could clearly make out the pinkness of my aureoles and the scarlet of the breast tips themselves in contrast to the ivory of the flesh through the material. The gauzy cloth billowed around my small waist but hugged my hips and was tight across my belly and groin. Indeed, it was so tight that my mound of Venus was plainly outlined and so too was the auburn shading of the silky hair covering it. When I turned on my side to dissemble this view, the transparent harem trousers clung to my high, plump bottom and to my rippling thighs.

Carried away with the idea of playing the houri, I untied my braids and allowed my chestnut hair to fan out over my upper body in a most provocative fashion. My fine-etched visage was too aristocratic by far for the part, but Nature's camouflage is frequently like that. The alabaster and the delicacy atop the swanlike neck are oft disguise for strumpet lust. And in truth, *mes amis,* hashish had provoked mine own passions beyond usual restraints.

There was a sudden clanking. I raised my eyes from beneath long webbed lashes. Emperor Manuel had donned the entire suit of armor. He had even put on the boots, even the helmet with its visor closed to a mere slit. He was covered with metal from head to toe.

"The houri costume suits you, Queen Eleanor." His voice was hollow inside the armor like an echo in a sea cave.

"How do you ever move inside that," I wondered, "let alone fight battles to the death?"

"One gets used to wielding a sword or a lance."

"What do you do when you have to—? You know."

"There is a hinged flap at the rear. Here. See for yourself." Manuel guided my hand.

I found the hinge. Curious, I worked it. The flap creaked downward. Manuel's bare, olive-skinned bottom appeared. It was round and smooth and gleaming like the cheeks of his face. It was very tempting. I did not resist the temptation. I pinched it.

"Vive L'Aquitaine!" Manuel turned around with a terrible rattle. "No false restraint."

"It is the *kif*." Having given in to the impulse, now I was embarrassed.

"I know." He took off one mailed glove and reached for my breast. "I too am affected by it." His manicured hand explored my bosom through the gauzy houri bodice. "You are warm," he observed.

"Being touched thus makes me so." In truth, I was breathing quite hard.

"Some cool wine," he suggested. His thumb strummed one of my nipples through the material.

"I fear it will but make me warmer, more feverish." It had been a long march, and an even longer time since I had been with a man. My nipple strained uncontrollably to his caress, and I was too excited to be ashamed.

"Then perhaps another hit?" He had taken off his other mailed glove and now was fondling both my breasts.

"Oui. I would like that." I had but to turn my face and the mouthpiece of the hookah was between my lips. I drew on it. A sense of well-being overlaid the passion within me.

"When you make a move like that to suck the hookah, your mouth is irresistible," Manuel told me.

"Then don't resist it." The hit had made me bold.

Manuel raised the visor of the helmet and bent to kiss me. It was like putting one's head inside a container. Nevertheless, it was worth it. His lips were warm and sweet with fig wine and moved over mine with a sort of sensual knowingness that set my very toes to tingling. His tongue moved in my mouth with phallic stiffness. His hands pushed aside the gauze and kneaded my heaving, naked breasts as the kiss continued.

I put my arms around him and felt the cold metal of the armor he was wearing. Resonating to the deep, intimate kiss, I lowered my hand and found the hinge at the back of the suit of armor. I opened it again and caressed the smooth, muscular, naked flesh of his bottom. We continued to kiss and I sucked on his hot, hard tongue and fondled his receptive ass.

"Now I am really warm!" I murmured when the kiss was finally over.

"*Oui.*" He stroked my naked, bright-red, upstanding nipples. "I can see that." He puffed at the hookah and then handed the mouthpiece to me.

As I was inhaling, I felt his hand sliding down from my breast to my belly to my thighs. Both of his hands were on my thighs then, and he was separating them. The copper color of my silky pubic triangle was more visible with my legs parted this way. Sucking on the hookah and watching his hot, dark eyes as they pierced the thin material of the harem trousers and ferreted out the cleft of my mons veneris made me suddenly wild. I reached deeper inside the suit of armor, forced my hand between Manuel's legs, and squeezed his balls from behind.

They were very smooth and he had not very much hair there. They were also swollen with passion, and the skin of the sac holding them was stretched very tight. As soon as my hand closed around them, Manuel reached down with both of his hands and parted my thighs widely and investigated the opening of my quim through the skimpy peach-colored material over my crotch.

"Play with me!" I whispered. "It's been so long! Touch me! Put your fingers inside me! Play with my pussy!"

When he heard these words, Manuel's balls swelled even more in my hand. He shuddered inside the armor and there was a hollow, metallic ringing sound. The fingers of both his hands curled around the gauzy material at my crotch, and he ripped it wide apart. He palmed my honeyed bush, and then his fingers slipped inside me.

"Mon Dieu!" I clutched and pumped over his wriggling fingers and with sudden inspiration sucked deeply and quickly at the hookah. "Is there no way to open this armor from the front?" I gasped.

"But of course. Do you think every time a man must pee he has to take it off? There is a cylinder of metal that slides away so. And then—"

As soon as Manuel slid the disk out of the way, his naked prick sprang free of the armor. It was thick and stiff. There were shiny black curls at its base. Its texture was smooth and olive like his bottom. The swollen head peeking out of the foreskin was like a ruby.

"Ahh!" I took it in my hand. It throbbed. I pressed it to my cheek. It throbbed again. I licked the shaft quickly. This time it bucked. I stroked it to calm it a little.

Manuel stroked the silky chestnut hair over my pussy. He slid a long, manicured figure up inside me. He found my clitoris and teased it to hardness with his fingertip. He stirred my honey and stroked the sensitive spot behind the clitoris and then began deep, pumping strokes that brought him to the very mouth of my womb.

Shaking, I took a deep suck of the hookah to calm myself. Then I took Manuel's burning, erect cock in my mouth and sucked at the ruby head. I took another short puff from the hookah, then another swift suck from his prick. This time I licked the head with my tongue. There was a drop of man-cream at the little hole at the tip, and it tasted delicious. I sucked more smoke-of-paradise from the hookah. I sucked the delicious man-cock deep into my mouth and down my throat.

Reacting, Manuel shook the armor so that it clanked loudly. One of his hands spanned my breasts and he toyed with both the long, hard nipples at the same time. His other hand played between the cheeks of my bottom at the same time that his long middle finger pumped like some cock on the verge of coming deep inside my hot, wet, writhing pussy.

Time out for one more drag on the hookah. Then I took his stiff prick in my mouth and curled my tongue around it like a snake. I sucked hard. My head was spinning with the excitement of the sex and the effects of the *kif*. I extended my tongue full length and licked under his cock, touching the ridge of flesh just behind his balls. I sucked. I felt the ridge forming up the length of his shaft. I sucked harder. . . .

Manuel forced me wide open with a second finger and began pumping hard with both of them. Looking down, past the stiff cock in my mouth, I watched my cunt, open and raw and meaty and pink as it writhed over Manuel's hand. I was going to spend. I could feel it. I couldn't stop myself. And as the orgasm began, I sucked and licked the hard, jism-throbbing cock in my mouth with all my might

"I'm going to come!" No sooner had Manuel shouted

the words than his cock began spurting globs of delicious cream down my quick-swallowing throat. I was delirious with spending myself as I feasted on this nectar and sucked and licked his prick until I had squeezed the last delicious drop from it!

My head was spinning and it seemed to go on forever. The spurting cock in my mouth . . . my quim exploding over his expert hand . . . a vision of my husband praying in bed, sleeping in bed, doing everything in bed but that which my hungry flesh cried out for him to do . . . an image of Manuel's wife baking pastry, cleaning the pan, eating sweets instead of supping on that wondrous morsel still geysering between my warm, wet lips. . . . And soon all of these crazy visions were merging and there seemed nothing to do about it but take another hit from the hookah!

Fantasy? Reality? It was a different scene from any I'd ever known before. It wasn't Aquitaine. It wasn't France. It was Byzantium.

Ahh, Byzantium!

Chapter Six

"I don't trust that Byzantine!" my husband, King Louis, snarled, referring to the Emperor Manuel Commenus. "I would not put it past him to betray me!"

"Betray you?" A small, nervous finger of guilt twanged my heartstrings. "In what fashion?"

"I know not. I only sense that Manuel's own selfish interest, whatever it might be, would take precedence over any loyalty to me, and that in such a case he would not weigh my status as leader of the Holy Crusade."

"But he has pledged fealty to the cause," I reminded Louis. "And he speaks constantly of his support for you personally."

"His language is too flowery. The words he uses are like snakes twisting through vines. I sense Byzantine irony. I sense a mocking of that which is not Greek."

"It is not to be heard in his tone," I pointed out.

"Nevertheless, I sense it. Back in France it would be

recognized as the manner of the seducer toward the poor fool of a husband he has cuckolded. But Manuel is a Byzantine, and so of course it might be viewed as political.''

''Of course,'' I murmured, agreeing. ''What else?''

''But just exactly who,'' my husband wondered, ''is he consorting with against me?''

I swallowed hard, still tasting the sweetness of Byzantine nectar. . . .

Suspicions of Manuel's duplicity were not Louis' only concern. As immediate commander of the combined French and Aquitainian armies, he had to deal with the results of the enforced idleness imposed on the troops since their arrival in Constantinople. This idleness had exacerbated the prejudices of the two groups toward each other and increased the friction between them.

''Frenchmen eat live lizards and frogs,'' was the folklore upon which Aquitainian children cut their teeth.

That ''Aquitainian peasants sprinkle sheep dip on their morning gruel,'' was well-known to the dwellers of the French city slums.

Aquitainian soldiers warned one another against catching the ''French disease'' in the brothels of Paris.

French recruits were firm in their belief that the source of syphilis was Aquitainian sheep.

''Treachery is in the nature of the Frenchman! He carries a club! He attacks from behind!''

''Slyness is bred into the Aquitainian! He hammers his sickle into a dagger and carries it in his boot! He falls upon the unwary sleeper!''

''The King is a Frenchman! He feeds his army beef while we Aquitainians subsist on roots and maggot flour!''

"The Aquitainian Queen is in charge! Her countrymen live on fresh produce and mutton while good French soldiers die with the dysentery from the sour wine the Aquitainians have discarded!"

"The French live off the fat while we poor Aquitainian crusaders watch our teeth rot and fall out for lack of the lean!"

"The Aquitainians are spoiled, the French deprived!"

"The frogs cheat at cards!"

"The Aqui-dungs load their dice!"

"The frogs pick their noses!"

"The Aqui-dungs scratch their asses!"

"Better the smell of a latrine than the stench of a frog's armpit!"

"Better a fishmonger's aroma than the foul body odor of unwashed Aqui!"

And that, *mes amis,* was the attitude of the two groups, one toward the other, before we even got to Constantinople. Our arrival there, needless to say, did not change things. There was no outcry of "Christians all! Crusaders all!"; no launching of Brotherhood Week. On the contrary, with no day's march to tire them out, the crusaders had ample energy to convert their bigotry into action.

The French raided the Aquitainian commissary and made off with four sides of beef.

The Aquitainians plundered the French of six casks of wine.

A platoon of French soldiers castrated an Aquitainian for ogling a French camp follower.

Six Aquitainians revenged their countryman by raping a French sergeant's mistress.

French lancers slew three Aquitainians in a barroom brawl.

Aquitainian cavalrymen rode down and murdered a quartet of drunken Frenchmen.

Soon swordplay between the two groups was a daily occurrence. Tempers were short. Blood was shed freely. Death resolved many a quarrel. The rivalry was fierce, the hatred bitter, the infidel forgotten, the purpose of the Crusade lost to immediate revenges by Aquitainians and Frenchmen toward each other. As yet, the war for which they had come was out of reach, and so they fought the war at hand.

But it was an undeclared war and unapproved by their mutual sovereign, King Louis VII. Indeed, it was being carried on in direct opposition to his orders. He was, therefore, obliged to put a stop to it. In this cause, still more crusader blood was shed.

The punishments imposed by Louis were both brutal and public, much to the amusement of the Byzantine citizens of Constantinople. Crowds of laughing, cheering, olive-skinned men and women would gather to watch the hanging of an Aquitainian soldier who had run through a French officer with his sword, or the cutting off of the hands of an Aquitainian who had stolen from a French comrade. They particularly seemed to enjoy the death by fire of two Aquitainians who had buggered a young French priest, as well as the traditional drawing and quartering of a French nobleman who had forced his will upon one of my Aquitainian ladies-in-waiting.

Not only did the Byzantines enjoy these spectacles, they profited by them. The crowds were good for business and the prices of foodstuffs and baubles in the marketplaces soared. The value of the local currency rose with what might be characterized as the "tourist influx" of the crusader army.

The problem was that the army's pay was devalued by comparison. Soon there was grumbling among both French and Aquitainians about the gouging of Byzantine merchants. With plenty of time on their hands, the soldiers roamed the city in small bands in search of wine and amusement and souvenirs and local women. The problem was that when they found them, the prices being asked were, by their simple soldier standards, exorbitant.

This gave rise to a new problem, the increasing friction between the crusaders and the citizens of their host city. Louis was forced to object to Manuel that Byzantine merchants were taking shameless advantage of his soldiers and that their prices were inflationary. "Not in the spirit of the Holy Crusade!" he protested.

Manuel promised that something would be done about it. But nothing was. All that happened was that the prices mounted and the situation grew worse and more and more of the French treasury and the gold I had raised to finance the Crusade found its way into Byzantine coffers.

It worked out this way because Manuel raised the taxes of the merchants. This caused them to raise the prices they charged crusaders to even greater heights. And this squeezed the last of their meager pay into Byzantine hands and then, ultimately, into the Emperor Manuel's royal treasury.

"It's really not fair!" I protested to Manuel once when we were alone together.

"Shh!" was his reply. "Keep sucking!"

Finally matters came to a head with an incident that occurred on the Mese, the famous Constantinople square lined by the stalls of goldsmiths and jewelers, silversmiths and money changers. A Flemish knight—drunk, it is true— was evidently carried away by the open display of wealth. He and his troop swept through the Mese on horseback, stooping to gather up trays of precious gems and bars of gold and silver and baskets of coins and currency. There was a near riot on the part of the Byzantines as the invaders rode off with this booty.

The riot spread over Constantinople and bands of citizens began falling on small groups of crusaders and assaulting them. Blood flowed and many were robbed. There was further looting, blamed on the crusaders but more likely the work of enterprising young Byzantine hoodlums who saw their opportunity and seized it. In the end, Manuel had to call out the Byzantine guard to bring the populace under control. They accomplished this objective swiftly and brutally and left over one hundred of their fellow citizens dead in their wake.

At the same time, Louis was forced to accede to Manuel's demand that the Flemish knight who had started the riot with his raid on the Mese be punished. The culprit and his band were seized and their loot was returned to the Byzantine merchants. Then the Flemish knight and six of his horsemen were publicly beheaded on a platform built adjacent to the Mese. The execution was cheered openly by Byzantines, but French and Aquitainians alike stood around sullenly and muttered their disapproval. Indeed, the incident served to do that which Louis had not been able to accomplish. It submerged the feelings of hostility between French and Aquitainians in their mutual hatred of Eastern peoples.

"Their instinct may be well-grounded!" was Louis'

reaction. "The Byzantine is devious by birth. He is not to be trusted. He is a cheat and a backbiter and a seducer of wives!"

"Surely your judgment is too harsh," I protested, probing with my tongue at a Byzantine pubic hair which had become lodged between my teeth earlier that evening.

"Too harsh? You are naive, Eleanor! My informants tell me that Manuel is treating behind my back with the Turks!"

"The Turks?" I was confused. "I forget, Louis—are they Christians or Muslim?"

"Both."

"But are they on our side, or the side of the enemy?"

"Both."

"Then what exactly does it mean if Manuel is treating with them behind your back?"

"I wish I knew," Louis sighed. "I really wish I knew!"

"There has been a great victory!" the Emperor Manuel announced.

The occasion was the latest in the never-ending series of banquets he and Empress Bertha had hosted in our honor since we arrived in Constantinople. The announcement came somewhere between the serving of the stuffed kid with artichokes and the sautéed frog. (I had learned to stay away from these and other heavy Greek dishes and usually nibbled lightly on thin crackers with caviar washed down with an anise-flavored red Greek wine.)

"And who has won this victory?" The Abbot Bernard pawed with one intolerant foot at the rose petals strewn on the floor. He had no patience with Byzantine ostentation, not with the food and drink, not with the decorative effects.

"Why, the Holy Roman Empire, of course," Manuel informed him.

The Abbot glowered. He couldn't stand the Emperor and made little effort to hide his feelings. "I wonder why?" the Emperor would remark on those occasions when he laid his Byzantine wand lengthwise on my tongue. "After all, I have such great respect for the clergy."

On this occasion, it was left to Louis to ask for details of the victory.

"I have received word from your lieutenant," Manuel replied diplomatically, "the Emperor Conrad. There has been a great battle at Anatolia. The Germans have killed more than fourteen thousand of the enemy."

Louis and the Abbot Bernard exchanged sharp glances. Such a victory for the crusader army under Conrad was decidedly a mixed blessing. It meant that the Germans would have first claim on the infidels' booty. They had fought for it, they had won it, and they were on the spot to seize it. Both King and cleric recognized that it was going to be very difficult to separate Conrad and his Germans from the share due French troops under the agreements reached by all of the crusader leaders with the Pope. Indeed, it was going to be particularly difficult since Louis, as leader of the Crusade, was entitled to the largest share of all—whether he participated in any given battle or not.

After the banquet that night, Louis and the Abbot conferred almost until dawn. More disturbing rumors concerning Manuel's dealing with the Turks had reached their ears. These added to the urgency of their decision to leave Constantinople. Their armies must march; they must reach Antioch and launch the Crusade from there under Louis' command before his authority was completely usurped by any more unauthorized German victories led by Conrad.

Three nights later, I sucked the nectar from the Byzantine spout for the last time. The following morning, at the side of my husband, I rode at the head of our army as we marched out of Constantinople toward Nicaea and the deserts of Anatolia on our way to northern Syria and, ultimately, Antioch. This was the same route that had been followed by Conrad on the advice of the Emperor Manuel. In light of Conrad's great victory, it was obviously one where we could now expect to encounter little enemy resistance.

That expectation underwent a radical change when we reached the outskirts of Nicaea, less than twenty miles from Constantinople. Here we encountered a ragtag battalion of German soldiers and knights in the full panic of retreat from the enemy. The story they told was quite different from the tale of victory that Manuel Commenus had passed along to Louis.

Conrad had followed the route recommended by Manuel, the same route we were now following. Manuel had provided him with Byzantine guides who led him into the deserts of Anatolia. These guides had misled him about how much food and water would be needed to cross the desert without hardship. Halfway across the desert, these Byzantine guides had deserted the Germans. Beginning the next morning, the latter had been under constant attack from infidel bands which never engaged them in battle but simply showered them with arrows from one hidden defile or another and then rode away to repeat the maneuver from behind the next ridge of dunes. In this fashion they had destroyed half of Conrad's army. As to the other half, they had fled in disorderly retreat and we were encountering them now. Somewhere to the rear of them, Conrad had managed to maintain some discipline over a small part of his army and was fighting a holding action while these fellows fled.

"That Byzantine bastard laid the trap, and the greedy Hun walked right into it!" Louis summed up what had happened. "Manuel dealt through the Turks and set up Conrad for the Muslims. And now he is repeating this treachery with us. Never trust a Byzantine, Eleanor!"

True! In my heart I agreed with my husband. Still, when they betray, their nectar is most delicious! And sometimes a *fille* has to take the short view.

Louis and Abbot Bernard conferred as still more whipped Germans straggled into our encampment. The result of this conference was the immediate execution by hanging of the Byzantine guides Manuel had provided us. Following this, Louis and the Abbot pored over their maps of the region and worked out an alternate line of march.

The plan now was to circumvent the desert where the bands of Muslim rebels had inflicted such heavy damage on the Germany army. Instead, we would take a longer route through the hills to the Gulf of Smyrna and from there to Ephesus and on to Antioch. This terrain, Louis hoped, would be more conducive to keeping his army in closed ranks than the desert was.

It was my fault, I suppose, that Louis was weighed down with so much extra baggage. This was a matter of more than little concern to him on this march. The defense of his troops dictated that the line of march be foreshortened as much as possible, but the slow-moving wagons bearing my clothes and jewels and personal supplies were constantly straggling and forcing a choice between stringing out the army and slowing it down. As we moved deeper and deeper into enemy country, this became a major concern.

The greatest danger—thanks largely to the treacherous, sweet-tasting Manuel—came from our rear. As more and more fleeing Germans caught up with us, it became obvious that the enemy was not far behind. If there was to be a battle, then it would be a rear-guard action. Recognizing this, Louis and the Abbot Bernard took joint command of the main part of the army and deliberately positioned it behind the slow-moving wagons. Ironically enough, the vanguard was placed under the command of my Aquitainian vassal and erstwhile lover, the knight with the scarlet birthmark emblazoning one cheek, Sir Geoffrey of Rancon.

If there was to be a battle, Louis wanted men around him he could trust. For that reason the rear guard was made up overwhelmingly of French knights and foot soldiers. Mingled with them, because they had always been forced to march to the rear of the wagons, were the camp followers and pilgrims bound for the Holy Land. There were also some of Conrad's defeated Germans, now directly under Louis' command.

The Aquitainians, whom the Abbot Bernard didn't trust and whom French Louis likewise had doubts about, marched at the front of the column with their leader, Sir Geoffrey. For safety's sake, however, all of the French noblewomen, along with their Aquitainian sisters—my ladies-in-waiting and my servants—also stayed in the vanguard. It was agreed that any attack would probably come from the rear, or—less likely—from one of the flanks, but surely not from the front. Like the other women, I too remained at the head of the column under the protection of the Aquitainians and Sir Geoffrey.

This was the arrangement on the morning of the feast day of Epiphany in the year of Our Lord 1148 when our army began the ascent up Mount Cadmos. Before we started up, Louis rode the length of the column to the head to personally deliver his orders to Sir Geoffrey. The orders were for the vanguard to proceed to the summit at top speed. Geoffrey was to take this high ground, set up camp on the plateau there, and wait for the rest of the army to catch up. The idea—not spoken, but surely taken for granted—was that the advance force of Aquitainians would be standing guard over the slope as the rest of the army, slowed down on their upward climb by the heavy-laden wagons, made their ascent. Louis judged that the main force should be two to three hours behind the vanguard and should join them before dusk at the latest.

It was a crisp morning, sunshiny but breezy. The nip in the air quickened our progress. Our Aquitainian vanguard reached the flatland at the summit of Mount Cadmos much earlier than had been anticipated.

The sun was directly overhead when we dismounted. It was noon. The morning breezes had died away. The temperature was rising.

"We will fry here on this rocky plateau," Geoffrey judged. The blemish on his cheek flared ugly in the blazing daylight. "There isn't a tree; there's no hint of shade to be found."

"My ladies are already beginning to freckle," I agreed.

"Look you there, Sir Geoffrey." One of his knights called his attention to the slope opposite the one by which we had ascended.

A gentle, narrow stream trickled down this side of Mount Cadmos. It was rambling and crooked, but nevertheless it pointed like an arrow to a second plateau about a half-mile below the one at the top. This plateau was very different from the sun-baked clay and rock surface on which we were standing. Fed by the stream, it was grassy and surrounded by leafy trees. It looked pleasant and inviting, shady and shielded—a perfect campsite.

"We will set up the tents and the kitchen there," Geoffrey decided, "and await the rest of the army."

And so we moved down the opposite side of the mountain and left the slope behind us unguarded!

Much has been made of this decision because of what followed. Some see it as a deliberate betrayal of a French monarch by a disloyal Aquitainian vassal. Some see it as sheer military stupidity. And some even see it as the fruit of adultery between the royal French victim's wife and her ambitious lover.

In truth it was all of those things and none of them. Surely there was deep resentment of the French by the Aquitainians, and surely Geoffrey felt this as much as any of his countrymen, but the role it played in his selection of the campsite was at most subliminal, and even then negligible. Nor was it quite as brainless a decision as it seems in retrospect. The site he selected was far superior to the apex, not just for his own forces, but for the ladies entrusted to his care and—ultimately—for the French army as well when it arrived. It would be much easier to draw up a defense perimeter for the supply wagons in the grove of trees than out in the open on the upper plateau where they would be completely exposed. And as for the decision's being the result of adulterous plotting between us, that is a logic arrived at by the addition of apples and oranges.

It is true that on that fatal afternoon Geoffrey and I made love—if such it can be called. It is also true that this circumstance had nothing whatever to do with the fact that the slope by which the French army was ascending Mount Cadmos was left unguarded. It is absurd to think that I would have conspired with Geoffrey against Louis.

What would I have had to gain? Certainly not position. My husband was King of France and Geoffrey of Rancon had been my vassal even when I was merely Duchess of Aquitaine.

Passion then? Ludicrous! Louis may have chosen chastity and thought to impose chasteness on me with his choice, but Geoffrey, endowed with the amatory staying power of a moth in flight, was scarce enough of an improvement to tempt me to treason.

No. The truth is that we were in the East, the realm of Kismet. It was Fate which led us down the far side of the mountain while Louis and his army were still struggling in the hot sun to ascend. And it was Fate which cruelly coupled the events that followed.

It was midafternoon by the time the camp was set up and we finished lunching. At the same time, the French were having trouble negotiating the trail with the heavy wagons, and in order to deal with this situation more comfortably under the hot sun, Louis' knights took off their armor. An hour later, along with certain of my ladies and favored Aquitainian knights, I was sipping wine and watching the antics of the jugglers and acrobats we had brought along on the Crusade to be sure that we would not lack for amusement. Simultaneously, Louis was frantically urging his lieutenants to close ranks along the line of march which was now strung out most indefensively along the exposed mountain trail. At dusk, alone in my tent, languid with wine, I remembered the texture of Byzantine cock filling my mouth and allowed my hand to drop to the burning spot between my restless thighs. The same twilight saw the distance lengthening between the foot soldiers in the forefront of Louis' army and the wagons and servants and pilgrims and camp followers and knights trying to speed their progress in the rear.

A short while later—the sun still not set—I gave in to lust and summoned Three-Minute Geoffrey of Rancon to my tent. As Geoffrey was entering, a large force of Muslims—Turks and Arabs—fell upon Louis' army from behind and successfuly split it in two with the very first assault. Geoffrey quickly fathomed the reason for my summons, stroked his crimson birthmark, and knelt to the demand of my outstretched arms. The smaller part of the attacking force laid siege to the knights guarding the wagons, the pilgrims, and the camp followers while the main assault of the infidels was leveled at the exposed foot soldiers on the upper trail who were bottled up in such a position that they could neither go higher nor retreat. Geoffrey put his tongue in my mouth, stroked my right breast, and raised my skirt. The foot soldiers were caught in a crossfire and fell by the dozens in a hail of arrows and spears. Sir Geoffrey took out his familiar stable boy prick and inserted it in my warm, wet, willing pussy. King Louis, along with his knights and the Abbot Bernard, were trapped behind the supply wagons in a gully. Sir Geoffrey lasted for two minutes forty-seven seconds; the battle went on all night.

With darkness, however, while the foot soldiers in their exposed position still could not organize anything like a reasonable defense, many of them were able to escape the trap they were in by slipping past the enemy and making their way to our encampment. Thus it was that around midnight the Aquitainians learned of the French predicament. What followed was a great deal of discussion among Sir Geoffrey's advisers as to just what he should do about it and—more important—when.

I was not privy to this discussion. Indeed, I was sound asleep at the time and knew nothing of what was happening. It was only when morning came that I was made aware of the desperate predicament of the French army and particularly of my husband.

When I did learn what was going on, I immediately asserted my authority as Queen. "You will counterattack immediately!" I told Sir Geoffrey.

He and his knights exchanged glances. They were decidedly unenthusiastic at the idea of shedding Aquitainian blood to rescue the French. They began muttering and weighing the means by which my order might be implemented.

"IMMEDIATELY!" I roared.

"It is not practical, Highness." One among them began drawing a map in the dust with a stick. "The enemy is entrenched here. What is left of the French foot soldiers are here. Even if we could reach them, if we continued down the mountain to the gully where the wagons are under siege we would be completely exposed and at the mercy of the infidel."

"Are you Aquitainians or are you cowards?" I demanded.

"We are only trying to be prudent, Majesty."

"Prudent!" I looked at the speaker with the utmost contempt. "Very well, then," I decided. "I will lead the attack. I will mount the assault that will lift the siege pinning down my husband, the King, and his French knights."

"Please, Highness." Geoffrey looked pained. "You don't understand the situation. It may be possible to drive off the attackers closest to us on the hillside. Those bowmen and spearmen still face a considerable force of French foot soldiers, and if we attack them, our combined efforts should prevail against them. But the siege of the supply wagons is another matter. The infidels are dug in there. They control the approach down the mountain and the defile is very narrow. Once past this gorge"—he drew a line in the dirt with his sword—"we would have to regroup. They would surely not allow us the time to do that. Thus we would be at their mercy."

"A troop of cavalry," I suggested. "A cavalry charge."

"That would be better." Geoffrey looked at me with new respect. "Momentum would cause a certain confusion. But even so, it would not be enough."

"It will." I disagreed firmly. "My cavalry troop will confound the enemy beyond belief."

I was their Queen, and although they disapproved, they had no choice but to go along with the plan I outlined. When I was done, I returned to my tent and summoned my ladies-in-waiting to me. The majority of them were French, not Aquitainian, from my Paris court and romantically involved with one or another of the French knights who were trapped with King Louis.

"Ladies," I began, "do you remember at Vezelay when this Crusade started with us dressing in crusader tunics and mounting our white horses and riding like fierce amazons to inspire men to enlist in the cause? Well, ladies, the time has come now for amazons to ride again.'' I continued to explain exactly how I proposed to use my women's cavalry as—quite literally—shock troops to dispel the infidel.

Less than an hour later some forty beautiful young women were assembled under my command at the head of the Aquitainian relief force on the plateau atop Mount Cadmos. Each of them, like myself, rode a snow-white horse bred in far-off Hungary. Each was wrapped in a long crusader cloak with a bright-red cross emblazoned on the front of it. Each wore gilded silver boots and a silver helmet with a white plume. Each held high a naked sword.

We moved off down the mountain, our hair, by prearrangement, worn loose and streaming out behind us in the morning breeze. Shortly we heard the sounds of battle in front of us. The infidels had cut off a small party of fleeing Frenchmen and were slaughtering them with a crossfire of arrows from behind sheltering boulders. At my command, Aquitainian knights moved up and rode to the rescue of the beleagured Frenchmen.

My amazons and I bypassed this battle. We also circumvented the next one, which was far more violent and which pitted the main force of Aquitainian foot soldiers against a large body of Muslim Turks. With me at their head, the women kept riding. Our task was to lift the siege of the King and his knights.

Finally, from above we saw the gully with the French wagons and the hapless pilgrims and camp followers and the King leading the small band of knights attempting to protect them. Daylight had brought them under direct attack, and only the utmost valor enabled them to maintain their defense. Even as we watched, the infidels crept from the surrounding walls of the escarpment and began to move in openly on the tiny encampment. It would only be a matter of moments before the defenders were overrun and slaughtered.

"Mademoiselles!" I gave the command. "To arms!" I flung off my crusader cloak and stood stark naked in the stirrups, waving my sword and urging my white stallion to charge.

My ladies, one and all, emulated my example. As I had planned, upon my command, with one sweeping gesture, they doffed their cloaks, the only garments covering their flesh, stretched nude in their saddles, dug in their spurs, and attacked. Keening like Valkyries, long, loose hair streaming in the breeze of the gallop, we materialized out of the morning mist lying over the defile and rode to the rescue of our trapped Gallic knights.

To the infidels it must have seemed as if we were some sort of superbeings—pagan warrior-goddesses—who appeared out of nowhere. One moment they were engaged in a mopping-up operation against an enemy under siege and the next they were facing an apparition of naked Furies with their breasts moving in the wind and their bare buttocks bouncing as we descended. The chorus of our hackle-raising screams had turned them from their objective in order to face us. But their eyes, filled with so much unexpected naked pulchritude on the hoof, stared uncomprehendingly, and they made no effort to position themselves in a defensive posture. They stared at our streaming manes, our wildly swaying breasts, our lightly muscled, naked thighs clutched round our mounts, our cushiony bottoms pounding in our saddles, our excitement-moistened, fear-widened pussies thrusting forward with the momentum of the charge. They stared with awe and surprise and—*oui!*—a certain amount of lust. They stared, but at first they made no attempt to do battle with us.

Perhaps it was because initially the manner of our appearance and our wild nudity made them take us for supernatural beings. Or perhaps it was because their macho indoctrination was such that they could not let themselves do battle with women. Or perhaps it was because the sight of so much bare female flesh so unnerved them, so aroused their lust, that they were swept up in a sudden tide of desire to make love, not war. In any case, their hesitation to engage us in combat was their undoing.

We were naked and screaming and riding hard, and our blood was up. At the head of the charge, I let my upper lip curl into a fierce snarl and I did not hesitate to strike with full force the first infidel unlucky enough to step into the path of my charge. My sword pierced his belly even as his eyes were admiring the long, red, stiff nipples at the tips of my wildly bouncing naked breasts. His hand reached up supplicatingly and clutched my bare jogging behind as I pulled the blade free of his flesh and rode past him. His tongue licked his lips appreciatively at the pucker of my pussy as I wheeled my horse just in time to watch him twirl around and die. His dead staring eyes still admired me as I turned to my next victim.

The enemy was in complete disorder now, but here and there were pockets of quite active resistance. A well-aimed arrow shot the horse out from under the brunette *jeune fille* at my side and I had to ride around her in circles to fight off the Turks intent on carving up her slender, naked, small-breasted figure. I crossed swords with two dark-skinned infidels at once—huge, bare-chested fellows wearing white burnooses—and it was only the distraction of my glistening naked parts that saved me from being hacked to pieces. One made the mistake of letting his eyes fall to peruse the pink inner meat of my pussy, and I carved a second mouth under his chin. The second man was obsessed with running his blade through my heaving bosom, and once I realized this, it was a simple matter to parry and separate him from a large section of his groin.

The blood began to flow freely. Death and agony were everywhere. My husband, Louis, and his French knights had been fighting with their backs to the wall and anticipating defeat before we arrived. Now they came out from behind the wagons and joined in the fray. Soon it was obvious that the tables had been turned. The infidels were being beaten and started retreating down the mountain.

It was my first experience with war. I was frightened, of course, but beyond fear, I was thrilled. I had not dreamed that the shedding of blood could be so exhilarating. My naked body gleamed with perspiration. My blood seemed to boil with a sort of lust I had never known before. My reaction was to the violence, of course, but the experience was also very erotic. And each time my nostrils widened with the scent of fear emanating from the enemy—an aroma I had perhaps inspired with my merciless Valkyrie hellions—a surge of hot lust oiled my pussy and made it clench like a fist seeking a target or a hand seeking the hilt of a sword.

So this was what battle did to men. This was why they went from the battlefield straight to the brothel, from ravage to rape—the bastards! And yet I felt the base appetite twisting deep between my hungry thighs.

The enemy was in flight now. From the enthusiasm with which they gave chase, it was obvious that my ladies were as aroused by battle as I was. These were noblewomen, aristocrats, but they rode down the foe like savages now, striking them, smiting them, shedding their blood with un-Christian glee and killing them with the naked satisfaction of so many farm girls slaughtering chickens for Sabbath dinner.

I confess that I joined in this slaughter all too willingly. Each time I rode down and struck a fleeing enemy, the blood lust would build and I would chase wildly after another victim. In this fashion, I galloped farther down the trail from the wagons, leaving my husband and his knights behind me. They were safe now, rescued, but that did not stop a dozen or so of us amazons from continuing the pursuit. These women, as aroused as I, hurtled down Mount Cadmos wreaking havoc and seeking—let us be truthful!—Eros.

In this fashion my dwindling troop of naked noblewomen reached the base of the mountain. Here the enemy scattered. And we, carried along by the exhilarating momentum, scattered after them.

Spying a burly fellow with a scarred naked chest the size of a wine cask, I guided my mount into a grove of trees in an effort to ride him down. I was perspiring. My breasts were heaving. My blood was hot. Perhaps I would run him through. Perhaps I would hold a dagger at his throat and force him to grant me the traditional reward due the victor.

Would that be a problem for him? I wondered. Would

fear keep him from getting hard? Would it interfere with his performance? Or would it make him too hasty? By God, if he left me unsatisfied, he would die a nasty death! I would see to that!

But so obsessed with the itch was I that I became confused in the woods and lost the fellow's trail. Then, having wheeled my mount around one too many times, I became even more befuddled and unsure of the direction from which I had come. I dismounted. I shielded my eyes with the flat of my hand and tried to spy the sun through the pattern of leaves over my head so that I could get my bearings.

It was no use. The branches were too thick. I could only guess. Leading my horse by the bridle, I walked naked through the woods in search of some familiar landmark.

Perhaps ten minutes passed. Then, abruptly, the forest gave way to a meadow of high grasses. So high, indeed, that as I crossed it the tips of the blades of grass tickled my stiff, sun-worshiping nipples.

My steed and I approached a slight rise. The grass was thinner where this knoll was. I let my horse graze there and strolled to the top by myself.

The sound of bleating alerted me to the herd of sheep before I saw them. They were grazing on the other side of the knoll. It was a pretty scene, peaceful and pastoral after the carnage, and I gazed down on it for a moment. Then I saw him.

He was dozing under an olive tree, his shepherd's crook lying beside him. He was a very young man, scarcely more than a boy, and his skin was very dark. He was wearing a brief loincloth of the type that herdsmen wear in

Turkey, and nothing else. He was young and his body was muscular even in respose. He was beautiful.

I studied him for a long moment. His eyes were closed and his long black lashes were like an intricate scrollwork over his strong cheekbones in the sunlight. He was clean-shaven and he had a strong jaw with a cleft in it. His lips were very full and his dream must have been pleasant, for he was smiling a little. It was a pleasant smile, with the promise of a dimple at one corner. His hair was long and straight and black and rumpled by the wind.

My eyes kept returning to the young body. It was layered with the sinews of outdoor living. Even in his sleep the muscles rippled. His gleaming pectorals were particularly exciting. The silky hair on his chest didn't hide them. His arms and thighs were sleek with this sinew, but when he moved in his sleep the bulge of hard muscle was immediately apparent.

Silently, my naked sword in my hand, I approached him. I stood directly over him and looked down at the hard, dusky flesh. I was breathing quite heavily now—the battle, the blood lust began to come back. Nearby a sheep baa-ed. The sleeper stirred. The muscles of his abdomen rippled above his breechcloth. I caught my breath.

He quieted. Slowly, I reached down with my sword and inserted the sharp, still-bloody tip into the knot at his waist. Slowly, with infinite patience, taking great pains not to wake him, I worked it loose. I folded back the triangular breechcloth in much the same way as one might peel an onion. His belly was ridged with muscle. His prick was unaroused, but long and thick and dark and beautiful nevertheless.

I knelt beside him and looked at it closely. His balls

were quite large and resting in the grooves made by the muscles of his thighs. The tip of the prick was covered by the foreskin. His pubic hair was black and silky and not very thick. He seemed young and vulnerable, but his cock—its potential—was wicked. Truly wicked, *mes amis!*

If a *fille* does not take care of herself, then who else will? Holding the sword poised over his groin, I touched my breast with my free hand. I stroked my long, hard nipple. There was fresh blood on my fingertips and I smeared it over the swell of my breast. I caught the aroma of it and it made me gasp. My cone-shaped breasts rose and quivered. I dropped my hand between my legs. I was looking out for number one.

The insides of my thighs were sullied with the hard riding, the hard fighting I had done. There was dust on the silken, chestnut hair over my mons veneris. I could feel a welt—the result of a blow I had sustained in battle—swelling up on one buttock. The lips of my pussy were very sensitive when my fingertips touched them.

I stirred the honey there, the syrup roiled by battle. Gently, I rubbed the raw, pink inner meat. I pushed my finger up the tight, hot tunnel and sighed. I touched my clitoris. I looked at the pretty, long, thick prick stretched up along the muscle-ridged belly. My clitoris stiffened. I strummed it. I moaned aloud. The eyes of the young shepherd fluttered open.

"Who—?" He stared to sit up, but the threat of my sword blade at his groin held him in place. "What?"

"Eleanor," I answered his first question. "Duchess of Aquitaine." I deliberately frigged myself and watched his dark eyes widen. "Queen of France." I strummed my clitty for him to see and became even more exited when he licked his lips with a long, red, youthful tongue. "And you are my prisoner."

"Your prisoner?" He reached down as if to draw his loincloth back over his prick.

My sword stopped him. "*Oui*. There has been a great battle," I told him. "We are the victors."

"We?" He looked around him. There were only sheep to see. Sheep and me—naked me.

"And to the victors belong the spoils." I reached out with my hand, the fingers sticky with my syrup, and walked the fingers up and down the length of his cock.

My reward was instant. It stiffened and grew longer. The young shepherd made another futile effort to cover himself with his loincloth, and again I stopped him with my sword.

"You are embarrassed," I smiled at him. "Your desire betrays itself. But why this lust, young shepherd?" I teased him.

"You are naked!" he blurted out. "Why are you naked?"

"So are you," I reminded him. I slid my hand under his balls and made small circles with my fingertips there.

His cock quivered and stretched for the sky. "Because you unknotted my loincloth while I was dozing," he said.

"Well, I am a soldier," I told him. "That is why I am naked."

"I never heard of a woman soldier," he replied, his upright cock throbbing as I continued to squeeze and fondle his balls. "Or a naked soldier either, for that matter."

"Soldiers are frequently naked when they rape those they have conquered," I told him. "And I have conquered you."

"Are you going to rape me?" He sounded both curious and frightened.

"I am," I assured him. "I owe it to myself."

"It won't work," he told me. "I'm the man and you're the woman. A woman can't rape a man."

"That's what you think!" I nicked him under the chin with my sword tip to show him that I was still in charge.

"If you hurt me, or even if you just scare me enough, I will lose my erection. How can you rape me then?"

"By making sure you get it back," I told him. "Like this." I demonstrated. I held his hand to my breast and let him feel the heat and the hardness of my nipple and the breathless softness of my flesh. Then I put it between my legs so he might feel my readiness.

His cock stood up like the pole from whence flew the royal banner over our castle back in Paris.

I reached into my boot and took out a dagger. I tossed my sword to one side and held the dagger poised just below the juncture of his legs. "And now for the rape." I knelt, a knee on either side of his hips, and slid my gaping pussy toward him.

He watched with wide, disbelieving eyes as I transferred the dagger to my other hand and held it within easy stabbing distance of his throat. "Fuck, lackey!" I told him.

"Help!" he bleated weakly, sounding not unlike one of his sheep. "I'm being raped."

I took his stiff cock in my fist and bent it so that I could insert the tip in my quivering pussy. The head was dark, purplish, very swollen. He was very excited and the shaft throbbed in my grasp. I mounted him then.

Delicious! The stiff hard-on slid all the way up my

honeyed cunt. It was thick and it filled the cavity to the fullest. I pinched at his balls with the lips of my pussy.

"Kiss me while you fuck me!" I ordered him, still holding the dagger to his throat. "Play with my breasts. Suck the nipples. Put your finger between the cheeks of my ass. Play with me there. That's it! That's it! Now fuck me! Fuck me!"

I slid up the length of his hard prick. I slammed down so that my pussy spread out over his groin. I squealed with excitement. I held the knife to his throat. I reached behind me, under his balls and clawed at his hard, savage bottom with my free hand.

Muscles surging, his body rose and he rose inside me at the same time. He squeezed my breasts and sucked at the nipples. He played with my anus. He fucked me with long, deep, powerful strokes. His muscular body was just right for the feral appetite the battle had given me.

"Harder! Faster!" I clawed at him, feeling myself starting to spend. "Oh!" I writhed, grinding down on him. "Ahh! I'm coming! Now!" I grabbed his balls and squeezed. "Give it to me now!"

There was a powerful upward push and his body rose under me. He held me in place and an instant later I felt the lava exploding from the tip of the prick deep inside my climaxing cunt. Clutching the dagger in my hand, I squeezed his erupting cock with my orgasm. I came and came and came. . . .

When it was over, I climbed off him. His cock flopped out of me and lay limply on his belly. I stood and looked down at him. I was naked and perspiring, but I felt very good.

"I've been raped!" He turned his face away from me. He looked horribly ashamed.

"You're not the first one," I told him. "Women are always raped by the victors in war."

"But I'm not a woman!"

"Well—" I considered. "Now you know what it feels like to be one." As I continued to look down at him, I felt a little chagrined. "What's your name?" I asked the young shepherd, attempting to soften the brutality of the moment, perhaps even of the rape. "What do they call you?"

"Saladin," he replied. "They call me Saladin."

Chapter Seven

The most casual acts have the most far-reaching results. An unplanned rape, no more really than a chance release from the tensions of battle, engenders such resentments in the hapless victim as to create a larger-than-life monster of vengeance. A soul has been seared, a hatred intensified, and a leader is forged from the defiled flesh. And this leader's will burns so hotly that its flame ignites a *Jihad*, a holy war. Thus do the atrocities of one Crusade, one holy war, create the vengeful climate justifying the evil acts of the next holy war.

Saladin! He was the ogre I created. A humble shepherd lad when I ravished him, the crime against his person propelled him into joining a Muslim band dedicated to driving the crusaders from all of the Eastern lands they occupied. His bravery and savagery were such that he quickly rose to prominence in the armed forces. While still quite young he became a General, and his successes were so spectacular that he was able to unify Turkish and Syrian and Iraqi and Armenian and even Egyptian armies under his command and to face the crusaders with overwhelming force. Some years after our encounter, during the Third Crusade, he would lead his armies in a climactic battle against my young son, Richard Coeur de Lion, and defeat him so decisively that the crusaders would be forced to flee back to Europe and for the first time in eighty-eight years the Muslims would control not only the Holy Land, but all of the countries contiguous to it which the Europeans had tried to colonize.

My defeated son would tell me terrible, terrible stories of the rapes committed by Saladin's soldiers. The most heinous of these concerned Richard himself and how, taken prisoner, he was buggered by bestial Turks. "An atrocity!" he termed it. But I, older by then, and remembering, was of the opinion that atrocities are often a matter of viewpoint.

Certainly at the time, I viewed my ravishment of Saladin as no more than a meaningless interlude in the progress of the Crusade. Without so much as a backward glance, I left the shepherd lad with his sheep and rode back up the mountain to rejoin the main crusader force. They were gathered on top of Mount Cadmos, secure in having driven off the enemy. Aquitainians and French were now joined together once again.

They were not, however, together in spirit, and morale was low. The French were convinced that the Aquitainians had deliberately left them vulnerable to the enemy. And despite my role in rescuing King Louis and his French knights, they suspected me of being the leader of the Aquitainian plot against them. The absurd theory was that

I wanted to replace my husband both in bed and as leader of the Crusade with the Aquitainian Sir Geoffrey of Rancon. Crude drawings of us copulating—the rutting figures easily identifiable by the crown on the woman's head and the scar on the man's cheek—were distributed among the French rank and file.

Circumstance forced us to march together, but we were truly separate and hostile armies. Nor did hardship heal our differences. Crossing the mountains to the seacoast, we encountered raging storms that blew our tents away and tipped over our wagons. Two loads of my personal finery were lost to a mud-filled ravine. Autumn turned to winter and the rain to snow. Provisions were lost to the blizzard and we were forced to slaughter and eat our spare horses. On the rare occasion when we reached a mountain village, our need was such that we bartered weapons and armor for food. Fever, dysentery, starvation, frostbite—all took their toll.

When we finally descended to the sea, we found only enough ships waiting to transport the nobles and their ladies to the port nearest Antioch. The rest of the army had to go over land, across more brutal mountain terrain. Almost a third of them deserted, giving up not only the Crusade, but Christianity itself in exchange for Muslim vows and Muslim bread.

Nor was our voyage exactly a pleasure cruise. The seas were choppy, the weather most inclement, and both the King and myself were miserably seasick. The three weeks it took to reach the port serving Antioch were an eternity.

When we disembarked, however, it was like arriving in Eden. The trees and fields we passed through on the short ride to the city of Antioch itself were green and verdant and abundant with fruit. I was reminded of my native Aquitaine and my spirits lifted immeasurably at finding myself in such a setting after all the hardship we had passed through.

This feeling was enhanced by the warm greeting we received from my Uncle Raymond, once of Poitiers, now Prince of Antioch. Indeed, he embraced me with such Aquitainian fervor as to bring a scowl of disapproval from the Abbot Bernard and an echoing frown from my husband, Louis. But then, neither of them had yet forgiven me for riding naked with my ladies during the Battle of the Feast of Epiphany. No matter that I had saved Louis' skin by the maneuver; the blatant nudity had endangered his soul and the souls of all who served with him, and that put me in a category that was very close to unforgivable.

Uncle Raymond did not share their view. "You are your father's daughter," he enthused, "brave and bold, a true Duchess of Aquitaine."

"She is the Queen of France," Louis reminded him, his scowl deepening.

"Of course, Sire." Uncle Raymond's elongated face nodded soberly, but there was a twinkle in his dark eye. "And surely as beautiful as ever graced the throne."

"Why, thank you, Uncle." I shielded my blushing cheeks modestly with my fan and looked at him reminiscently over the top of it. I remembered that day in my girlhood back in Poitiers when I had watched him deflower my younger sister, and my disappointment when he had been too noble to perform the same service for me. I had been sure then that I would never forgive him for that insult. Indeed, I was not sure now that I had forgiven him.

What I was sure of was that I did still find Uncle

Raymond most devilishly attractive. His figure slender as a sword blade, his long, mournful, sensitive face, the memory of his unexpectedly plump penis—I knew without consultation with Petronilla, who had been his mistress, why these facets attracted. I could guess what delights she had experienced in his bed.

Ah, but that was in the past. This was now. And it was now, in the present, that my thighs rubbed contemplatively together when I considered Uncle Raymond. *Oui.* This was now. And what would be would be!

"What will be?" The question was raised in another context quite soon after our arrival. "What is the best course of action for our Holy Crusade?"

"We must reconquer Edessa." Uncle Raymond was clear and firm. "The threat of the infidel army surrounding Antioch must be removed. Only that way will the Holy Land itself be safe."

Louis and the Abbot Bernard both raised doubts as to the wisdom of this course.

"You are dubious because you have not heard the latest news," Uncle Raymond told them. "The Emperor Conrad has rallied his German army after the defeat he suffered and even now is on the march to the Holy Land itself."

I noted the troubled glances exchanged between my husband and the Abbot. I understood them well. Once again Conrad had acted without waiting for orders from Louis, who was supposed to be in charge of the Crusade. Once again he had put himself and his men in the forefront of the quest for infidel booty. And if he was allowed to set himself up as the protector of Jerusalem, there would be no stopping him and his Germans.

It may have made perfect sense to Uncle Raymond to attack the infidels in Edessa while they were being forced to redeploy part of their strength to deal with Conrad's march to Jerusalem, but to Louis it would have meant accepting defeat in the most important struggle of all—the battle over leadership of the Crusade.

"No!" Louis was adamant. "I will not further battle the pagan until I have myself made my pilgrimage to the Holy Land."

"It is God's will." Piously, the Abbot Bernard backed him up.

Uncle Raymond looked from one to the other of them in amazement. "But surely the whole point of this Crusade is to secure Antioch and lift the threat to all of the East," he reminded them, "not to forgo battle for the sake of pilgrimage."

The argument went on far into the night, but Louis and the Abbot would not be moved. Piety came first. Only after having secured God on their side, would they smite the infidel and save Antioch.

After breakfast the next day, strolling through the Moorish-style palace with its sun-drenched patios and parlors alternating with dim, high-ceilinged rooms slit by narrow windows covered with hallowed, geometric tapestries, I encountered Uncle Raymond lying in the shadows of a small chamber on a low Arabian-style divan and staring disconsolately at the dust motes floating in a stray patch of light near the rafters far above him.

"Why so pale and wan, fond Uncle?" I greeted him teasingly. "Prithee, why so pale?"

"Your husband, the King," he told me frankly. "I don't understand him. The opportunity to act and to win has been thrust under his very nose, and he refuses it. Tell me frankly, Eleanor. Is he still holding that business with Petronilla against me? Is that why he refuses to save Antioch?''

"I doubt that Louis thinks of it. The Abbot Bernard, however, may be another story. He is not likely to forget immorality. Also, he has no fondness for Aquitainians.''

"I thought I noticed some tension between the Aquitainians and the French. Why is that?''

I explained it to Uncle Raymond.

"And it extends even to you, their Queen?'' He was surprised.

"*Oui*. Particularly to me.'' I was seated on the edge of the couch upon which he was lying. We were all alone, and so I decided to change the subject. "You have not inquired after Petronilla,'' I chided him.

"How is she?'' He sighed.

"Very well.''

"I am glad. There are still times when I miss her very much.'' His moody face took on a mournful aura.

"You could have stayed with her.''

"And renounced Antioch? Rejected the opportunity to be its Prince? Truly, that would have been asking too much of love. It would never have survived such a sacrifice. Believe me, my way was kinder. A quick end. A new beginning for both of us.'' Again Uncle Raymond sighed. "But I will tell you truly that I have not found Petronilla's like here in Antioch.''

"The daughters of Aquitaine are a rare breed.'' I looked him quite directly in the eye.

"Why, so they are, Niece.'' My meaningful glance had

lit a gleam. "And none are more rare, surely, than your sister and you."

"How odd that you should pair me with her when it was Petronilla that you embraced while rejecting me," I reminded him.

"Rejected you, my Queen?" Uncle Raymond looked blank for a moment.

"The stables. Poitiers. When I was but a girl." I refreshed his memory.

"Ah!" His narrow face lit up with a fleeting smile of remembrance. "But I was only protecting you, protecting Aquitaine. You were the oldest daughter, in line to be the Duchess. Your maidenhead was a precious national asset."

"Nevertheless I perceived it as a rejection and became so angry that I surrendered that national asset to the very first stable boy I encountered."

"My loss!" Uncle Raymond sighed ruefully. "My very great loss. I wish you hadn't told me. Now I shall always regret my chivalry."

"It was indeed the sort of action that gives chivalry a bad name." I smiled at him. "But nothing in this life is irremediable, Uncle. The courier always jangles his spurs twice."

"Does he?" Uncle Raymond sat up beside me on the couch. "Does he, indeed?" His deep-set eyes moved over my body approvingly. "It occurs to me, Niece," he said carefully, "that perhaps my greeting to you yesterday may have seemed lacking in enthusiasm. I was distracted by political matters. I should like to take this opportunity to welcome you more wholeheartedly now."

"That would be lovely," I told him. "That is, if you are sure. . . ." I paused.

"If I am sure?"

"If you are sure that politics will not again distract you, Uncle." And I moved just enough so that my thigh brushed his through our clothing.

"I am sure." Uncle Raymond took me in his arms then. His beard fell softly over my face and tickled my cheek as he kissed me. His breath in my mouth was quite warm and exciting. His hands moved freely, squeezing my breasts, my hips, my buttocks through the high-necked taffeta afternoon gown I was wearing.

His lips forced mine to part. His tongue entered my mouth. Its rhythmic thrusting prompted me to suck at it.

"Welcome, Eleanor," he murmured when the kiss was over. "Most welcome."

"As welcome as if I were my sister, Petronilla," I teased him.

"Welcome for your own beautiful sake." He ran both his hands over my body, fondling my breasts, my belly, my thighs. Then he reached to the top of the bodice of the high-necked dress and began to undo the buttons. "I have heard that your husband has vowed chastity until the Crusade is over," Uncle Raymond remarked.

"It seems all Christendom knows of this vow of his." I sat with my head bowed, looking down at his long, graceful fingers as they turned back the taffeta and laid bare the top swelling of my quick-breathing bosom.

"Surely this must work a great hardship on you." He stroked the warm, heaving, naked upper mounds.

"I feel the deprivation keenly," I admitted, wriggling under his firm caresses.

"He took this vow when he first left France." Uncle Raymond dipped a long finger inside my bodice and toyed with a long, burning nipple. "That is a very long period of deprivation for you indeed, my poor Eleanor." The tip of his finger was like satin against my quivering, sweetly tormented breast tip.

"A very long period," I agreed breathlessly.

"And how have you occupied yourself during this period?" His hand moved between my breasts, a long, insinuating finger rubbing up and down in the perspiration-moistened cleft there.

"I have taken care of myself," I moaned. "I have looked out for number one."

"Ahh, Eleanor." He bent his head to my breast. "You are your sister's sister." He freed one breast completely from my bodice and took the long nipple between his lips.

At first he sucked it gently, then more strenuously. My pear-shaped breast jiggled against his mouth, the flesh warm, excited, heaving. His long, straight black hair tangled in my fingers as I pressed his head to my bosom. His mouth opened wider and encompassed more of my panting breast. His tongue licked and teased the throbbing nipple. I had a sudden vision of his thick, hard prick moving in and out of my sister Petronilla's wide-spread quim just after he broke her maidenhead on that long-ago day in Poitiers.

I writhed with this memory as he transferred his mouth to my other breast. I slid my hand inside the loose neck of his tunic and over his chest. The hair there was surprisingly bristly and curlier than the hair on his head. His nipples were sensitive and rose to my touch.

"Let me kiss you there." I pulled up his tunic from the bottom and bared his chest.

Uncle Raymond stood in front of me, now fondling my naked breasts instead of kissing them. The top of my dress was unbuttoned to the waist and both orbs were completely exposed. Sitting on the couch, I leaned in to him and licked his chest, his risen nipples, with a hungry tongue. I trembled as I tasted the flesh over his slender frame. His very boniness excited me. I slid my tongue down, dipped it into the waistband of his drawers and probed his navel.

"You are making me very excited, Eleanor!" His hands became a bit brutal on my breasts.

Looking down, I saw that it was true. His drawers were distended in front by an irresistible erection. It poked them out in front and its pulsing was clearly visible.

"Poor Uncle Raymond." I patted the brazen lump. "Calm down." I laughed, but being none too calm myself, it was an excited laugh.

Needless to say, he ignored the suggestion. Instead, he bent swiftly and raised the hem of my gown. He caught my chemise with it and bared my legs entirely. He stood back and looked down at them.

I shifted position and stretched my legs straight out on the couch so that he might better admire them. It was shadowy there, but somehow they looked even more alluring with the striated sunlight speckling the white skin. Their shapeliness seemed in itself an invitation. The muscles of the pale inner thighs were clenched with erotic promise.

"Lovely!" Uncle Raymond ran his hands over the naked thigh flesh.

"*Merci.*" I traced my fingers up the insides of his thighs to the juncture of his drawers. There, through the material, I felt the heaviness of his nectar-filled balls.

When he felt me touch him there, Uncle Raymond was inspired to caress me through my bloomers. I was already quite damp there, and this made him smile. He rolled his fist over my groin and caused my body to heave upward and to writhe uncontrollably with the caress.

"You are sensitive," he observed.

"Like Petronilla?" I asked, continuing to squirm.

"The heat is in the blood." Uncle Raymond did not deny the similarity.

"Indeed it is." I reached out with both hands and squeezed his erection through his drawers. "And the same hot blood runs in your veins as mine, Uncle."

"True." He drew me to my feet, holding the skirt of my gown and my chemise up and out of the way. "Very true." He kissed me. His tongue pumped hotly between lips that I purposely kept tight around it. His hands slid around from my hips to my derriere. He fondled the burning cheeks through my bloomers. His fingertips explored the flesh and the cleft and even the little entrance to my bunghole—all through the silken material.

His playing with my bottom this way while he kissed me was very titillating to me. I was unused to being handled in this fashion. As with all that is new and innovative in erotic practice, I found his hands on my bottom doubly stimulating for that reason.

Sucking on his tongue, I let my hand drop between us. I slid it down inside his drawers and found the diamond-hard shaft of his aroused prick. I fisted it and squeezed. The naked flesh-rod burned and throbbed in my grasp.

The long, deep, hot kiss continued. I became dizzy and feverish with its effects. I pushed down Uncle Raymond's drawers and forced his erect cock to stand horizontal to his flat belly. Then I rose up on tiptoe and moved forward to settle myself astride it.

Although it was not inside me, the sensation of the rod

stretching between my legs from my pussy to my ass was most pleasurable. I moved over it slowly, sensuously, enjoying the feeling through my silk bloomers. At first I rocked over it and then I sawed back and forth. The silk was pushed up inside my cunt, and I could feel the heat of the stiff prick between the swollen lips of my pussy. I sucked his tongue and I kept on sawing.

Finally the kiss ended. "Ah!" I gulped air and rubbed my cheek against Uncle Raymond's soft beard. "This feels so good." I slid up and down the length of his prick without allowing it to enter me. My silk bloomers were still in the way.

"You are a true voluptuary, Eleanor." He slid his hands inside my bloomers and separated the squirming cheeks of my ass with his fingertips.

"Like Petronilla?" I teased, gasping at the multiplicity of sensations—his thin, hard chest against my swollen, sensitive nipples and heaving breasts, his fingers tormenting the equally sensitive cleft of my ass, his hard prick moving between my thighs against the mouth of my pussy.

"Petronilla was just a bit more impetuous, just a little more in a hurry. I prefer lingering."

"Then let us linger." I forced my hand between us as we stood in front of the couch and found his balls. The nest of hair surrounding them was crinkly, like the hair on his chest. Deliberately, my fingertips pushed the hair aside and tickled his balls.

"Witch!" Both hands closed hard on the naked cheeks of my ass. "You'll pay for that!"

"Will you spank me?" I asked, half hoping. "As you did that day in Poitiers when I caught you deflowering my sister?"

"You'd like that!" He stepped back and his drawers fell down around his ankles. He stepped out of them. He was completely naked now. His body was thin, but wiry and athletic. His prick was fat and juicy looking.

Uncle Raymond removed my gown and chemise. I stood before him dressed only in brief bloomers and slippers. The bloomers were still pushed down in back to reveal the plump, high-mounted, flushed cheeks of my derriere. "Perhaps," I admitted. "Perhaps I would."

Abruptly, he sat down and pulled me across his lap. He forced me to lie face down. He arranged my body so that the juncture of my thighs was positioned directly over his upstanding prick. "Bad girl!" he said, his voice hoarse. He once again pulled down my bloomers behind. "You must be punished." And he brought the flat of his hand stingingly down on one of my quivering bottom cheeks.

My auburn hair tickled as I craned my head to look over my shoulder. His hand had left a red welt on my derriere. Somehow the sight of this aroused me more than anything that had gone before. "Again!" I squeezed his prick between my thighs. "Do it again!"

The stinging hand struck again. The impact widened the space between the wriggling cheeks. I felt an added tickle of air there from the breeze of the blow. I thrashed wildly over the shaft of his cock. "Again!" This time after he struck, the tip of his organ became visible, poking up below my bottom. "Again! Again!"

Uncle Raymond began spanking me in earnest. The flat of his hand established a rhythm as it reddened the receptive flesh of my bottom. Soon I was rising to meet each blow, and with the rising, I was squeezing the shaft between my legs.

In this way, my climax quickly came. I felt it deep inside me, but I also felt it no place more intensely than in the exposed anus the spanking presented. "I spend!" I cried out at last, sobbing and laughing at the same time. "I spend!" And I clenched Uncle Ramond's hard prick with the lips of my pussy through the silk of my bloomers and wrenched it as I came.

My uncle did not come with me. He deliberately held back. He lent his hardness and the thrill of his spanking hand to the cause of prolonging my orgasm, but for himself he had other joys in mind. Even as the last shudders drenched his obliging but not imbedded cock with honey, he made these appetites known.

"Stand up, my dear." He lifted me from his lap, stood himself, and then drew me to my feet. His cock stood out hard and red in front of him. There was a strange expression on his face. His eyes glittered.

As I stood, I became aware of how my behind chafed from the spanking. "What are you going to do?" My green eyes were open very wide.

"You will find out soon enough, my darling niece." There was just a hint of menace in Uncle Raymond's voice. He took my hand and led me around behind the low-backed couch.

Movement made me even more aware of the damage he had wrought to my hindquarters with his spanking. My heart began to pound in anticipation of some new violence. I would not allow him to really harm me, but there was an odd sort of thrill to playing with the fire of the cruel side of his nature.

"Bend over the couch." Again he positioned me.

The couch back caught me just at the tops of my thighs.

I braced my hands on the couch itself. My long chestnut hair hung down, all atumble. The nipples of my pear-shaped breasts tickled me under the chin.

As I had before, I craned my head to look over my shoulder. My bottom jutted upward. My bloomers had once again been pulled down in back. My cunt and my anus were both completely exposed. Both were quite red and moist and looked abraded from the activity they had just undergone. My most intimate interior was opened wide, gaping and vulnerable.

"Are you going to spank me again?" I was panting in spite of myself.

"Should I?" He slapped one of my naked buttocks lightly. "Have you been naughty?"

"No naughtier than you, Uncle."

"Well put!" He threw back his head and laughed. Then he stepped up close behind me, and I felt his silky beard and straight black hair against my naked shoulder. "Then let us be naughty together," he whispered in my ear. His tongue followed the whisper, licking the inside of my ear, sending shivers up my spine.

"Oui!" I was so eager, it was all I could manage by way of reply.

His hands slid to my hips and gripped them. Then they slid around back and caressed my burning buttocks. Finally they were between my legs, rubbing the sopping silk of my panties which still clung to my crotch in front. Soon the silk was turned into a glove finger and the finger it encased was pushing up the clutching slit of my pussy.

"Oui!" I repeated again. *"Oui! Oui!"*

Uncle Raymond reached down with his other hand and used it to rip the silk. He pushed the remains of my panties out of the way. He stroked my naked pussy with his hand. "Do you like this, Eleanor?" he inquired.

"Very much."

He traced the cleft from my pussy to my anus and back. I shuddered with delight. He worked the tip of his finger between the swollen lips of my pussy and stirred the honey there. The pleasure made me moan. He moved the fingertip to my anus and lightly probed my sphincter. I ducked my head and caught one of my nipples between my lips and sucked it hard.

"You like the way that feels?" The heat of my body was his answer. "My Queen," he murmured in my ear, "you are a hot wench!" His white, even teeth sank into the fleshy part of my shoulder.

I pushed back against him with my flaming bottom and my gaping cunt and bunghole. My reward was to feel the hard, hot tip of his prick against one cheek of my ass. I reached behind me and fisted the shaft. He let me pull the foreskin back and forth for a moment, but then he took my hand away.

"What do you want me to do?" I asked breathlessly. "What do you want to do to me?"

Uncle Raymond didn't answer me. Instead, he put both hands on my upthrusting bottom and drew the flaming cheeks wide apart. He left one hand there to secure them in this position. Then, with his other hand, he reached under and in front of me and raised my gaping cunt. When it was tilted just as he wanted it, he laid the swollen tip of his cock between the lips. He paused and then gave a mighty thrust. His cock penetrated me to the hilt.

There is no way that I can describe how that first full, powerful thrust of Uncle Raymond's cock made me feel.

One moment my cunt was hot and empty and hungering, and the next it was stretched full of swollen Aquitainian cock. My response was not ladylike. I think what I said was "Oof!"

But directly the rude syllable escaped my lips, I began rolling my bottom under the hand still holding it and squeezing the cock inside me with the enthusiasm that a thirsty Arab uses to squeeze the juice from an orange. Pounding with my fist on the couch, still mindlessly sucking one of my nipples, the blood rushing to my upside-down head, I ground in small, tight circles over the impaling cock with such energy that quite soon my naked alabaster flesh was all agleam with perspiration.

"Oui!" I rose up on my toes and then bent my knees as I came down again. "Fuck me!" I rotated against the bristly hair of his groin. "Fuck me hard!"

Suddenly Uncle Raymond pulled back and then rammed his cock into me full force again. I let out a yelp and managed to reach behind me with one hand and clawed his naked buttocks with it. This, however, merely inspired him to repeat the maneuver. And then I was pinned over the back of the couch with his full weight on top of me, and he was ramming his cock into me over and over again with all his energy.

"No! Wait! *Oui! Oui!*" It was too much for me. I could not withstand the assault. I could only surrender to it. That pumping cock drew the first long, agonizing shudder from my sore pussy, and then I was wrenching violently and spending again with a force I couldn't control.

When it was over, Uncle Raymond was still inside me, still hard. Sore as my pussy was from his violent assault on it, I nevertheless felt a new thrill with the realization that he was not done with me yet. I reached behind me with a trembling hand and stroked the underside of his balls.

Immediately, his weight doubled me over the couch again. His hands were on my hips and he began slowly pumping inside my pussy. It was different from before. These were long, slow, deep thrusts, not violent but lingering, filling. My consciousness focused on the feel of his hard-on as it drew across my aroused clitoris the way a minstrel's bow draws across his fiddle. His balls rolled hotly against the lips of my pussy and my backside. He was purposefully arousing me again, and he was doing it slowly, carefully, and with great finesse.

"Ahh," I moaned. "So nice. *Oui.* . . . That's it . . . slow and hard . . . easy and so-o-o-o nice. . . . Ahh! . . . That feels— That feels—"

I was conscious of every calculated movement of his prick inside me. I was conscious of the rustle of his balls and the tickle of his pubic hair. I was conscious of his lips nibbling my ears and of his hands reaching around to play with my down-hanging breasts and hard, burning nipples as he fucked me. I was conscious of it all, and most of all I was conscious of another slow, extremely intense orgasm starting to build deep inside me.

"I think I'm going to spend again," I gasped.

"You think?" Uncle Raymond fingered my anus and moved his cock in knowing circles that covered every interior inch of the clinging, honeyed walls of my cunt.

"I am!" I was sure. "I'm going to spend!"

Suddenly he pulled his cock all the way out of my sopping pussy. Both his hands went to my flaming cheeks and he pulled them wide apart. Then he laid the shaft of his cock in the cleft between my bottom cheeks.

"What are you going to do?" I was suddenly fearful.

"Just relax." He reached between my legs with his hand and caressed my gaping pussy.

"But—"

"Shh!" He fondled my naked breast with his other hand. He turned my head and kissed my lips and licked their inner surface with his tongue.

I did indeed begin to relax. And as I relaxed, my lust reasserted itself. I pushed against the fist at my quim and by so doing pinched the hard-on between the cheeks of my ass.

As if it had been a signal, Uncle Raymond slid his prick up and down in the perspiration-slicked cleft. His hot balls bounced along behind. The bristly hair of his groin abraded the sensitive pink flesh between the cheeks of my ass.

"I like that," I heard myself moaning. "I like that very much."

"You'll like this even more." He backed off a little, and then I felt him insert the head of his prick between the wide-spread cheeks. He moved it around with his hand, obviously looking for the anus.

"You'll hurt me!" I was suddenly afraid again.

"Not if you relax. Just relax."

Once again I made a conscious effort to do as he said. This time my reward was to feel the head of his prick at the entrance to my anus. He pushed carefully, holding my cheeks apart with his hands. I pushed back and felt him slide into me.

It was very tight, but the sensation was excruciatingly

thrilling. By concentrating on not tensing up, I was able to make myself push back a little more with my ass, and I felt his prick sliding up. A moment later I relaxed my sphincter muscle and Uncle Raymond was up my ass to the hilt.

"That feels marvelous!" I said, and I could not keep the note of wonder from my voice.

"It's going to feel even better," He promised, starting to move.

He was right. As his cock moved out of my bunghole and then all the way back in, I instinctively used my sphincter muscle to grip it. The sensation was even more thrilling than before. Soon he was moving faster and faster and his balls were bouncing against my eager ass as I thrust back against him.

"Can I come this way?" I babbled. "*Oui!* I can! I can! I can feel it! I'm going to spend!"

"And I'm going to come inside you when you do!" Uncle Raymond declared, clutching my breasts, pressing me down with his weight, thrusting into my ass, breathing like a blacksmith's bellows.

"God! God! God!" I slammed my ass back against his cock. I could feel the ridge of jism mounting to the tip, getting ready to discharge. "Give it to me!" I shrieked. "Give it to me now!"

"Up the Aquitainians!" Uncle Raymond bleated. A moment later, the fiery nectar of his passion geysered into my very bowels and I started to come with him.

Together we drew it out to the last lovely drop. When his limp organ finally was withdrawn from my bottom, the effect was like removing a cork and his lotion splashed out of my ass and over the fronts of his thighs and the backs of mine. Only then did I straighten up and turn around to face the lover who had introduced me to such ecstasy by the rear door.

I straightened up. I turned around. I looked at my lover. Then I looked over his shoulder.

And that, *mes amis,* is when I saw my husband, the King, standing in the doorway and looking at his naked, buggered, semen-spattered wife in the arms of her anal lover!

Chapter Eight

It put a crimp in the Crusade. If Louis had been stubborn before about putting pilgrimage before battle and the salvation of his own soul before saving Antioch from the infidel by force of arms, now he was adamant. There is nothing like discovering that someone is cuckolding one to firm up one's resolve not to stick one's neck out for him.

"We depart Antioch immediately," Louis told me a day later. These were the first words he spoke to me since finding me in flagrante in my uncle's arms. "You will accompany me to Jerusalem and beg God's forgiveness for your sins."

"If we leave Antioch undefended now, it will be a virtual declaration of our willingness to surrender it to the Muslims," I pointed out to him.

"You have the audacity to plead your incestuous lover's case to me!" Louis' voice quivered with outrage.

"My behavior and his are irrelevant to the cause that

197

brought us here at such great cost, such great hardship," I answered him. "As head of the Crusade, you are charged by His Holiness the Pope himself to save Antioch and to protect the gateway to the Holy Land. Surely you will not let our marital difficulties stand in the way of this."

"You are incredible!" Now Louis' fair face turned a mottled red with rage. "Do you feel no shame at all for your adultery?"

"You took a vow of chastity and denied me your husbandly attentions," I reminded him. "And so I did what I had to do. I looked out for number one."

"Jezebel!" His voice rose to a screech. "Hussy!" He took a deep breath and brought himself under control. "We leave for Jerusalem at cock's crow," he added in a low, somber, final tone.

"No, Louis." I found the courage to be firm. "I personally rode the length and breadth of Aquitaine to recruit warriors for this campaign. I told them that we would fight for Christendom and to hold Antioch and secure the Holy Land. I am still Duchess of Aquitaine and I cannot betray my soldiers and knights now. If you will not, then I must remain here in Antioch with my Aquitainians to protect the city."

"That is two-thirds of my army!" Louis was shocked.

"*Oui*. I beg you to stay here and command it. But if you refuse, these are my vassals and they will do as I order them to do."

"And you are my vassal!" Louis reminded me, his voice quivering again. "You must obey me! You are my Queen and my wife!"

"I would gladly give up the crown in exchange for my freedom." I gazed at him steadily with my green eyes.

"What are you saying, Eleanor? Do you know what you're saying?"

"I am suggesting that we get a divorce!" I told Louis bluntly.

"You would have me publicly brand you an adulteress?"

"That would not be necessary. Abbot Bernard has frequently charged that we are not married in the eyes of the Church because we are fourth cousins. All we have to do is grant the legitimacy of the charge. We can simply admit that we have been living in sin, and I feel sure that the Abbot himself will secure a divorce for us from the Holy Father."

"Never!" Louis turned abruptly on his heel and left me. "Never!"

I thought about our conversation after he had gone. My suggestion of a divorce had not been made hastily. I had been thinking of the possibility for a long time. Louis was a total disaster as a husband as far as I was concerned.

Indeed, I had not been able to help recognizing the emptiness of my marriage from the very first time I had surrendered to Bernard de Ventadour. More than any other man I had known before or since, Bernard had brought home to me what it could be like to be a woman in the arms of a man one loved. *Oui*, I loved him still. I thought of him constantly. I always would. And such interludes as I had enjoyed with the Emperor Manuel, Saladin, and Uncle Raymond were as nothing compared to my memories of ecstasy with my lost Bernard. And, oh! how wonderful it would be to be free—unmarried—if ever we should find each other and that rapture again.

The timing of my suggesting divorce, however, was not wise. Catching me in the act of adultery had shaken Louis' confidence. Now my suggestion shook it further. Without my vassals, his crusader army would be reduced to a mockery. And an acrimonious divorce might also mean the loss to France of Aquitaine, its wealthiest province. He was pushed into a corner, and he had to act.

Act he did! The next morning, before dawn, I was rudely awakened by the forcible entry into my bedroom of the Abbot Bernard and four armed guards. "Seize her!" He commanded them.

"What is the meaning of this?" I demanded to know.

"You are under arrest, Majesty," the Abbot told me, unable to withhold a note of gloating from his voice.

"By whose order?"

"By order of His Majesty Louis Seventh, King of France!"

"On what charge?"

"Many possible charges spring to mind, Majesty." The Abbot allowed himself a thin smile. "But no formal charge has been drawn up as yet. When it is, you will be informed. Now please be so good as to put on your clothes. We are leaving."

"Leaving Antioch?"

"*Oui.*"

"But—"

My protests were in vain. Within the hour I was marched from Uncle Raymond's palace under armed guard. This guard was surrounded by the bulk of the crusader army on the outskirts of the city. Vulnerable, unguarded Antioch receded into the distance behind us as the march to Jerusalem began. We had come as the protectors of the Prince of the city, but we left with no word of farewell and no concern for his welfare. . . .

*   *   *

What followed was an exercise in the divine right of Kings to self-destruct. With no regard whatsoever for the Muslim armies making conquests at his heels, Louis let nothing distract him from reaching Jerusalem. When he got there, rather than deploying his forces to defend the Holy City, he neglected his command to go every day to the tomb of Christ, where he prayed for forgiveness for his sins. Thus, precious time was squandered while he and the Abbot Bernard spent their days praying instead of planning for battle.

When the pair finally did resume command of their forces, they demonstrated a lack of knowledge of elementary strategy and tactics unparalleled in modern warfare. They received word that Antioch was under heavy siege but chose to ignore the circumstance. (Doubtless my peccadillo with the Prince of Antioch had something to do with that decision, but I ask you, *mes amis*, should such a trifle have been allowed to destroy the main purpose of the Crusade?) Instead, they decided to attack the enemy in his strongest bastion, the thick-walled, stoutly defended city of Damascus. And so the army marched through Syria like lemmings to the sea.

Reaching Damascus, our first all-out attack was driven off with no breaching of the enemy walls, few enemy casualties, and much French and Aquitainian blood shed. During the next four days several more such attacks were mounted against the Syrian stronghold. None succeeded.

Sir Geoffrey of Rancon and some of my other Aquitainian Barons began taking issue with the strategy of King Louis, the strategy that seemed to consist only of hurling large numbers of exposed troops at the city walls for the bowmen behind the barricades to shoot down. Also, the Aquitainians, although kept in the dark as to the exact nature of my custodial status, were growing more and more suspicious and asking more and more embarrassing questions regarding my whereabouts and welfare. (It never occurred to them that I was actually being held in Louis' encampment under arrest. If they had known, there might indeed have been an open mutiny.) They argued against Louis' stubbornness and demanded that he give up the siege of Damascus.

His refusals became immaterial when a large army of Muslim reinforcements arrived to relieve the defenders of the city. When they attacked from the rear, the result was panic and chaos. That one battle—if such the bloody rout can be termed—broke the back of the entire Second Crusade. The army fled Damascus in disorder, with the infidels wreaking havoc at its heels.

They continued to devil us all the way to the coast. The cost of that retreat in men and equipment was truly horrendous. And if there was justice in the loss of the wagons loaded with my frippery, what sense was there in the sacrifice of all the men and money I had labored so hard to raise in Aquitaine?

But there was no time for such questions now. The enemy had driven us to the coast, and we were trapped here with the sea at our backs. There was no longer any doubt that the Second Crusade was a complete catastrophe. The only question was how to get out of it alive.

The answer was ships. There was no other way to flee the mopping-up operation of the foe. And so we commandeered vessels and set sail for the safety of Europe.

I was still persona non grata with my husband and the

Abbot Bernard. These two devoted religious zealots did not have it in their hearts to forgive my sin. This was the reason, I suppose, that I was assigned a separate ship from theirs.

The vessel on which I sailed was a small two-master with a pert stern that rode high in the water. She was yare, a craft built for speed, but not for comfort. Once aboard, I was no longer under guard. There was, after all, no place for me to run to in the Mediterranean Sea.

In its way, the Mediterranean was more dangerous than the battlefields of the East. It was often buffeted by brutal storms. As a route much frequented by trading ships and wealthy pilgrims on their way to the Holy Land, it was constantly being preyed upon by swift, heavily armed pirate corsairs. I would be unlucky enough to encounter both on my voyage.

The seas were rough, but the weather was not yet stormy when we rounded the tip of Greece. We were entering particularly dangerous waters. There had been a war going on for many years between the King of Sicily and my one-time lover Manuel, the Emperor of Byzantium. This war was fought mainly at sea, and for the most part in those waters of the Mediterranean between Greece and Sicily. It was an odd war, for more important than the fleets of naval vessels were the pirate ships on both sides. These fought major battles and flourished from the booty they captured.

As we turned the Peloponnese Peninsula, our small convoy found itself making straight for just such a battle. A Greek pirate fleet was in the very act of attacking a smaller force of the Sicilian navy. We tried to turn to avoid the fray, but the wind was against us and the maneuver came too late.

As soon as they saw us, the Greeks dropped their assault on the Sicilians and turned toward our weaker vessels. Immediately there was panic, and our convoy broke up with craft making off in every direction. It was every ship for itself.

Toward nightfall, a fog rolled in and further complicated the situation. Now our ship completely lost contact with the others in the convoy. It was almost dusk when the fog lifted slightly and we found ourselves completely surrounded by Greek pirate ships. We were outnumbered and to give battle would have been suicidal. The captain of our vessel had no choice but to surrender to them.

An armed party boarded our ship. The leader of the Greek pirates headed it. Phebo by name, the leader was dressed in a short leather tunic and a leather jacket. Phebo had long hair and a patch over one eye, wielded a wicked, naked blade, and displayed a well-turned leg in the silken hose of a body stocking. Phebo was a woman.

With a sneer on her face and a sword at his throat, Phebo commanded our captain to change course to due north and proceed at full sail. The corsairs of her pirate fleet would fall in around and behind us. Even as this was done, from the afterdeck, I could see the original Sicilian naval fleet, reinforced now, reforming, and bearing down on us from the distance, as it sped to the rescue.

Alas! The wind was with us. Soon we would outrun them, and doubtless our pirate captors would find haven in some hidden Greek cove.

Night fell. To add to our troubles, a sudden squall blotted out the stars and moon. The Sicilians must surely lose us now. We were at the mercy of the pirates and the mounting storm.

The howling wind and the sudden sheets of rain seemed to exhilarate Phebo. She took over the captain's cabin with two of her burly lieutenants and had me brought there to join them. "He says you are an important person," Phebo said, jerking her thumb at the captain.

"Not so very important," I demurred.

"He says you are a Duchess of some kind."

"He exaggerates."

"He says you are a Queen."

"Merci, chéri." I smiled sweetly at the captain.

"Queen of France."

Fear lit up the captain's eyes at the smile I now bestowed upon him.

"You must have a drink with me!" Phebo ordered. "I have never had a drink with a Queen. Not, in any case, with a Queen of France."

"I will be honored," I told her. "I have never had a drink with a pirate Queen."

"A pirate Queen!" Phebo guffawed and jostled each of her lieutenants in turn with an elbow. "Do you hear that, buckos? A pirate Queen!" She turned to the captain. "Bring rum!" she ordered.

"I have retsina." His tone was ingratiating.

"I said rum!"

"I only thought that since you are Greek you might prefer—"

"RUM!"

"Of course! Of course!" He scampered to the door of the cabin and ordered one of the sailors to fetch a cask of rum.

A jagged streak of lightning lit up the sky outside. Rain fell in sheets to the deck. The wind was mounting a gale force. The captain was compelled to order all sails trimmed lest the force of the wind capsize us. There was a low, ominous rumble of thunder, then a loud clap like an exclamation from Hades itself. It ushered in two sailors with the keg of rum.

Phebo poured two tankards, one for herself, one for me. She ignored the captain. Her lieutenants cupped their hands under the spigot of the keg and slurped the liquor from their palms. Phebo raised her mug to me, drained it in one quaff, and then refilled it.

I drank my own portion more slowly. It was the first time I had ever tasted rum. It had more bite than wine and more sweetness than whiskey, but I liked it better than mead, which was what it was closest to in my experience.

"Not bad grog!" Phebo pronounced.

"Quite good, really," I agreed.

I looked at her with curiosity as we continued drinking. I had never encountered a woman remotely like Phebo before. I had known ladies and scullery maids, Queens and peasant wenches, but this was the first time I had ever met a lady pirate. She was—there is no other way to put it—an experience!

Despite the patch over one eye and the masculine-seeming leather apparel, Phebo was not at all unattractive. As tall as I, her figure was more sturdy—more voluptuous, I suppose. Certainly it was more athletic.

Where my skin was pale, alabaster, ladylike, Phebo's reflected her outdoor life with a sort of rosy duskiness. Her flesh glowed and her bronze Greek complexion had been both flushed and tanned by the elements. She seemed somehow to brim over with vitality and health. There was that peculiarly Greek quality about her of savoring life to its fullest.

It was easy to see that she was not the sort of person to make any bones about her appetites. She would eat with lustiness and not too much concern for the niceties of the table. Right now she drank with a fierce thirst that seemed unquenchable and smacked her lips with each tankard of rum she drained. A good guess was that she would satisfy her erotic needs in the same vigorous, uninhibited fashion. As it turned out, this surmise was to be confirmed with an immediacy I could not have anticipated.

Phebo set down her mug and ran both her hands through her long, curly jet-black hair with an abandon that left it in swirling disarray. She stretched and the leather of her bodice crinkled and bulged with the expansion of her large breasts. She pushed back from the table and scratched her belly through the leather. Balancing on the back legs of the chair, she rolled on her cushiony bottom and wiggled her fleshy, jutting hips. She was. *mes amis,* to put it crudely, a lot of woman!

"Sex!" she said in such a low, throaty voice that for an instant I thought she had merely burped. "I want sex!" Rum, it seemed, had clarified her objective for her.

Now, I had always looked out for number one, but I had never before met a woman who gave voice to my philosophy quite so blatantly. I could not help but admire her. "Bravo!" I murmured. "Bravo!" I repeated in a slightly louder tone.

"Men!" Phebo demanded. "Bring me men!"

"Delicious!" I approved her specificity.

"And more rum!" She pounded the table. "Bring more rum!"

"BRING MORE RUM!" her lieutenants chorused, also pounding the table. "BRING MORE RUM!"

And now all chanted—all, including me—"BRING MORE RUM! BRING MORE RUM!"

The rum was brought. So too were the men. They were handsome lads, all three Aquitainians, a blonde, a brunette, and a redhead. Phebo had evidently pointed them out as being to her taste before. She had good taste. All three were robust and had a quite lusty look about them.

She looked them over and turned to me. She grinned. And it *was* a grin, broad and lascivious. She drained another beaker of rum. She smacked her lips. She spoke.

"I'm into leather," Phebo said.

"I beg your pardon?" I wasn't sure I had heard her right.

"I said I'm into leather."

"Oh." I had no idea what she meant. I thought about it. "You mean you dress in leather," I interpreted finally.

"Well, yes. But that's only part of it."

"What's the other part?"

"This is." She reached her hand over her shoulder and one of her lieutenants inserted the butt end of a long snake-whip into it.

"Oh!" It suddenly dawned on me what Phebo meant. "Oh, dear!"

Outside, the storm was raging with new intensity. The ship was being tossed crazily from side to side by high and violent waves. Some of them were breaking over the prow and some of them were crashing down on the decks. There was something savage loose outside. And now it was inside the cabin as well!

Phebo ordered the blonde Aquitainian brought face-to-face with her. He was a strapping specimen, bare chested with golden fur covering him from shoulder to belly. He had huge arms and a neck thick as an oak tree. His face was perhaps not too expressive, even dull, but sweet, very sweet.

"Your name?" Phebo demanded of him.

"Victor. Victor Darlan."

"And what do you do, Victor, when you are not posing as a soldier?" Phebo asked with a touch of sarcasm that was wasted on him.

"I am a smith. I shoe horses."

"Do you brand them as well?"

"If that is what the owner wants."

"And cattle? Sheep?"

'Calves and lambs. Twice a year."

"Is that not very painful for the animals?" Phebo inquired, her breasts rippling with the quickness of her breathing under the leather.

"I don't know." Victor looked at her with mild blue eyes that didn't understand.

"Bare his bottom!" Phebo instructed her minions abruptly.

They obeyed. At a gesture from Phebo, they turned Victor away from her and bent him double. His ass, substantial, beefy, jutted out.

Phebo reached out and stroked one of the cheeks, then the other. She pinched them each in turn. "This one!" she said finally. "We'll put the brand right here." She smacked the buttock and the white flesh pinkened. "Then," she informed Victor, "you will find out if it is painful or not."

Victor was dragged to the opposite side of the cabin and flung to the floor. He was naked from the waist down, and he crouched there with his large hands clasped over his genitals. He watched with large, frightened eyes as Phebo turned her attention to the second Aquitainian, the brunette, who admitted to the name of Marcel.

"I was a baker before I enlisted in the Crusade," he answered her question.

"And did you beat your dough before putting it in the oven?" Phebo asked.

"But of course." Marcel was wary. His small eyes darted about. He was not unhandsome, but there was a decidedly sly look about him. The impression he gave was somehow of speed rather than strength. His smile was an ancient shell game.

"And of course the dough did not protest the beating."

"Of course not." His puzzlement made Marcel even more suspicious.

"And if the situation were reversed?" Phebo's smile was voluptuous. "You would not protest, would you?"

"I—" Marcel was still trying to formulate an answer when he was seized from behind and struck three times hard on the posterior with the butt of the whip. "Ow!" he cried out.

"You disappoint me." Phebo nodded for her lackeys to drag Marcel over beside Victor and deposit him there.

Now the redhead was brought before the pirate leader. He was a sun-freckled farm worker, still young, but already quite stooped from working in the fields. His name was Antoine.

"Stand up straight!" Phebo commanded him.

He tried, but was unable to satisfy the order.

"You are a shambler!" She was amused.

It was true. Antoine was a loose-limbed, rawboned sort of fellow, lanky and bony and uncoordinated. His smile was frightened and one of his red, work-calloused hands kept straying to his forelock to tug at it.

"A serf," Phebo realized. "Tell me, my man, does your master beat you?"

"Betimes, ma'am."

"Then you know what it is to be on the wrong side of the lash?"

"Aye. Such was why I joined the army."

"But were you never beaten in the army?" Phebo persisted.

"Aye." Antoine sighed. "Whipped there too."

"And what do you do when you're whipped?"

"Do?" Antoine looked at her blankly.

Suddenly her arm snapped forward and she caught him on the side of the head with the doubled lash of the whip. A bloody bruise parted the sea of his freckles. He flung both hands up in front of his face and crossed them at the arms, trying to shield himself from a second blow that might be forthcoming.

"I see." Phebo's voice was soft, reflective. "You cringe, Antoine. That is what you do when you are whipped."

Antoine hung his head as if in confirmation of her judgment.

"But what if you were to do the whipping?" Phebo suggested. Her shapely thighs quivered through the thin material of her body stocking. The leather she wore moved as if it were skin. "Spread them here!" she commanded her men. She handed Antoine the whip. "Here is your chance," she told him softly. "Whip well, and who knows what your reward may be?"

A loud clap of thunder punctuated her words. The ship rolled violently, virtually flinging her victims to the table where she had indicated they should be spread-eagled. A jagged streak of lightning lit the scene cruelly. The drumming rain and howling wind commented on the sadism that was about to occur.

Victor and Marcel were positioned side by side on their knees in front of the table. Their upper bodies were stretched prostrate across it so that their heads hung down over the far edge. They were bent at the waist so that their naked bottoms stuck up in the air just where the table caught them in the midriff. The table was low and so they were able to kneel, but not so low that it didn't strain the muscles of their thighs to stay in that position.

The pirate guards arranged them according to various gestures from Phebo. Their legs were parted widely so that their balls were visible hanging down below the naked, wide-spread cheeks of their asses. Marcel had a surprisingly long prick, and it was visible from behind, hanging down in front of his balls. Victor was very hairy, and his large balls were encased in a nest of golden fur.

Phebo positioned Antoine behind them with the whip. Then she walked around in front of them where she could see their faces. Her good eye glittered as she brushed back her unruly black hair. "A fellow Aquitainian will punish you," she told Victor and Marcel. "Surely that is fair."

"Queen Eleanor!" Marcel appealed to me. "Surely you are not going to let her do this. We are your vassals! You owe us your protection."

"She cannot help you," Phebo assured them. "Like yourselves, she is a prisoner. Strike!" she instructed Antoine.

He laid the whiplash across Victor's furry behind, leaving a pronounced welt behind.

"Queen Eleanor!" the burly blonde blacksmith bleated. "My Duchess! Help me!"

"I cannot," I told them both. "You must bear your

chastisement. You must remember that you are Aquitainians and soldiers. You must stiffen your upper lips.''

"You don't want to leave, I trust." Phebo was quivering with excitement.

"No. These are my subjects. I owe it to them to stay and lend what support I can.''

"Besides, you just might enjoy this entertainment." Phebo turned to Antoine. "Again!" she instructed him.

He whipped each of his fellow Aquitainians in turn.

"It is warm in here." Phebo undid the strings securing her leather bodice. The upper halves of her large, round, full breasts bobbled into view. "Again!" she instructed Antoine. As the whip struck Marcel's jutting, naked, sparse-haired buttocks, she bent to look into his eyes as if in an attempt to apprehend the fleeting instant of maximum shock and pain caused by the lash. Moving in this fashion, the leather fell away from her bosom and Marcel was granted a clear view of her wide, round copper aureoles with the little nipple-buttons standing up in the center of them.

Phebo caught his eyes looking at them. She smiled with satisfaction. The look she saw there—the mixture of agony and lust—was the expression she had been seeking. She was panting hard against the loose leather as she straightened up.

"What is the condition of this one's épée?" she inquired of one of her minions.

"Stiffening," was the reply.

"Whip Victor." She instructed Antoine to switch targets.

She positioned herself in front of him and lifted one of her swollen, heavy breasts from her leather bodice. The red-brown aureole was the size of a doubloon. She lifted her breast toward her mouth, extended her tongue, and licked a wide circle. "What do you think, my blacksmith?" she murmured.

"Hard as iron!" was the verdict of the lackey.

"Mmm." Phebo left the one impressive breast hanging nakedly and obscenely outside her tunic as she walked around behind the hapless victims to see their tumescence for herself. Satisfied, she then turned to Antoine. She took the whip from his hand. Then she took the hand and held it against her naked, heaving breast. "Do you like whipping better than being whipped?" she asked him.

"Yes, ma'am."

"And do you like the way this feels?" She rubbed his hand over her breast, over the perspiring, heavy flesh, over the wide copper aureole, over the hard, risen nipple.

"Yes, ma'am." Antoine's freckled face was perspiring now too.

"How much?"

He looked at her dumbly.

"Let me see how much." Phebo reached between his legs. "Mmm!" She approved what she found. "That much!" She stood on tiptoe and kissed him, licking his lips with her tongue. "But I want to see it," she decided. "It's not fair. Your countrymen are revealed and you are not. Lift your tunic, Antoine. Remove your body stocking."

Blushing, he did as she told him. His prick sprang out like a spare limb. It was thick and hard and pulsing and—

"Why, it's freckled!" Phebo realized. "You've got freckles all over your cock! And you're a real redhead too!" Her long nails tangled under his fat balls. "What do you think of that, Queen Eleanor?" she called to me.

"Remarkable!" What else was there for me to say?

"I shall keep my eyes on it while you continue whipping," Phebo assured Antoine. She walked around in front of the table and ran her fingers through Victor's curly blonde hair and then chucked Marcel under the chin. "Proceed!" she ordered Antoine.

He striped Victor's large beefy ass. The blonde writhed and grunted. At the same time, his blue eyes clung to the sight of Phebo tracing her naked aureole with one long fingertip while at the same time she ran her other hand up and down the insides of her shapely, squirming, silken thighs.

Laughing, she came closer to Victor. "It hurts, but it's exciting too." She pushed the leather out of the way and showed him where the moisture of her passion was darkening the crotch of her bloomers. "It excites me," she told him. "And that hard cock of yours between your bleeding bottom cheeks—that excites me too."

I was not immune to the rising temperature of lust in the room. My vassals were being demeaned, and I could not allow myself to be party to that, but nevertheless, secretly, under my chemise, my thighs were grinding together and my pussy was sucking my sopping bloomers deep up inside it. It took a conscious effort to keep my hands away from my aching nipples, my pulsing quim.

Phebo was back behind the victims once again. She was holding up her leather tunic and rubbing against their bleeding bottoms with her bloomered cunt. Laughing, she reached under the kneeling Victor and squeezed his balls as she moved against him. With her other hand she traced the wide cleft of Marcel's hairy behind. When he began to tremble, she leaned over and reached between his legs and tugged on his erection. She was becoming more and more excited and the look in her one good eye was becoming wilder and wilder.

"Come here, Antoine," she called to the redhead with the whip without turning around. "Lean into me while I lean into Victor," she instructed him when he answered her summons. And she reached behind her and positioned Antoine's erect prick lengthwise up the cleft of her behind as she pumped against Victor and jerked at Marcel's and Victor's cocks by turn.

When she finally pushed Antoine off her and moved away from the two kneeling men, her body stocking was smeared with blood. She grimaced and took it off. She also dispensed with her bloomers. Now when she lifted her short leather tunic, the long blue-black hair of her pussy flashed in and out of view.

"Violence excites me!" She stood there illuminated by a sudden jagged streak of lightning and laughed at the clap of thunder that seemed to challenge her to act on her words. "Give me the whip!" She pulled it from Antoine. "Spread him on the table face up!" she ordered her men.

Antoine's freckles shone with fear as they obeyed. She stood over him and wrapped her free hand around the shaft of his thick, throbbing, erect penis as it pointed toward the storm-torn skies above our battered ship. Holding it, fondling it, squeezing it, Phebo lashed out with the whip in her other hand and brought it down hard over Marcel's already ribboned posterior.

"Oww!" The dark man with the furtive eyes cried out.

Phebo fondled Antoine's nectar-fat balls and brought the lash down on Victor's chunky rear.

"Oof!" He too reacted.

Panting, Phebo tore off her tunic altogether. She stood

naked a moment, holding Antoine's hard-on, whipping Victor and Marcel by turn, her large breasts swinging like ripe melons, her shapely, fleshy thighs shiny with perspiration, her blue-black bush parted by the meaty pink slit of her hungry pussy. Her generous ass shook like the expensive guava jelly sold to European traders in a Persian market. She was like some primeval force—sensuality given life by lightning—and the storm of passion bursting free from inside her was every bit as spectacular as the one raging o'er the ocean outside.

She mounted the table now. Her lackeys were holding Antoine's wrists and ankles wide apart. His throbbing cock was sticking straight up out of the forest of his red groin hair. She straddled him, her magnificent bottom swaying over that reaching hard-on. Then she parted the lips of her pussy with the fingers of one hand and lowered herself down on Antoine's cock. "Fuck me!" she told him. And she struck him across the cheek with the doubled lash of the whip. "Fuck me hard!"

Antoine's middle rose as if the very earth had moved. His bottom rose from the table. His cock stabbed deep into the writhing cunt engloving it. His balls forced their way between the swollen pussy lips. He grunted and thrust upward and pulled out and stabbed again. He fucked. He fucked hard. He fucked Phebo as hard as he was able.

Laughing wildly, she rode the rampaging cock as if it were a steed not yet broken to the saddle. At the same time she snapped out with the whip and brought the lash across Victor's meaty, bleeding, naked haunches. She laughed with excitement when he cried out. "Bring him to me!" she told her guards, twirling the whip over her head, continuing to rise and fall on the thick prick pumping deep inside her clutching quim.

They dragged Victor in front of her. His clothes were in tatters. She reached out for his cock. It was semihard. Laughing, she ran her tongue around it, under his balls, up and down the shaft. It stiffened. She took it in her mouth. It started to pump deep between her lips. Victor's balls bounced against her rounded chin.

I was very hot now. I was hovering on the edge of an orgasm just from watching. If I could only touch one of my burning nipples— If I could only squeeze my thighs together in a certain way— Even if I could only move my bottom just so against the seat of the chair— *Oui!* I was caught up in the erotic scene and it took all of my will-power not to join it!

Phebo rose up and down the length of Antoine's cock, her heavy, large-nippled breasts bouncing. She sucked Victor's cock, her tongue extending beyond the shaft buried in her mouth to lick at his dancing balls. And at the same time, she contrived to reach over Victor with the whip and to lash his bleeding behind, thereby inflicting the pain of punishment at the same time as she gave him the exquisite pleasure of sucking his aroused member.

After a little while passed in this fashion, she remembered Marcel. She left off whipping Victor to lash Marcel instead. Soon he was sobbing, for the lust she was experiencing gave Phebo a heavy hand.

"An inequity." She took notice of his sobs. "Victor and Antoine have pain and pleasure, but poor dark Marcel has only pain. Show him where to lay his pike for pleasure." And Phebo slid forward on Victor's thrusting cock and provocatively wriggled her large, generous, perspiring, gaping bottom.

A moment later Marcel had mounted her. Victor grunted under the added weight and thrust upward into the impaling gash with even more energy. He was rewarded when Phebo wrenched his shaft in a variety of titillating directions under the new inspiration of Marcel's prick reaming her anus.

I was—I confess it, *mes amis*—both envious and curious. What must it feel like to be triply and simultaneously penetrated in this fashion? What must the sensations be of one hard cock filling one's mouth and reaching for one's throat whilst another rode deep in one's bowels and a third stirred the honey of one's fiery quim? What sensations the fortunate Phebo must be experiencing! I identified with her as I watched, and as I identified, I felt a phantom fist seem to reach high up inside my throbbing quim and tickle me beyond restraint.

And then Phebo was making uncontrollable animal noises around the cock in her mouth. Her ample bottom was a golden blur of motion around the shaft buried in it. Her hairy quim was wrenching fiercely as it rode up and down on the third cock penetrating her. Shudders began to sweep over her body and her big naked breasts swung wildly. She started to come.

Her grinding movements captured the balls of the redhead between her and squeezed them. The freckled cock heaved upward and then began geysering its nectar deep up her clutching cunt. Feeling the eruption inspired Marcel to let loose deep in her bun. His groin vanished between the cheeks of her ass and he started to come with an intensity that shook his entire dark body. That, finally, was what triggered Victor. The chunky blonde ass began rotating wildly, and he held Phebo's head with both hands and shot copious spasms of cream down her hard-swallowing throat. Thus the four of them came together.

Watching, I surrendered to my own abandonment. I did not so much as touch myself, but I quivered long and hot in the throes of an orgasm I could not control. Squeezing and panting, I sat and watched and spent. All by myself I spent and watched the three men empty themselves into the sucking, hungry, grateful orifices of Phebo's body.

Just as we were all of us subsiding, a very strange thing happened outside the cabin. The storm abruptly ceased. The rain stopped. The sea grew calm. There was neither lightning nor thunder. And swiftly the clouds passed by and a bright full moon lit up our vessel.

And more than our ship!

"Sicilians to starboard!" That was the first warning cry.

"Sicilians abaft!" That was the second.

"Coming up on the port side!"

"We're surrounded!"

Phebo flung off her hapless Aquitainian lovers and leaped to her feet. She grabbed up her sword and made for the deck at top speed. There was already a savage Sicilian boarding party and the pirate leader would be in the forefront of the Greeks forming to repulse it.

Naked she would fight! Nectar dripping from her lips, her bottom, her quim, she would fight! Still hot with passion, she would fight!

But are nudity, nectar, and passion the stuff it takes to win?

Chapter Nine

No.

In the final analysis, lust wearies. Passion crimps the fighting muscle. Rutting depletes, spending tires, and the sport of love is not fit preparation for the sport of battle. Which is why the jousting knight abstains from such activity prior to the tourney, why the warrior forgoes willing thighs before the onslaught, and why if Phebo had foreseen the attack, the pirate leader might not have opened the moist petals of her various orifices quite so eagerly to the victims of her leathery lashings. Because of this lack of foresight, Phebo's game was sadly off in the swordplay that followed.

She and her Greek pirate crew were no match for the Sicilian boarding party. The Sicilians were a picturesque group of sailors dressed in homespun blue uniforms with square white caps made rakish by a blue tassel hanging down in front of each. They were curly headed, with long, single braids down their backs, and gold nuggets screwed in the lobes of their ears. Their eyes flashed and their teeth flashed and their swords flashed. When they saw the naked Phebo, they spouted erections in their tight body stockings, but these made them no less fierce. With knives in their teeth and throbbing hard-ons, they swung through the rigging and shed Greek pirate blood as if it were so much brine with which they were washing down the decks.

In the end, Phebo was fortunate to be able to abandon the prize she had captured, fleeing in a longboat with six bleeding members of her band. Behind her she left two dozen Greek pirate corpses. And three flayed and wearied Aquitainians with stories to tell—a blonde, a brunette, and a redhead with freckles on his épée. The last I saw of her was a naked, Juno-esque figure standing in the stern of the longboat as it sailed off into the moonlight. Her heavy naked breasts seemed to flash defiance at the parting barrage of Sicilian arrows which sped her on her way.

"Queen Eleanor of France, Duchess of Aquitaine?" The man bowing before me in the captain's cabin was short and round and wore the tunic of an officer in the Sicilian navy.

"*Oui.*"

"I have the honor to announce that your rescue is completed and that you will be restored to your husband, the King of France."

Returned to Louis? Perhaps Greek pirates were not so terrible after all. "*Merci,*" I told the rotund Sicilian officer. But my heart wasn't in it.

"Allow me to introduce myself." He bowed again. "I am Captain Alfonso Caponini of the Royal Sicilian Navy." His eyes flashed like those of his men during the attack.

So did his white teeth. Except for a belly like a small melon, he was not unattractive. "At your service, Majesty," he added.

"I am in your debt." I held out my hand for him to kiss.

His own hand, when he took mine, was very soft and warm for the hand of a man. He had a flowing black mustache and it tickled my knuckles. His brown eyes were soft and limpid and strangely sentimental. "How may I best insure your comfort, Majesty?" Captain Caponini inquired.

"A long, undisturbed night's sleep," I told him. "Then breakfast. And after breakfast, a bath. A steaming hot bath."

"All shall be as you wish, Majesty." He clapped his hands and the cabin was cleared. "Sleep well, Majesty." And then he too was gone.

I retired. In my bed, after I had blown out my candle, only once did sounds disturb my quest for sleep. Two sailors exchanged some words in Italian that sounded like either the menu for a banquet or plans to go to a brothel when they had shore leave. The voice of Captain Alfonso Caponini, soft but firm, remonstrated with them. I could almost feel their chagrin in the silence that followed. And then I felt only sleep, deep, blessed sleep.

Drab daylight eased me into wakefulness. Once again the sky was overcast. The clouds varied from gray to somber black, and there was not a sun ray to be seen. The sea looked mean, brooding, rough, and ready to get rougher. The sails were billowed out like lust-filled breasts by a wind both strong and nasty. Like the sea, this wind seemed but preparing to become meaner. To sum up, it was the sort of a day at sea when one knows well why one has chosen life on land.

Things looked brighter with the arrival of Captain Alfonso Caponini. He knocked, bowed himself in, and announced that my breakfast was ready if I was. I replied that I was famished.

A smile of approval lit up his dark, round, mustachioed face. He clapped his hands loudly over his head. Again the door to the cabin was flung open. This time a parade of seamen from the galley entered, each with a white apron over his naval uniform tunic, each with a chef's hat in place of the sailor cap, each holding high a covered tray from which escaped a variety of the most deliciously steaming aromas.

"Hot antipasto!" Captain Caponini announced. The tray was lowered to a point just below my nose, and he removed the cover with a flourish. I saw shrimp in green sauce and hot sausages in tomato sauce and eggplant under melted cheese and spaghetti rich with hot clam-and-garlic sauce. My nostrils dilated as the tray was re-covered and placed on the serving table across the cabin. "Minestrone!" A cloud of steam rose from a tureen thick with vegetables and pieces of ham and diced crusts of hard bread. "Salad!" A crisscross of tomatoes with anchovies and hard salami, olives and lettuce and celery all dressed with olive oil and the magic hint of vinegar was shown me. "Pasta." There was both fettuccine alfredo and ravioli. "The entrees." There were three—*scungilli* with whole stewed tomatoes, veal Parmesan, and chicken cacciatore. "And for dessert," Caponini concluded, "tortoni, spumone, and our own special pastry tray." The pastry tray was unveiled to present a testament to chocolate, whipped cream, and custard fillings.

"I personally recommend the cannoli," he couldn't help adding.

"What is all this?" I was stunned.

"Breakfast."

"Breakfast?" I looked at the food heaped on the table across the room, and then back at Caponini. "Breakfast?"

"*Si*. Breakfast." He beamed at me. "You said that you wanted a good night's sleep and then breakfast, Majesty. And so here is breakfast."

"I meant coffee and a *brioche*. Perhaps a croissant with some strawberry jam. But this—"

"It is a Sicilian breakfast, Majesty. Just try it. I beg of you. Let me fix you a plate. Just a taste of this and a taste of that."

Well, after all, *mes amis*, he had saved me from pirates. I didn't want to hurt his feelings. And to be truthful, I was hungry. And getting hungrier as I inhaled those aromas. "Very well," I said, "just a small plate."

And so Captain Alfonso Caponini fixed me a plate. And then a second. And—I blush to admit it—a third. The food was absolutely delicious and I wolfed it down with an appetite like none I had ever known before.

"Try the cannoli." He brought it to me with espresso.

"I couldn't possibly."

But I did.

Captain Caponini watched me with a broad smile on his moon face. "French ladies do not eat a healthy enough breakfast," he told me. "It is why they are so slender."

"We are poor skinny wenches, I suppose, compared to your Sicilian women." I amused myself by agreeing with him.

It was warm and cozy inside the cabin. Outside it was

becoming more and more ominous. A major storm was gathering.

"I only said slender, not skinny. You are well formed, to be sure. Only not so—" Here words failed him, and he used his hands to describe an amplitude of flesh. "The way our women of Sicily are."

"I suppose it is only natural that Sicilian men prefer their women that way," I observed.

"Sicily is a rocky place." He shrugged. "A man needs something soft between himself and the ground."

"You look as if you have something soft." I nodded at his round belly.

"This? No, Signora Queen Eleanor. This is a hard rock. I will show you." He came around in front of me and took my hand and pressed it to his belly.

It did indeed feel quite hard.

"Hit it."

"No. I—"

"It is all right, Majesty. I am Sicilian, not French. You can't hurt me. Go ahead." He winked at me conspiratorially and his next words were obviously a translation of some sort of Sicilian idiom. "Go ahead. Take your best shot."

I shrugged and punched him in the stomach.

"Harder."

I struck him harder.

"As hard as you are able, Majesty."

I swung from all the way behind my shoulder and hit his stomach with my fist with all my might. It gave hardly at all. It felt tight and hard, not flabby.

"You see, Majesty. I am a man of stomach, of substance. But I am not soft."

"No," I agreed. "You are not soft."

"Have another cannoli, Majesty."

"Oh, no!"

And then he laughed. And then I laughed. And then we split the cannoli between us.

There was a low rumble of thunder. Captain Caponini cocked his head and raised an eyebrow toward the sky. "If you wish to have your bath, Majesty, I would suggest you do it now," he said. "You'll not enjoy it so much once this storm really gets under way."

I did indeed want to have my bath. It was at the head of my list of priorities. I bade Captain Caponini make haste to clear the cabin of the breakfast dishes and have a tub and hot water brought to me. All this was done, and no sooner had the captain bowed himself out to leave me alone than I stripped off my night clothes and lowered myself into the waiting tub.

Ahh, how good it felt! The steaming water was balm to my flesh. As I sank deep into it, letting it cover me, a feeling of total well-being—despite all I had been through—spread over me. Not even the increasingly angry sounds of the storm outside the cabin could lessen the feeling.

It sounded even angrier than it had the night before when Phebo had played counterpoint to the howling wind with her singing lash. The waves were pounding the hull like a hammer. Jagged streaks of lightning rent the harsh gray-black fabric of the sky. The ship rolled violently, pulled one way by the wind, pushed the other by the persistent seas.

Still I ignored all this beyond my cabin. I lay back in my hot tub, stretched out full length, let the water wash over my naked body, luxuriated in the sensations of the bath. And inevitably I thought of Bernard de Ventadour and touched myself as I so pondered.

Bernard my love! My own true love! I closed my eyes and saw his poet's face, the ridiculous scarlet cockade sticking out of his cap, the rakish tilt of his head. I heard his deep poet's voice, the unashamed Gascon lilt, his expressions mirroring his emotions as they tumbled over his craggy face. I smelled his peasant poet smell, that man-smell, that aroma he gave off of wanting me, of passion rising, that virile scent that originated square between his sturdy thighs. And I sighed deep from my breast and touched myself there to feel the pain of memory.

Bernard! Bernard my troubadour! Bernard who put it in me, held it in me, used it in me as no other man ever had or ever would!

I squeezed shut my eyes and told myself that the two fingers squeezing my nipple below the surface of the hot water were his lips, Bernard's expert sucking, kissing lips. I felt them drawing the heat and the fire from my pear-shaped breast. I lived again the pleasure of his suckling—his pleasure, my pleasure.

Bernard! Bernard! Why did you leave me? Why did I let you go?

Writhing in my bath, I remembered and longed for my lost love. I squeezed my hot, submerged breasts and played with the nipples and teased the aureoles and pretended that the hands arousing me were Bernard's hands. I remembered his naked, broad shoulders looming over me as I spread myself to him. I remembered his clean-shaven face and his deep chest and his own sensitive nipples and how I used to love to torment them with deep, tonguing kisses. I remembered how he would lay his thick, hard prick on top of my trembling white belly and rest it there while he aroused me, played with me, with my breasts, my bottom, my pussy, before he finally mounted me and put it all the way inside.

Bernard! Bernard!

The waves were crashing over the deck now. The tiller was out of the water; steering was impossible. The ship was being buffeted in crazy circles. Outside, on deck, sailors were scurrying about in confusion, in panic.

I was not aware. Both my hands were deep in the bath now, between my legs, drawing wide the portals of my pussy. *Bernard! Bernard! Put it in me, lover! Don't tease! Do it! Do it!* One long finger crept under me. I rose. The tip found my anus. I settled to the impalement. *You drive me crazy when you do that while you fuck me, Bernard!* Two fingers of my other hand entered my honeyed, gaping pussy and twistd.

Water splashed from the tub. I laughed aloud. I frigged myself deeply, fully!

Bernard! Bernard! Bernard!

De Ventadour!

The ship gave a sudden wild lurch. A wall of water crashed against the side of the cabin. The cabin wall gave way. *I'm coming, Bernard! I'm coming! I'm coming. I'm coming.* The tub with me in it went skidding across the floor. A wave lifted it over the deck. *I spend, my darling! I spend! I spend!* Tub and all, I was tossed over the rail of the ship and into the sea as I clutched my climaxing pussy.

Now! Now! NOW!

And as the Mediterranean swallowed me up, I remembered the feeling of the hot lotion of Bernard de Ventadour spurting powerfully into my pussy as—on one memorable occasion—I sat on his lap making love in a bathtub filled with warm water! And then I was sinking . . . sinking . . . sinking. . . .

Calm rather than storm, light instead of darkness, life, not death—such was my awakening. The vortex that had seized my tub had spun it in such a way as to hold me inside it. And now it was floating, bobbing like a cork, a miniature boat if you will, atop a placid blue-green Mediterranean sea under a smiling midafternoon sun. Like myself, the elements had spent, and all was languid.

I congratulated myself on being alive. Indeed, buffeted as my naked body had been, it was unharmed. Aside from a pleasant ache in my loins—the price of erotic nostalgia—I felt as fit, as they say, as a fiddle.

Raising myself up on my elbows in the tub, I looked around me. The seas, though rolling gently, were flat, and I had a clear view in all directions. There was no sign of the ship that had disgorged me. None of the ships of the Sicilian navy that had rescued me from the pirates were anywhere to be seen. There was no ship of any sort in view, nor on the horizon. Nor was there sight of any land.

There was only the sea.

Only the sea and me.

And then—

"O sole mio—"

I heard the rich baritone long before I was able to perceive the source of it. The voice seemed to be coming from the blinding sun itself, the late afternoon sun sinking now in the west. Only by looking straight into the sun and squinting was I finally able to see the hazy shadow appearing and disappearing behind a distant swell of sea.

"O sole mio!"

"Ahoy!" I found my voice. "Avast!" A creature of the land, I was unsure of the proper nautical terminology. "Yo!" I began paddling my little bathtub furiously toward the setting sun and the shadowy singer.

"Avanti!" My cries were heard and answered. "A mermaid!" Even with the sun behind him, the afternoon light was deceptive. "A naked mermaid!" Paddling toward me, the baritone picked up enthusiasm and speed.

I saw now that the singer's situation was no more promising than mine. He was perched on a large, jagged chunk of wreckage, a piece of ship deck turned by circumstance into a life-saving raft. He was the only one on this large piece of flotsam which also held a table covered with a damask cloth and set with silverplate for two. To one side, there was a second table, this one in the shape of an oblong, and there were several covered serving dishes on it. As the distance between us narrowed, I saw that the plate in front of the baritone was piled high with food.

"Clams *posillipso*," he called. "And a good chilled Chianti to wash it down. Do me the honor to join me."

"I am not dressed for dinner," I demurred.

"Nor I." He stood to demonstrate that the storm had torn his clothes to tatters. "So let us dine *au naturel*."

The sun was blinding me and he was still only a hazy figure, but I accepted his declaration of lack of formality. It was a little tricky on both our parts maneuvering my tub and his makeshift raft into a proximity that would allow me to join him. Therefore it was only as his hand pulled me up beside him that I had a really clear look at the baritone who had saved me from the isolation of the sea.

"You!" I was startled to find myself facing Captain Alfonso Caponini.

"Majesty!" He sank to one knee.

The courtesy was an error. He had not exaggerated the punishment his garb had taken from the storm. Now what was left of his body stocking split down the rear and his bare fundament popped out from under the tatter of his naval officer's tunic. Indeed, the rotund Sicilian was as close to nude as he could get without being in the same state as I was, by which I mean, *mes amis,* jaybird naked.

"*Scungilli.*" He rose and held a chair for me to be seated. "Some *scungilli* to start, I think, Majesty, and then perhaps you will try the lobster Fra Diavolo."

"I am not really hungry," I told him, and proceeded to consume three heaping plates filled with delicacies garnished with a variety of pastas.

By this time, the sun had set and the moon had risen.

"*O sole mio—*" Alfonso serenaded me. (Circumstance had put us on an informal basis; I called him "Alfonso" and he called me simply "Majesty.")

"You have a lovely voice." I trembled with the chill of the night air.

"You are cold," Alfonso noticed.

"The ocean climate."

"Put this on, Majesty." He took off his tattered tunic and offered it to me.

I was touched. There was not enough left of the garment to cover more than a portion of my anatomy. I was faced with a choice of arranging it above the waist or below. My pussy was still warm with memory, and so it was my breasts I chose to shield. I smiled my thanks to Alfonso.

He, poor fellow, was shivering now in much the same

way that I had been before. His body stocking was in such tatters as to leave him little protection against the cold and even less pretense to modesty. Besides the rent behind, it was so destroyed in front as to reveal his bare melon of a belly and the admirable equipment beneath it as well.

"I should not take your tunic," I told him. "Now you will freeze your *cojones* off."

"You speak Spanish, Majesty."

"Just enough to make myself understood." I watched him trembling in the moonlight a moment. "We must bundle," I decided. "It is the only way."

"Bundle, Majesty? What is that?"

"It is what we do in Aquitaine to counter the cold." I sat down on the planking on which we were floating and patted a spot beside me. "Sit here," I ordered Alfonso.

He obeyed, making a lap like a Buddha.

I stretched out full length. "You too," I commanded.

Alfonso stretched out beside me on his back. His naked stomach rose like a hillock. Beneath it his Sicilian marbles were fat in their tight little sac. And his Sicilian dagger quivered at a rakish angle along one naked, muscular thigh.

"On your side."

He turned on his side.

I snuggled against him. I curled my naked body around his protuberant belly. It felt hard and very warm against my flesh. I entwined my limbs with his. "This," I told Alfonso, "is bundling."

"In Sicily," he replied, his dagger stiffening against my thigh, "we have another name for it."

"The purpose is for two people to keep warm by merging their body heat."

"In Sicily we have other purposes as well." His erection extended out beyond his substantial belly and between my thighs.

"Hush now." I stroked his fleshy haunches. "We must get some sleep."

"Sleep!" He was breathing quite heavily. "Of course, Majesty. Sleep."

His body was like an oven. Clinging to it, I absorbed its warmth. In this fashion, wearied by the strenuous day, I drifted off to sleep. . . .

"Land ho!"

Alfonso's excited cry awakened me. Simultaneously, I felt myself bouncing off his hard belly as he leaped to his feet. I opened my eyes and looked up at him standing there and shielding his eyes against the sun as he gazed into the distance.

"Land ho!" he repeated.

"You're being redundant, darling." I yawned. I squinted against the bright sunlight. I found myself focusing on the dagger of flesh beneath Alfonso's belly. It was still deliciously hard.

"Sicily!" He began jumping up and down.

The movement certainly did enhance my view. "You're so excited, darling," I murmured.

"Sicily!" So happy was Alfonso to see his native shores that I half expected him to ejaculate on the spot.

Instead, he picked up a piece of board and began to furiously paddle with it. Caught up by his enthusiasm, I found another board and helped him. In this fashion we moved swiftly through the water toward a small horseshoe cove.

Too swiftly. We had forgotten that not all the rocks were where we could see them. Some of the worst, the sharpest and most jagged, were beneath the surface of the water.

About a hundred yards offshore, one of these hidden crags attacked our makeshift raft from underneath and ripped it asunder. The surf had brought us crashing down on this hidden knife-sharp outcropping, and when the froth cleared, Alfonso and I were floundering naked in the water while what was left of our raft was being swept back out to sea in a dozen pieces. Flailing furiously, we managed to half swim and half wade in to shore where we collapsed on the dark, hard-packed wet sand.

"Are you all right, Majesty?" Alfonso was the first to recover.

"Except for the skin I lost being dragged on the bottom," I told him.

We stood. He took my hand. We walked farther inland to where the sand was drier and fluffier.

"What now?" I wondered.

"Food."

"Don't you ever think of anything but your belly?"

"You will be glad I thought of it later, Majesty. You will be hungry."

He was right, of course. By noon I was famished. And I was very glad to join in eating the fish that Alfonso had caught and cooked. And I wolfed down the olives and the berries he had found as well.

By then we had determined that the spot where we had washed up was not Sicily proper, but only a small deserted island somewhere off its coast. There were, according to Alfonso, many such islands. They were uninhabited because nobody had ever been able to come up with a good reason for living on one of them.

Alfonso was disappointed. "Nobody ever comes to these places," he sighed. "We could be here forever without being found. What"—he sighed again—"are we going to do?"

"Vous faites ce que vous avez à faire," I told him.

"I beg your pardon?" Alfonso stared at me as if he suspected that a great truth might suddenly have been revealed to him. "What did you say?"

"I said that we will do what we have to do," I translated.

"That is very profound!" Alfonso said slowly, nodding his head. "Very profound!"

"Merci."

"Did you just think of it?"

"It's an old Aquitainian saying. 'You do what you have to do.' "

"Heavy!" Alfonso was quite impressed. "Very heavy."

"Merci," I thanked him again, flattered by the depth of intellect he ascribed to me.

"I must bring that back to Sicily with me, if I ever get there," he mused. "It's very important to learn from other cultures."

"Oui," I agreed.

"You do what you have to do." Alfonso repeated it as if making sure that he had it exactly right. "But in our present situation," he asked as an afterthought, "just what is that?"

"We should build a large fire," I told him, "and keep it going all the time. That way it will be seen by any ship passing by, and they will come for us."

"But suppose that it is a Greek pirate ship?" Alfonso worried. Suppose it is Greek pirates who come for us?"

"Pensez à numéro un!" I advised him.

"What?" His dark Sicilian moon face was illuminated as if by some wondrous philosophical dawning. "What did you say?"

"Look out for number one," I repeated.

"My God!" Alfonso was visibly shaken. "That is deep! So deep!"

"*Merci.*"

"Do you mind if I write it down along with 'You do what you have to do'?"

"Go right ahead."

" 'Look out for number one.' Taken together they almost form an ethos," Alfonso observed. "Still, something is lacking."

"Of course," I agreed. "All great philosophies come in three parts. You are lacking the third part. But I will tell it to you."

Hearing this, Alfonso became so excited that he responded with a rough translation of the Sicilian idiom. "Lay it on me," he said.

"All right," I replied. "Here it is." I pronounced the words slowly and forcefully as they deserved. "Don't get mad, get even!"

"Of course," Alfonso whispered, his eyes shut. "Of course."

"Don't get mad, get even," I repeated.

"Of course." He was so visibly moved that he had no other words.

"And now you have all three parts," I told him.

"I have never heard anything so cogent!" Alfonso carefully wrote down the last of the three phrases. "It is a complete philosophy. It will have the most profound effect on my country. We will embrace it and then—then— Why, the whole history of Sicily may be altered!" Slowly, he read the words he had written down: "You do what you have to do. Look out for number one. Don't get mad, get even. Tonight, Majesty," he added in a voice fraught with emotion, "the Sicilian Credo has been born!"

This conviction gave Alfonso great energy. He gathered kindling and firewood and soon had a roaring signal fire going. I don't know whether it was the words or the blaze, but he also was wagging a most impressive erection beneath his melon belly.

"Shall we bundle, Majesty?" he suggested.

"It is still daylight," I pointed out.

"Nap time for Sicilians."

"But the fire provides much warmth and there is no need to bundle."

"It provides no warmth equal to that of Sicilian blood."

"You forget yourself!" I tapped the drum of his belly to remind him. "I am the Queen of France."

"And I am a Sicilian!" He curled a leg behind me and pushed hard so that I tumbled to the sandy dune beside the roaring bonfire. "I do what I have to do!"

"You learn fast!" I gasped.

"It is only that I look out for number one." Alfonso fell to his knees beside me, his cock outstretched, and reached for me with both hands.

I kicked out hard with one foot and caught him neatly in the groin. He fell back with a cry of pain. It was several minutes before he recovered. When he did, he spoke.

"I don't get mad," he said. "I get even."

I laughed in spite of myself. I had planted three seeds in hard, fat Sicilian soil, and they had flowered. "Did I hurt you very badly?" I inquired solicitously.

"It did not tickle, Majesty."

"Let me see."

Alfonso came to me, his rotund stomach preceding him, both hands supporting his injured gonads. The redness was receding to pink and the swelling was going down. "The pain is easing," he admitted grudgingly.

"I should not have kicked so hard," I apologized.

"True, Majesty. It was something of an overreaction."

"Sit down." I patted the sand beside me.

He sat.

"You should take off a little weight," I said after a few minutes.

"Why? A stomach is a mark of prominence, of success."

"Is it not also an obstruction at times?" I asked delicately.

"Not at all. One adapts."

"And one's partner? One's lady?"

'She also adapts."

"Indeed?" I murmured, fluttering my long eyelashes.

Alfonso caught my hot-eyed look. His prick rose. "You seem—"

"*Oui?*"

"—friendlier."

"Do I?" I let my hand fall casually on his naked thigh.

"I don't understand." Alfonso was blunt. "When I made advances a few moments ago, you rejected them most violently."

"I just don't like being forced," I told him. "But I am open to persuasion." I squeezed his tensed thigh muscle.

In truth, the fire was warm. The sun was warm. My

blood was warm. And as to that old Norman dictum "Nobody loves a fat man"—why, *mes amis,* circumstance makes its own exceptions.

Alfonso was most persuasive. His long mustaches flowed over my cheeks and his sensual lips enveloped mine. There was the bite of Sicilian seasoning as his tongue dueled with mine. His hands stroked up my long, naked thighs with slow, lingering expertise.

I put my hands on his large, hard, round stomach. In the circumstances, it began to feel warm, sensual, tough, manly. I kneaded it as we continued sucking at each other's mouths.

"Lovely." The kiss over, Alfonso reached for my breasts. He cupped them in his hands and then traced their upward curve. His fingertips stroked the blood-red nipples to hardness.

"You are arousing me," I told him frankly. I kissed his chest, my auburn hair fanning out over his belly.

Alfonso responded by stroking my back and my milk-white bottom. While I sucked one of his nipples and then the other, he became more probing. He parted the cheeks of my bottom and stroked the delicate inner flesh there with his soft, velvety fingertips. The heat spread over my naked body in the heat of the fire and the heat of the sun. I groped for his penis. My way was blocked by stomach.

"Have you ever thought of going on a diet?" I murmured.

He did not answer. Instead, he took my hand in his and guided it. My fingers trailed down the mound of belly into a lush tangle of curly black hair. An instant later I was grasping a thick shaft of throbbing flesh.

"Oh, my!" I exclaimed.

"No," he replied. "Mine."

"But may I beg the use of it?" I squeezed appreciatively.

"At your service, Majesty." Alfonso rose up and leaned back so that his erection was thrust forward. At the same time his hand reached between my legs and stroked the swollen, honeyed lips of my quivering pussy. "Oh, my!" he explained.

"No, mine," I countered. "But yours to dally with if you desire."

He desired. His satiny fingertips spread wide the entrance. His other hand paid obeisance to the sensitive, pink, meaty flesh inside. His fingertips swam in the moistness, in the syrup.

I gasped. I squeezed his balls. I wrapped both hands around his shaft as around the hilt of a broadsword and pulled back on the foreskin until I was rewarded with the sight of the large red ruby head with its little hole gleaming from the premature drop of nectar nestled there.

"I want it!" I moaned, rolling to my back, flinging my long legs wide and to the sky. "I want you!" And I tugged him urgently atop me.

Alas! I was too hurried! No sooner was he on than off! The curvature of his belly was such that he rolled away even as I pulled his weight to press me down.

Some different position was needed, I decided. I turned on my belly and rose up on my elbows. "Mount me thus!" I suggested, panting.

But his belly bounced off my burning posterior before I so much as felt his cock's tip nick my nook. Once again my mounting lust was foiled. "Standing?" I suggested. But one look told me that wouldn't work.

In the end, my impatience had to concede to Alfonso's

superior experience of the situation. After all, it was his belly. And it was, therefore, his solution.

A tad novel this solution, mayhaps. He lay down on his back, looking like a beached whale with his naked belly rising. He guided me to straddle his belly. And then he put his hands on my hips and pushed me backward so that my gaping pussy slid neatly onto his waiting hard-on. The belly heaved, and we were off and running.

"Oh!" I hammered his belly with my fists and rode up and down that hard cock with my breasts and buttocks bouncing wildly. "Oh!"

"Ahh!" He squeezed my perspiring breasts, squeezed the cheeks of my behind, moved inside me with mystic Sicilian circular movements that were driving me to the point of hysteria. "Ahh!"

"*Oui!*" I reached low behind me and found his balls and squeezed them. "*Oui!*"

"*Si!*" He began rolling from side to side, his stomach heaving like a mountain in an earthquake, his balls bouncing wildly in the palm of my hand, his prick a live flame searing unexpected pockets of sensitivity deep in the recesses of my squirming pussy.

"I'm going to come!" I bleated. "Fuck me!"

"Come!" He slapped my bottom and rose to new heights inside me. "Come!"

"I'm coming!" I couldn't wait. "I'm coming!" I raked his heaving belly with my nails. "I'M COMING!" And I squeezed down so hard over his groin with my clutching pussy that I felt his balls rise up inside me.

After a very long time I slumped over him, my breasts on his belly, perspiring, exhausted. I was still impaled on him. He was still hard inside me.

"But you didn't spend," I remarked finally.

Instead of answering directly, he moved his prick in an unusual manner inside me. Then he spoke. "How does that feel?" he inquired.

"Different," I granted.

"But not exactly titillating, right?"

"That's right."

"But not exactly not titillating either?"

"True," I agreed.

"It tickles."

"*Oui.*"

"But that is not the overwhelming sensation."

"*Oui.*" Again Alfonso was right.

"And the overwhelming sensation is—"

"I have to go!" I started to rise, sliding up and off his still-stiff prick.

"I know," Alfonso told me softly. He held my wrists firmly with his hands so that with my ankles digging into the sand and in a half-risen position, the entrance to my pussy was still enclosing the tip of his erection. He wiggled. He smiled. He wiggled again.

The sensation was abruptly insistent. "I have to go," I repeated. "Let me go."

"In Sicily we say 'rinse a kidney.' Is that what you mean, Majesty?"

"*Oui. Oui.*"

"Wee-wee." Alfonso smiled. "In Sicily we spell it differently."

"Please—" I struggled to free myself.

"In Sicily"—he held me firm—"the man spends best under the reward of the Golden Shower. Do you know what that is, Majesty?"

"No." I tried to wrench away. My need was becoming more urgent. "What is it?"

Alfonso explained.

"You mean you want me to—?"

He nodded.

"On you?"

"*Si.*"

Well, *mes amis,* the fact is that I had run out of time. By holding me in place above him, Alfonso had rendered the esthetic of the act a moot point. I did not so much comply with his wishes as surrender to a pressure I could no longer resist.

"Ahh!" The first drops of the shower made Alfonso shudder from toe to top. His hand went to his erection just in time to catch the baptism. And then he pulled me forward and enjoyed his ultimate wish at the same time that his flailing fist claimed the reward of geysering nectar from his thrusting cock. "Ship ahoy!" he bellowed. "SHIP AHOY!"

"I beg your pardon?" It seemed a very odd cry under the circumstances.

But then I saw that his eyes were looking past the golden waterfall, beyond the frame of my inner thighs, past the shoreline, and to the mouth of the cove. I peered over my shoulder then and saw what Alfonso saw. A ship of the Sicilian navy, sails billowing, was making straight for our bonfire.

"SHIP AHOY!" I echoed his cry and splashed the last of my Golden Shower onto Alfonso's belly. "SHIP AHOY!"

And so we were saved!

Chapter Ten

"An eye for an eye!" Alfonso rephrased his new Sicilian philosophy.

"That's right, darling." I sat hugging my knees and watching the Sicilian bark settling at anchor.

"I'm glad that you agree." He strode toward me, naked, belly out, limp organ in hand.

"Of course I—" With a sudden shock, I perceived what Alfonso had in mind. "Oh, no!" I scrambled away from him.

"But to be enjoyed fully, the Golden Shower must always be reciprocal." He stalked me determinedly.

"No!" I spied the small boat rowing toward us from the ship.

"Don't get mad, get even," he reminded me, wielding his cock like a watering spout.

"Look out for number one," I reminded him.

"You do what you have to do," he reminded me.

I did. I kicked him again. It was a hard kick and it landed smack in the center of the under part of the sac holding his balls. Alfonso collapsed. Simultaneously he loosed his stream. But not on me!. . .

Alas, the incident quite spoiled the little time left to our relationship. In defiance of what I had taught him, Alfonso, unable to get even, got mad. And he stayed mad throughout the entire voyage from our little desert island to the mainland of Sicily itself where I was finally reunited with my husband, King Louis. Indeed, the last I saw of Alfonso he was walking away from me in a crouch (I really had kicked harder than I meant to, and to more lasting effect) with his large round melon belly pointing downward, his épée adroop, and his resentment still so strong that he refused to even bid me a proper good-bye.

There was not much more warmth to be found in the renewal of my relationship with Louis. I had not forgiven him for placing me under arrest and holding me a prisoner these many months since we had left Antioch. And now sorrow added another grudge to those I held against my husband.

A messenger had arrived from Antioch. When Louis had marched his army out of the city, the infidels had not waited long before laying seige to it. Uncle Raymond was a formidable adversary, and under his direction the city had withstood the siege for a long time. Finally, however, superior force had told. With the crusader army far away, Antioch had finally fallen.

Uncle Raymond was killed in the final battle. His head was cut off, placed in a silver casket, and sent as a gift to the Caliph of Baghdad. Subsequently it was placed high on a pole for all Baghdad to see.

His decapitated head was not the only memento Uncle Raymond left behind. In the wake of his death, there also came ample proof of the unwiseness of refusing to follow the strategy he had advocated. With Antioch, the Gateway to the East, in the hands of the enemy, the days of the Christian colonizers were numbered. One by one the Muslims retook not only the crusader fiefdoms, but the Byzantine territories as well. The end result of the Second Crusade was exactly the opposite of that intended. It drove Christendom out of the Holy Land and actually opened Europe to future invasions by Muslims under a very famous General named—oh, irony!—Saladin!

But that was later. For now it was shameful enough (and expensive enough in terms of both lives and material) that the Crusade had failed. My husband, King Louis, had failed the Pope!

This being the case, it was all the more peculiar that he chose to return to Paris via Italy so that he might stop off in Rome for an audience with His Holiness. The peculiarity was explained by the fact that he was acting on the advice of the Abbot Bernard. And the cause of that advice was me.

I made no secret of the fact that I blamed Louis for Uncle Raymond's death. I refused to temper this attitude with shame because we had been apprehended as incestuous lovers. My husband had bound me to his chastity, and I was damned if I would apologize for (as went the advice I had bequeathed to Sicily) doing what I had to do. Rather than the attitude of shamefulness which might have been expected from an unfaithful wife who had been caught in the act, I held my head high and continued to demand of Louis that he grant me a divorce.

This presented Abbott Bernard with a dilemma. On the one hand, he would have been delighted to be rid of me and to have the King completely under his influence with no distractions. On the other hand, he could not risk giving his monarch advice that might cost France its rich territory of Aquitaine. Finally, however unwillingly, the Abbot had come down on the side of Empire. And so he arranged an audience for us with the Pope on the theory that if anything could reconcile us, papal marriage counseling could.

I agreed to the audience for a different reason. I hoped that I might marshal strong enough arguments to convince His Holiness to grant a papal decree dissolving the marriage. I thought that the combined evidence of Louis being my fourth cousin (the very reason Abbot Bernard had himself used once to claim the marriage illegal), my husband's long-term vows of abstinence from marital relations, and his brutality in holding me under forcible arrest would surely be evidence enough to secure my purpose.

I was wrong. Louis pleaded his love for me so tearfully, so convincingly, that the Pope was visibly moved by his arguments. He freely forgave me my infidelities and pledged that in his eyes the slate was wiped clean and the marriage could begin afresh. Since the Crusade was over, his vows of chastity were at an end and he was now prepared to perform his husbandly duties. All he asked was for the marital breach to be pronounced healed and for the papal blessing for the marriage to continue.

He got what he asked. The Pope was our marriage counselor, and he decided that we should continue with our marriage and work at it. I did not really hear the little speech he made us—something about marriages being made in Heaven, I believe. In any case, Louis was delighted to give the marriage another chance. I, on the other hand, was in despair. I still wanted out most desperately. But rebellious as was my nature, I could not go against the Holy Father to his face. And so I smoldered.

And smoldering, returned with Louis to Paris. . . .

The city was caught up in a severe winter when we arrived. The Seine was frozen over. The bridges were packed high with snow and ice and frequently impassable. The temperature was frigid.

This frigidity greeted me inside the palace as well as out of doors. The French aristocracy, and also the hierarchy of the Church which was controlled by Abbot Bernard, was bitterly disappointed by the failure of the Crusade. It had cost them heavily in men and money. They needed someone to blame. They needed a scapegoat. They found one in me.

The story of my adultery with my uncle in Antioch was widely spread and interpreted so that I was the one to blame for the failure to defend Antioch which had led to its fall. An exaggerated version of the Battle of the Feast of Epiphany was circulated which postulated that not only had the French been betrayed by the Aquitainians when they deliberately left the summit of Mount Cadmos unguarded, but that the betrayal was by direct order of his treacherous Aquitainian Queen. Likewise, the rumor was spread that I had been in league with the Emperor Manuel Commenus to betray the Crusade to the infidels in exchange for certain territories which would be ruled jointly by Byzantium and Aquitaine. And there were other, lesser canards circulated in such variety that I found it useless to even try to keep track of them.

If my popularity was at a low ebb, however, certain courtesies nevertheless still had to be granted to me. I was the Queen. My King and I were reconciled. And so while chilliness was the norm, none dared open insult. This meant that I automatically received invitations to all of the parties given by the aristocracy.

Winter had passed and an early spring was pushing the buds up through the soil when I received one such invitation from a certain Countess Devereaux. She was giving a *bal masque* on her estate on the outskirts of Paris. There would be lavish costumes and music and dancing and champagne and caviar and platters of exotic foods and gaiety. Perhaps if I consumed and masked myself cleverly enough, I would not be recognized as the hated Aquitainian Queen and thus might be able to dance and enjoy myself for at least one evening. With this hope, I brought the engraved invitation to my husband, Louis, who disliked parties of all sorts and was always reluctant to attend them, and prepared to overcome his objections.

"It is not that I will not go, but that I cannot," Louis told me. There was obvious relief in his voice at being able to offer so justifiable an excuse. "I must hold counsel that evening with the Abbot Bernard and other advisers regarding this dreadful Plantagenet affair and what should be done about it. I am due to receive the scoundrels in court the following afternoon."

The Plantagenet matter had been the talk of the royal dinner table for some time, and so of course I knew all about it. "Plantagenet" was the nickname of Geoffrey the Fair, Count of Anjou, because of his rakish affectation of decorating his cap with leaves of the broom plant, otherwise known as the *planta genista*. Thus the de-Latinization "Plantagenet."

Geoffrey Plantagenet had become involved in a dispute over a strip of land called "Vexin" with an officer in King Louis' army. He had settled the altercation by attacking the officer's castle, battering down its walls, and taking his enemy captive. When Louis heard of this, he sent word to Geoffrey that this was no way to settle a quarrel, that the settlement was in any case up to him to decide as King, and that Geoffrey should immediately release his prisoner. When Geoffrey flatly declined to do this, the Abbot Bernard excommunicated him for committing "high treason against the Crown."

The excommunication was shrugged off by Geoffrey. Having no other alternative, Louis decided to try to reason with him. He summoned him to Paris to discuss the Vexin dispute. Publicly, to save face for the Crown, the summons was for Geoffrey to answer a charge of treason. Privately the volatile Geoffrey was informed that the King was prepared to mediate the Vexin dispute and settle it fairly, and with no punishment for anyone involved.

Summoned to Paris with Geoffrey was his son, Henry of Normandy. As Duke of Normandy, Henry was required to swear allegiance to King Louis. Because of his father's trouble with Paris, however, he had delayed in the performance of this important symbolic act. Now Louis was giving him the opportunity to do so without rebuke. But privately he said flatly that if Henry did not take advantage of the opportunity, it would not be offered again and his reign over Normandy would be ended by French arms if necessary.

This was strong talk for Louis, and dangerous talk as

well. Henry was not only Duke of Normandy and heir apparent to Anjou, he was also through his mother in the direct line of succession to the throne of mighty England! Louis and France had enough trouble controlling the territories of their rebellious vassals. A quarrel with England stemming from his disciplining of Henry would be a most undesirable result for King Louis and his country.

The many aspects of the Plantagenet affair weighed heavily on Louis. Every day brought a new story about father and son and how one or the other had given expression to his savage temper. This violence of family character was so well-known that long before the Abbot Bernard excommunicated Geoffrey, it was said of the Plantagenets that "from the Devil they came, to the Devil they will go!"

I had no choice but to recognize that the Plantagenet affair took precedence over the Countess Devereaux's *bal masque* and to accept Louis' decision not to attend. Still, I didn't fancy remaining alone in my room with a book while my husband conferred with his advisers and the rest of Paris danced. In this spirit, I chose my words carefully.

"We don't want to offend the Countess," I told Louis. "Perhaps I should attend without you."

"Attend without me?" His tone was dubious. Not that much time had elapsed since he had discovered me in flagrante with Uncle Raymond.

"Just to put in an appearance," I reassured him. "And then I will come straight home. I won't even dance." As to my intentions, it was a bald-faced lie. But I calculated that it would be a fait accompli before Louis found out. And then what could he do? Divorce me? One could only hope!

"All right." He gave his permission without much enthusiasm. "But just put in an appearance and come home. I don't like the idea of you running around by yourself at a *bal masque*. I'm told those affairs can get quite wild."

Again, one could only hope!

There are times—rare and wonderful times, *mes amis*—when reality outshines hope. The *bal masque* of the Countess Devereaux was one such occasion. I shall remember it always.

I chose to wear a Byzantine costume, perhaps a bit garish and somewhat daring by Paris standards, but undeniably becoming. The gown was of *cendal,* a closely woven silk of many colors with scarlet predominating. The tunic, tight across my hips, fell loosely to my ankles. The close-fitting bodice was slashed by a deep, revealing V outlined with embroidery of gold thread. The belt, loose at my waist and hanging in a sort of echoing V down my belly to the juncture of my legs, was woven of the same gold thread in thicker strands. I wore a golden Byzantine amulet with a jeweled ruby in its center on a golden chain around my throat. The amulet was suspended just above the naked top halves of my upthrusting pear-shaped breasts. A similar jewel decorated a tiara which crowned my chestnut tresses. These fell loosely to my bare shoulders and down my back, picking up an additional depth of texture from the scarlet woven through the material of the gown. The domino mask I wore was of a matching scarlet, as were my dancing slippers.

To some extent, the mask did hide my face. It could not conceal my identity indoors where the hundreds of candles were brightly reflected by cut glass. But outdoors, where the Oriental-style lanterns supplied only the most shadowy illumination and where the interlocking branches of the oaks coming into leaf blotted out the moon and stars, I could indeed manage to maintain a degree of anonymity.

A platform for dancing had been set up on one of the lawns. Tables with hors d'oeuvres and champagne surrounded it. The spot was particularly shadowy, and so I drifted over to it.

Halfway there, a young cavalry officer that I knew asked me to dance. I could tell by his manner that he did not recognize me. I used my fan to good advantage to be sure that circumstances did not alter. I danced with him and let him hold me close so that he could not see me too clearly.

Unaware that I was his Queen, and therefore uninhibited, he flirted outrageously. Amused, I flirted back. Soon he was shamelessly pressing the back of his hand against the naked top of one of my breasts each time the figures of the dance supplied him with an opportunity. I confess that this made me breathe somewhat faster.

When the dance was over, he coaxed me to take a walk with him in the gardens, but I declined. I knew him too well and was sure that further intimacy—a stolen kiss, for instance—would reveal my identity. I was tempted, for he was young and firm of flesh, but I dared not take the chance. So I sent him on his way and drifted over to the table with the iced buckets of champagne.

A liveried servant poured sparkling golden fluid into a crystal goblet for me. I sipped it slowly and enjoyed the feeling of warmth spreading through my body. When it was empty, I held it out and the servant refilled it for me.

He did that twice more as I stood there in the shadows and observed the other costumed guests strolling about and dancing.

Most of them were masked, and there was a wide variety of costumes. The men wore animal skins and ancient armor and togas, as well as more conventional attire. Some of the women dressed as jesters or clowns, while others wore Eastern costumes and still others emulated mythic goddesses with horned helmets or brazen feathers or even saucy tails. Those who wore ordinary ball clothing were in the minority, and few of them were without masks as well.

I danced again, and then again. There were similarities in these *danses royales,* as they were called, but there were differences too. They were rounds, but there were pairing movements, and in some of them occurred a repeated changing of partners. All—the *ductia,* and *estampie,* the *stantipes*—allowed to some degree the pressing of flesh.

These *danses royales* were also quite energetic. They left me flushed, patting the perspiration from my brow, dry of throat. I drank quite a bit of champagne to slake this thirst and to cool myself.

It did help the dryness, but I did not feel noticeably cooler. Finally I decided to take a stroll through the gardens in search of an errant springtime breeze. I was frankly tiddly with champagne and my legs were none too steady as I started out.

Although many of the flowers had not yet come into bloom, the gardens were quite lovely. They were banked and sculpted, set off by hedges and flowering shrubs. Also there were stone sculptures and small running fountains and high ledges everywhere.

It was at one of these ledges that I detected a breeze. I paused to rest and savor it. I sat on the ledge and enjoyed the mild dizziness of too much champagne.

"Ahh! *Oui!* That's the spot!"

I was roused from my alcoholic reverie by the sound of a breathless, throaty female voice.

"Then you must touch me here." The second voice was male, excited, insistent.

"There?"

"Oui!" His voice went up an octave.

"Like this?"

"Oui!" Higher still.

Amazing! As his voice climbed toward the soprano, hers became deeper, throatier. "Wouldn't you like to kiss it?" she inquired, an alto now.

"Oui!" Astounding range!

I turned around on the ledge and peered into the shadows whence the voices had come. I saw nothing. Then I realized that they must have come from directly below me. There was a steep embankment on the other side of the ledge and they were somewhere at the foot of it.

Bending over the ledge, I scrutinized the area below. Holding on to it with my hands, I leaned way over so that the ledge caught me at the waist. Now my feet were dug into the ground behind me and my hair was hanging down with my head. In this position, I finally spied them.

The first thing I saw was a leg. It was very shapely and naked to the garter high up on the thigh. I judged it to be a woman's leg and I judged the hand stroking it to be a man's hand.

Moving my head, I changed the angle of my viewpoint. Now I saw the upper half of the woman. She was quite young—perhaps only seventeen or eighteen—and pretty in a red-cheeked, tousled, curly-headed blonde sort of way. The top of her Grecian-style costume was pushed down and both of her breasts were exposed.

They were young-girl breasts, firm, high-piled mounds. Either the aureoles were very pale or I simply couldn't distinguish them in the dim light. Her nipples were the color of nutmeg and looked like little round buttons in the center of her breasts.

Then the breasts were blotted out. The man's head moved over them. It descended on one of them. I couldn't see him suck it, but I knew that was what he must be doing because the other one inflated so suddenly and sharply. Also the naked leg rose in the air and flailed for a moment.

"I should get back," she said, digging her hand into the back of his neck to hold his mouth to her nipple. "My fiancé will be wondering what happened to me."

"I didn't know that you were betrothed." He lifted his head up long enough to reply. "You're so young."

"Girls marry young these days." Her arms were moving as if her hands were unbuckling something—something of his, not hers—but I couldn't see below the wrists and so I couldn't tell for sure. "And I bring a very large dowry."

"And a very nice bosom." He was gallant. He kissed her nipple again.

Either the kiss or his words or what her questing hands had found decided her against the necessity to leave. She closed her eyes and lay wriggling and panting, her fiancé obviously forgotten. Every so often her tongue crept out between her lips and licked their redness all the way around.

I was getting dizzy hanging straight down, and so again I changed position. It just so happened that they also changed their position at the same time. Now my view was much clearer, much more entire, and much more stimulating.

Her skirt was all the way up above her belly and tucked in at the waist. Her bloomers were pushed down around her ankles. Both her fleshy, girlish legs were naked. So was her round belly. So was her blonde-haired cunt.

He stroked the sparse triangle of curls. He squeezed the insides of her fleshy thighs. He investigated the quivering lips in the act of opening between her legs.

I saw then that her hands were inside his body stocking. They were moving rhythmically, and he was rising and falling against them. Then she rolled down the top of the body stocking and the inflamed head of his cock came into view. An instant later I saw the shaft appear and disappear as she masturbated it.

For a moment I thought I would faint. Perhaps it was from hanging down over the ledge. Perhaps it was from too much champagne. Or perhaps it was from excitement at what I was seeing.

Straightening up, I gave myself a moment for the dizziness to go away. I pulled the V of my close-fitting bodice away from my breasts and fanned air into the deep, lightly perspiring cleft between them. I raised my skirts momentarily and cooled the overheated oven between my legs. Then, more cautiously so as to control the dizziness, I bent again to peep at the scene beneath me.

Matters had progressed in the short time my attention had been absent. The young man, a mere stripling, was seated with his back against the tree and his body stocking pulled all the way down. The young blonde sat on his lap facing him, straddling him, her legs extending widely around the trunk of the tree, her fleshy thighs flattening against his bony young hips. Her plump, naked young breasts were bouncing violently against his chest and her moist, clutching pussy was sliding up and down his erect penis.

"I shouldn't be doing this!" she was gasping as she squirmed and pumped and licked her red lips. "My fiancé would be furious!"

"It will be our secret!" he assured her, his hands kneading her generous bottom and guiding the heaving cheeks as he thrust deep into her cunt. "He need never know!"

"It is really evil!" she moaned. "Ooh! Fuck me! Fuck me!"

"All sin is relevant," he assured her, "Fuck, lady, fuck!"

Watching, I could not contain myself. Quite soon, without willing it, I was bouncing to their rhythm. My hand slipped inside the V of my bodice and I toyed with my aroused, swollen nipple. I sucked my own tongue and clenched my thighs under my gown and rubbed them together. I felt them grow slippery with honey as my pussy heated. Unable to stop myself, I reached down and raised the front of the loose-hanging multicolored *cendal* gown and reached under it. I tugged down my bloomers until they were around my knees.

Now the loose gown hung demurely down in back, concealing what my hands were up to in front. There, pressed against the low wall and leaning over, I had the gown raised and tucked and two fingers in my gaping, honeyed pussy, and was most industriously frigging myself as I watched the lovers' lust-filled joining. I hung over the ledge, hair atumble, breasts hanging almost free of the V of my bodice, hands moving deliriously between my legs, prolonging my own pleasure even as the young couple was prolonging theirs.

Suddenly I felt hands clasping my hips firmly from behind. A weight pressed down on me in such a way as to testify to youth and muscle and a broadness of chest and shoulder. I felt a certain hardness against my derriere through my Byzantine skirt.

My natural reaction was to whirl around. The hands holding my hips prevented me. A cheek pressed against mine. From the corner of my eye I could see a black domino and a few freckles where the mask ended. I could also see a tumble of bright red hair. "Don't move, Madame." The husky, low voice spoke directly and warmly into my ear. The intimate breath made me shiver.

"What do you want?" I was alarmed and embarrassed and—*oui!*—intrigued.

"Some activities are more enjoyable in company," he told me. "I believe that you are engaged in such an activity." I felt a throbbing against my derriere.

He was leaning over the ledge with me now, his cheek pressed to mine. I couldn't see his face in the dimness, but he could see what I could see in the bushes below.

The young blonde was moving up and down on the stripling's lap with blind, perspiring enthusiasm. He was sucking on one of her nipples as her pussy slapped wetly down against his groin and then rose up the length of his erect shaft. Her tongue was in his ear, and then her teeth in his shoulder. His hands were squeezing her writhing bottom.

"Voilà!" The freckled cheek beside mine moved behind me. The hands slid around from my hips to the front where my gasping breasts were pushing up from the V of my bodice. They squeezed my breasts firmly through the woven silk. The tips of his fingers investigated the firm consistency of the flesh of the upper half-moons. Then his hands slid inside the bodice, tracing the Anjou shape of my bosom, finding the risen nipples, lifting the hard red tips free of my gown, stroking them so that I gasped and wriggled and forgot myself and resumed the frigging of my pussy.

His hand slid down between my naked thighs. It found my hand and immediately he understood what it was about. My cheeks burned red with embarrassment at being thus found out. Then he lifted my hand and carried it over my shoulder to his lips and licked the syrup from it and I was shaking too hard with excitement to worry about being embarrassed. His hand replaced mine between the wet, swollen lips of my pussy.

"You take great liberty, sir!" I mouthed the protest with no great feeling.

"Look," he said, ignoring my complaint.

I looked. The blonde was on her hands and knees now, her gown flung up and over her back, her bare bottom and pussy sticking out and up and wagging impatiently. The stripling stood behind her, long, thin erection in hand. Then, as we watched, my anonymous lover and I, the young man below began to feed the shaft into her, inch by slow, pulsing inch.

"Ahh!" I moaned. "Ohh!"

My own gown was raised from behind then. Strong, round hands moved up the backs of my naked thighs. A tucked-up tunic brushed against the quivering upper cheeks of my behind. Then I felt naked hipbones and naked thighs encircling my own naked bottom in a singular fashion. I was puzzled for an instant, and then it struck me that the fit was like that of a carefully handcrafted saddle. And the legs circling my bottom cheeks were most pronouncedly bowed. They were the legs of a knight who spent much of his life in the saddle.

The hands moved around to the front of my body. One reached into my bodice to fondle my heaving, hard-nippled naked breasts. The other went between my legs to spread the honey, to part the swollen lips, to strum the stiff and brazen clitty. And at the same time, between the saddle-bowed legs gripping me from behind, a large, thick instrument rose, passed under the trembling cheeks of my naked bottom, and pushed into my pussy to join the finger already there.

Below us the blonde maiden with the fleshy thighs was crouching on all fours with her head down and her bottom up. The stripling was behind her, holding her by her ample hips, his shining, purplish cock moving in and out of her sparkling quim in the moonlight. Every fifth stroke or so, he plunged in to the hilt and fell on her fully, grasping her large, naked down-hanging breasts and squeezing them as he ground deep inside her. When he did this, she flung back her head and whimpered, bleated, sobbed with pleasure.

The full weight of my anonymous bowlegged lover was on me now as well. His flaming red hair pressed into my cheek as he leaned over my shoulder, looking down at the scene below with me at the same time as he thrust his prick in me to the hilt. I gloried in the thick heat of it, in the way his heavy, hairy balls bounced against my bottom cheeks. Now passion removed all shame and loosened my tongue.

"*Oui!*" I moaned. "Fuck me! Whoever you are, fuck me the way they are fucking! Only harder! Faster! . . . Harder! . . . Faster!"

"I spend!" The blonde below us whinnied, her impaled bottom moving in a blur of flesh.

"I too!" I could not hold back.

"Come inside me!" the blonde pleaded with her pumping lover as he sprawled over her in the fashion of beasts in the field.

"Now!" The youth's bare backside vibrated with the discharge of his lust deep inside her.

"Please to give it to me, sir!" I snarled to the bowlegged force which held me in its lust-pounding grip.

"As you wish, milady!" My naked thighs were pulled back cruelly and my bottom cheeks were gripped by the bowed thighs as by a vise. One long, thrilling plunge that filled my pussy with cock and the lips with swollen balls, and then I felt the hot geysering stream of my anonymous lover's lust spraying my writhing, wrenching, climaxing cunt.

"*Mon Dieu!*" I pushed back ass and cunt with all my strength and fell into a hysteria of sensation in which he came and I came . . . and I came . . . and I came . . .

At some point while this ecstasy continued between us, the other couple concluded their lovemaking and departed. The youth had not the staying power of my anonymous lover, nor, I am sure, his copious spending fluids. He filled me with his nectar and I heaved my bottom and howled like an animal for more and he supplied it until there came a point at which I simply collapsed leaning forward over the ledge in a happy exhaustion.

His thick, sopping prick was removed then. The effect was not unlike pulling a cork. Indeed, the liquids of our lust ran out of me and down the insides of my thighs below my knees. I cared not. I could not move. Ecstasy had drained me of energy.

I was only hazily aware that my skirts had been replaced behind. Dimly I knew that the weight no longer pressed me down. The bowlegs no longer gripped me. But it wasn't until some time later that I was able to stir myself and turn around. Only then did I find that I was quite alone.

My anonymous red-haired, freckle-cheeked, bowlegged lover had departed as silently as he came.

The following afternoon I joined my husband, King Louis, the Abbot Bernard, and a collection of the mightiest Barons of France in the great hall of the castle. The occasion was supposed to be—at long last—a resolution of the Plantagenet affair. Of course it was recognized by all of us present that before any such resolution could occur, Geoffrey the Fair must first release the King's officer with whom he had the land dispute from the dungeon in which he was holding him. Then the two men would stand before the King as equals and a compromise regarding Vexin would be worked out. It was also expected, of course, that Geoffrey would be suitably repentant toward the sovereign whose authority he had usurped, behaving abjectly toward the Abbot Bernard, who had excommunicated him.

It was an extremely warm day for springtime. The air in

the great hall was close. The murmur of discussion as to what might be fitting punishment for Geoffrey was more like a mingled snarl. He was not popular with the Barons or the priests or the King himself.

The events of that day did not increase his popularity.

There was a blare of trumpets. A herald appeared to announce Geoffrey, Count of Anjou, and his son, Henry of Normandy. What followed was most unexpected.

Sir Geoffrey appeared holding one end of a long chain over his shoulder. A man in tattered clothing was bound by the chain and was being dragged forward like a low-caste felon. The other end of the chain was held by Sir Geoffrey's son, Henry. But the chained man was no commoner, no criminal. He was the King's officer that Geoffrey had suffered excommunication rather than release.

Anger spread like wildfire among the assembled Barons. It was unheard of to flaunt the authority of the King in this manner. And the insult to the Church was even greater.

Abbot Bernard was the first to recover from the shock and to act. "You offend the Crown and sin against God!" he roared at Sir Geoffrey.

"If this be a sin in the eyes of Our Lord, then I will live in sin!" was the volatile Count of Anjou's outrageous reply.

"Blasphemy! Blasphemy!" First one voice and then all present raised the cry. "Blasphemy!"

The Abbot rose up then with pious fervor. His skull-like face blazed with wrath. The smoldering coals of his eyes took fire. When he spoke his voice was hollow and booming—almost otherworldly. "God will punish you for this heresy!" he assured Geoffrey. "If you do not release your prisoner immediately, I warn you, Our Lord will mete out to you the early death that you have earned!''

''Ha!'' Geoffrey smiled a ferocious smile that included Abbot, King, and Barons. Then he turned it exclusively on the Abbot. He extended the middle finger of his right hand and jabbed it toward Heaven. ''Ha!'' he repeated with the utmost contempt.

Then Geoffrey signaled his son, Henry. They yanked simultaneously at the chains, and their prisoner sprawled at their feet. They stepped around him and started to march out of the great hall, dragging him behind them. Before they vanished from sight, the son, Henry of Normandy, turned and looked me straight in the eye.

I gasped. That blazing red hair! That freckled cheek! That breadth of chest and shoulder! And most of all those saddle-bowed legs!

Henry Plantagenet of Normandy, son of Count Geoffrey of Anjou, claimant to the throne of England, was, without a doubt, my bow-legged anonymous lover of the previous evening!

And it was writ clear in his eyes that he knew me for the willing object of his brief but delicious dalliance!

Chapter Eleven

Henry of Normandy's dramatic and insulting exit with his father left me with much to think about during the days that followed. This rumination was in the nature of supplying—umm!—body to the memory of exquisite sensations I had enjoyed. A smattering of freckles glimpsed from the corner of my eye was now filled out to a freckled face, ruddy with the outdoors, flushed with the heat of young lust. A crinkling of red hair barely seen, hardly brushed against, now became a bright and flaming mane crowning a visage which while boyish was nonetheless handsome and virile. Those gray eyes, like the tempered points of lances, promised future joinings of a lust surpassing even our first encounter.

Pondering such possibilities, I closed my eyes and pictured how his bowed legs had curved under his short tunic when he marched from the great hall. I remembered how they had felt, surrounding my squirming bottom. I merged the two concepts and sighed for the time that I might once again encounter Henry of Normandy, heir to Anjou and claimant to the throne of mighty England.

Still, he was so young! I smiled to myself. I was surely not old myself at twenty-eight years. And if he was younger than I—well, surely the years had given me cunning to match the energy of his youth.

Oui, mes amis! I was smitten!

Not since Bernard de Ventadour, my poet lover, had a man so taken my fancy. Of course it was not the same with this Henry of Normandy. There can be only one true love in a woman's life, and then only when she is young and naive enough to believe in such a thing. As she grows older—not very much older; only a little bit older—she learns to value other qualities. These are less romantic perhaps, more tangible, but they tone one up better than morning exercises and, oh! how the skin does tingle.

There was no way I would ever be able to banish Bernard de Ventadour from my memory. Always my blood would run hot with the memory of him. Always I would long for his return. But in the meantime— Well, *mes amis*, freckled young Henry of Normandy certainly had a knack for surprise encounters. And a big cock and active balls and a marvelous wiggle as well!

There is romance and there is— Well, whatever name you put to it, Henry of Normandy was a most adept practitioner!

Would I ever see him again? That was the question in my mind as I languished and compared and remembered. I never dreamed how quickly the answer would present itself.

Three days after the dramatic scene they had staged, Geoffrey the Fair and his son, Henry of Normandy, returned to Paris and requested an audience with my husband, King Louis. Again the Barons were summoned. Again Abbot Bernard and his priests were present. Again I was there. But this time, my heart was fluttering quite shamelessly.

Their second entrance was as different from the first as it could be. Both father and son prostrated themselves before the King and voiced their homage to him. Then they genuflected to the Abbot Bernard and begged God's pardon and the Church's pardon and the Abbot's pardon as well. Finally, with a timid smile and cajoling voice, Geoffrey the Fair spoke.

"Highness, we have behaved abominably," he began, including his handsome, bowlegged, large-pricked, redheaded son in his apology. "We had no right to seize your officer. We had no right to seize the disputed land, Vexin. We wish to atone for these sorry deeds. We wish to free the officer and turn him over to Your Majesty. And we wish to restore the disputed Vexin to his properties."

Louis was so astounded by this change of heart that he had no words. He simply nodded. But then he remembered something and looked questioningly at young Henry.

My anonymous lover—no longer anonymous—stepped forward and knelt. His bent leg, bowed though it was, was muscular and sturdy. Remembering the feel of it, I caught my breath.

"I promise to be your faithful vassal, Majesty," Young Henry of Normandy said. "I promise to defend you against all your enemies, foreign and domestic. I promise always to be a true subject of France." And his gray eyes strayed to one side and met mine and one of them closed in a quick, hot, meaningful wink. He then placed his strong, round hands in Louis' palms, the traditional gesture of fealty.

Louis kissed him on both cheeks. "This is a kiss of peace," he announced. "And I, Louis VII, King of France, do now officially pronounce you Henry, Duke of Normandy."

Everyone at court was of course greatly puzzled by these developments. None could fathom the reason for the change in attitude by father and son. It seemed so strange that they had returned in this fashion.

Later that night, I could have enlightened them as to the reason for the change of heart. On Geoffrey's part, it was simply his wicked inability to resist seeing his son, Henry, cuckold the King who had decreed through his Abbot that Geoffrey should be excommunicated. And as far as Henry himself was concerned—well, modesty forbids my detailing all of the delectable reasons for his return. Suffice it to say that he was more interested in privately pleasing Queen than publicly pleasing King.

We spent the night together, my bowlegged lover of boundless energy and I. We explored each other's flesh and hyperventilated until the dawn. We exercised equestrian muscles, a practice most suited to the horseman's curve of my lover's legs. And so satisfied were we both that we made arrangements for another assignation on the very night following.

"I must have you!" Henry vowed that second night, his hand a riding crop on my flank, his gallop at top pace.

"You do have me!" I wrenched the épée my flesh was surrounding to remind him.

"I mean as wife!" And his punctuation was the hot spouting of Normandy nectar.

"But I am already married to the King of France!" I squeezed hard so as not to lose so much as one precious adulterous drop. "And besides, I am older than you."

"All France knows your marriage is a farce and that you want a divorce." There seemed no end to Henry's energy, his pumping, his delicious spending. "And I am very mature for my age."

Well, *mes amis,* he did have a point there. Henry was very mature. Very! A future without such nights as these would be bleak indeed. I must insist that Louis agree to divorce me!

And so it was agreed between us, Henry of Normandy and myself. We also agreed that it would be better if he was not on the scene when I reembarked on these delicate negotiations. I would be better able to handle them without the distraction of his erotic presence close at hand. And so Henry and his father once again departed for Geoffrey the Fair's castle in Anjou.

Their sojourn was to end tragically. Not far from Anjou, seeking refuge from an unseasonably hot sun, father and son paused for a swim. They stripped off their clothes and plunged into an icy stream. Young Henry took the chill in his stride, but Geoffrey could not make his teeth stop chattering even after they emerged from the water.

The next day Geoffrey's chills turned into a fever. The day after that the fever was raging. His castle doctors threw up their hands; there seemed no way to bring the fever down. Geoffrey became hysterical and violent, quite out of his mind. And three days after the fatal swim he vomited his last and died.

Thus was the damning prophecy of the Abbot Bernard fulfilled!

News of the death of Geoffrey the Fair receded in importance as far as Paris was concerned when it became known that King Louis and the Abbot Bernard had at long last agreed to grant me the divorce I wanted. My constant hammering away had finally achieved results. They had been made to see that it would be more advantageous to have a loyal vassal ruling over Aquitaine than a dissatisfied Queen in Paris whose Aquitainian subjects were more and more coming to look upon her as a martyred captive held in marriage against her will by a tyrannical French King. Of course I had made sure that there were rumbles and incidents in Aquitaine to back up my arguments. And so at long last, with the Pope in faraway Rome accepting Abbot Bernard's advice not to become involved, the Church discovered that King Louis and Queen Eleanor were actually fourth cousins, a relationship far too close in the eyes of God to constitute a lawful marriage. We went to the royal castle at Orléans, and there our marriage was officially annulled.

I was twenty-nine years old and a free woman. I was no longer Queen of France, but I was Duchess of Aquitaine, the richest duchy in all of Europe. And besides the fact that my body was on fire for him, I had an understanding with Henry of Normandy—now, with his father's death, Count of Anjou as well and more and more spoken of as the logical choice to be the next King of England!

Merged, our holdings would constitute a mighty empire! Such a merger, however, would require the utmost finesse. It was sure to be opposed by King Louis, who could never countenance two of his vassals wielding more power than he did himself, and who surely would never have granted me a divorce if he had had any inkling of my involvement with young Henry of Normandy.

A certain amount of time would have to elapse before Henry and I dared act openly on our passion. And it would be wisest for me to be in a stronghold where my security was assured. For this reason, as soon as the annulment was granted, I set out for Aquitaine. My Henry of Normandy— my eighteen-year-old Romeo—stayed in Anjou to straighten out his own tangled family affairs.

My Aquitaine-bound caravan got as far as the Loire River when trouble struck. I had accepted the hospitality of a local Baron and was spending the night at his castle. I had already retired when I was notified that a man wished to see me on a matter of the greatest importance.

The man was a knave. He was an informant with information to sell. The information, however, bore on the safety of my journey and so I had no choice but to buy it.

"The Count of Champagne," the knave told me. "He plans to ambush your party. His intent is to kidnap you and to force you into marriage."

I thought about that. The vendetta of the Count of Champagne was many years old by now. Still, I knew that time would in no way lessen the hatred of the stiff-necked old man toward my sister Petronilla, who had stolen his niece's husband, nor toward King Louis, who had visited the atrocity of massacre upon the Champagne city of Vitry, nor toward me whom he blamed for influencing both Crown and Church to act in behalf of my sister in such manner as to bring shame upon his family name. He had vowed this revenge, and it mattered not how many years had passed, he was determined to have it.

But marriage?

"To his son." Another gold coin had brought answer to my question from the knave.

His son! It was not hard to fathom the Count of Champagne's plan. He would kidnap me, marry me off to his son, escort the two of us back to Aquitaine, and then, after a decent interval, see to it that I met with an accident. A fatal accident! Once I was out of the way, through his son he would rule Aquitaine as well as Champagne. Like two slices of bread, they would make quite a sandwich, and France would be the filling caught between them! All by himself the Count of Champagne would have surrounded the man he hated most in all the world—King Louis!

Oui! It was a grand design! The prize was no less than La Belle France herself. And the first objective to be seized was me!

Late that night, when an obliging cloud blindfolded the moon, my party slipped from my castle and silently forded the Loire River by raft. Silently we floated downstream, passing right by the military encampment of the Count of Champagne. By the time the sun rose, we were many miles away and—at least for the time—well out of reach of his marital plans and his vengeance.

I was not, however, out of danger. Some things, *mes amis,* never change. A divorced woman is always fair game. Her very state, it seems, erases men's scruples.

It would be nice to believe that my beauty alone would have been temptation enough for young knights. The truth is, however, that if that had been the case, my flesh would have been the target, rape the unsavory game, and any follow-up at best fleeting. But when other factors were added to my beauty—a former Queen of France, a present

Duchess of Aquitaine, estates and holdings that made me quite the wealthiest unmarried woman in all Europe—the object was neither rape nor seduction nor dalliance, but marriage—which is to say possession in the sense of husbandly ownership.

The deeper I penetrated into Aquitaine, the more I was made aware of the ambitions of young knights who had decided that their future career would best be served by kidnapping and marrying their Duchess. I tell you, it was epidemic! Every piddling rascal with a suit of armor to his name had marital designs on my person and the intent to use force to secure them.

At the Creuse River, one such upstart attacked my caravan in force. Still wet behind the ears, he sat his steed with more cockiness than surety and counted his suit won when he penetrated my mounted guard and wrapped a clanking arm about my waist in my saddle. I tumbled to earth in his arms, his warriors and mine still engaged in hot battle all about us.

"You bruise me, sir!" I protested. "Your armor is too rough!"

And so the silly varlot opened his breastplate the better to press his intentions whilst his men mopped up around us. It was a fatal mistake. I inserted a small dagger in the aperture and slipped it neatly between his second and third ribs and into his heart even as he was pressing it on me in marriage. When his lackeys perceived his fate, they recognized that their cause was eliminated and fled the scene.

Thus beset and thus defending, I finally reached the sanctuary of Uncle Raymond's old castle at Poitiers. It was heavily fortified and any more would-be husbands intent on abducting me would have a hard time storming its battlements. Still, as strong and independent a woman as I was, I was also a practical one. I had been born into a time when the protection of a powerful man was necessary to a wealthy woman's survival.

I was fortunate: I had such a man. I sent word to young Henry of Normandy to come to me as quickly as he could.

It seemed an eternity, but in actuality it was not long before my lover came riding, bowlegged and handsome as always, through the gates of the castle. A Plantagenet like his father, he wore a sprig of *planta genista* in the brim of his cap. His red hair blazed out from under that brim, his freckles sparkled, and his gray eyes were as unfathomable as those of the falcon sitting on his shoulder.

I had been divorced for only eight weeks. A discreet affair was the most that should have been allowed to occur. But it was not merely that the sexual attraction between us was powerful. If Aquitaine were put together with Normandy and Anjou, the rulers would control an expanse reaching from Spain to the English Channel—not to mention the possibility of Henry becoming King of England and the woman he married becoming Queen.

Sometimes, *mes amis,* the attraction between two people is truly irresistible.

Protocol demanded that Henry and I, both vassals of King Louis VII of France, ask his permission before marrying. In point of fact, we had no right to marry at all without that permission. Common sense, however, informed us that the wild horses had not yet been conceived who could force such permission from the lips of good King Louis.

For one thing, to marry so quickly after my divorce from him was as good as pinning the horns of the cuckold to Louis' brow. That I should marry a vassal he disliked and mistrusted as much as Henry of Normandy, son of the hated Geoffrey the Fair of Anjou, was adding insult to injury. But worst of all was the prospect of Aquitaine and Normandy and Anjou with all their mighty armies under one rule, with France trapped in the middle. That, Louis could never countenance. Thus it would have done no good at all to ask his permission to marry.

And so we simply married without it!

I am told that in Paris, when he heard the news, Louis was apoplectic. Even the normally imperturbable Abbot Bernard was shaken to the quick. Without Aquitaine, Normandy, and Anjou, the Kingdom of France was a paltry country indeed. And if Henry and I could openly defy Louis in this fashion, insult him, ignore his authority, then it followed that his control of our lands was a thing of the past.

Louis sent a message to Aquitaine, summoning Henry to Paris. The message was strong, blunt, and most undiplomatic. It called my new young husband to task for marrying without the permission of his sovereign, for daring to marry that sovereign's recently divorced wife, and for swearing false fealty to the throne—the last being a sin before God. Summed up, the message ordered Henry to Paris to answer charges of high treason.

Henry and I conferred. It was decided that he would not go to Paris. (The Abbot Bernard would not have been beyond invoking a punishment such as burning at the stake for breaking the laws of divine rule.) It was decided that we would not even answer Louis' message. Indeed, we would prepare for war.

It was not long in coming. Louis—or perhaps his Abbot—

had anticipated our reaction. Now he massed his troops and rode at the head of them straight for Normandy. Alas! he was no more accomplished a military tactician now than he had been during the Crusade.

Henry, on the other hand, was a brilliant soldier. Young as he was, he had the knack for it, and the energy and speed to turn strategy into action. He embarked on a forced march with a mixed army of Aquitainian and Norman troops. They cut Louis off at the very Vexin that Henry and his father had ceded just a short time before. Here a pitched battle soon turned into a rout for Louis, and he was forced to turn tail and flee back to Paris. Henry had retaken the Vexin and a large chunk of France along with it.

And for a time, I was sure what they say is true: second marriages are truly made in Heaven.

Well, all maxims are subject to modification, are they not? Thus, my second marriage was—well, a marriage after all. My husband was young, given to tantrums over small matters, occasionally flatulent, and frequently drank too much. He was also unfaithful—but I am getting ahead of myself.

The first time he told me he would be away overnight— over quite a few nights—on business, the possibility of his unfaithfulness truly didn't occur to me. Why should it have? There was certainly no doubt that he had business— important business—in England.

"You don't get to be King of England by sitting at home on your kiester," was the way he put it. "If you want the big jobs, Eleanor, you have to go out after them."

"Go, darling," I told him. "Look out for number one."

"That's heavy!" He was young and he spoke as the young speak. "Did you just think of that?"

"No. It's an old Sicilian proverb."

"Really?"

"Well, actually it used to be an old Aquitainian proverb, but we gave it to Sicily."

"I don't get it."

"Go to England, *chéri*. Have a good trip. Bring back the crown."

Such was Henry's intention. His claim was just, but when in history has righteousness alone prevailed? Not so often as to stop Henry taking hundreds of knights in armor and expert bowmen with him to England.

Henry's claim rested on his direct descent from William the Conqueror. His grandfather was King Henry I, the Conqueror's son. His mother, Matilda, had been the rightful heir to the throne, but it was usurped from her by her cousin Stephen on the grounds that it was not fitting for a woman to rule England. She had fled to the arms of Henry's father, Geoffrey Plantagenet, while Stephen had prevailed upon the English Bishops to crown him King of England in her stead. Now, with Matilda long dead and Stephen getting on in years, Henry stood ready to reclaim the English crown.

There were, however, certain obstacles. Chief among them was Prince Eustace, son of King Stephen, who considered that his bloodline entitled him to succeed his father. But Eustace was an arrogant and greedy man who had managed to make himself thoroughly loathed by the English Barons and the English Bishops as well. More of an obstacle was the fact that King Stephen himself was still very much alive, was as popular with his English subjects as his son was unpopular, and was still lodged firmly on the throne to which my young husband aspired.

War was a decided possibility. In an effort to avoid it, the Bishops of England offered to arbitrate the dispute. It was a tricky question. On the one hand, it could be argued that if Henry I was the rightful King of England and the crown had been illegally taken from his daughter, then it ought to be restored to her son, Henry of Normandy. On the other hand, Stephen had been acknowledged as the legal King of England for many years, and so it seemed logical that upon his death the crown should pass to his son, Eustace.

"A family dispute involving uncles and nephews, aunts and cousins," one Bishop was heard to mutter. "A family dispute! And they are the most murderous kind!"

As it happened, Prince Eustace himself proved most helpful in resolving the dispute. The idea that the Bishops would even consider deposing him in favor of Henry Plantagenet threw him into a savage fury. He led his troops over the estates of the Archbishop of Canterbury and torched everything in sight. He didn't just burn churches, barns, and cottages, he burned peasants and priests as well.

It was in the wake of this terrible royal tantrum that Henry landed on the shores of England with his knights and bowmen. Never one to miss an opportunity to improve his image, Henry immediately marched to the rescue of the subjects of the churchman in charge of arbitrating his case. Before his army clashed with that of Eustace, however, Fate twisted the crank of history one more time.

Eustace was taken with a sudden illness and died within three days!

The aging King Stephen, grief-stricken at the death of his only son, gave up his opposition to Henry's claim. On November 6, 1153, he signed a decree that named Henry Plantagenet as the heir apparent to the throne of England. This meant that Henry would be crowned on Stephen's death. It also meant that Henry must pledge to cease all military activity to seize the throne before that event.

His cause won and without a war to wage, time now hung heavy on Henry's hands in England. King Stephen was ailing and his court was not a very active one. The obvious course was for him to return home to Aquitaine and to me, but there was a roadblock to this obvious course.

Her name was Rosamund Clifford—Fair Rosamund, or *Rosa-immundi*, which means "Rose of Unchastity," the designation depending on one's viewpoint. She was his age, younger than I by ten years. She became his willing mistress during that first trip to England when I was not there to do battle o'er my marital exclusivities. Word of this reached me long before Henry returned to Aquitaine, long before I myself journeyed with him to England and saw her for myself.

And word also reached me of the unsurpassed Anglican loveliness of Fair Rosamund!

Their affair was almost a year old when I finally was able to judge that loveliness for myself. It had not been exaggerated. Fair Rosamund—Rose of Unchastity—was beautiful and—*merde!*—so very, very young!

Seeing her, hating her, I could understand why Henry

had found it so difficult to tear himself away from England. He had come to Aquitaine only long enough to fetch me and return there so that we would be in place, he said, to accept our crowns as King and Queen of England when the ailing Stephen breathed his last. There was sense to his reasoning, but there was more real reason to the magnetic form and face of Fair Rosamund.

She spoiled London for me. The sights and sounds of Bonny Britannia, the storied isle over which I was to rule with Henry, were quite wasted on me. My young husband was philandering. Worse, he was neglecting me! And I was all afire with jealousy!

I did not conceal it very well. All London buzzed with stories of the Aquitainian green-eyed monster. Fact was embellished by rumor, and soon there were stories all over the city about how the tempestuous Eleanor was dealing with the situation. The most popular of these had me making repeated attempts to poison Rosamund Clifford's food in order to rid myself of her.

Oui! The perverse English sympathized with the mistress and not with the wife. They said I attempted to murder poor Rosamund, Fair Rosamund, with poison!

Well, I did no such thing!

I only tried to kill her with love!

Literally, *mes amis*. I lay awake and planned it out. I was just thirty years of age, still a magnificent figure of a woman, tall, voluptuous, passionate. Rosamund was not yet twenty, slight, slender, a raven-haired nymphet with pink Anglican cheeks and blue Anglican eyes and healthy Yorkshire breasts that were alive with the glow and bounce of audacious youth. It was not difficult for me to see what Henry saw, to feel the heat the wench gave off, the heat which raised his Norman saber in salute and stirred his Anjou juices to demand release between her milkmaid thighs. She vibrated with a passion for life, and what could be more erotic than that?

Of course Henry was attracted. Even hating her, I was attracted myself. And realizing that, my plan fell into place quite seamlessly.

I called on Rosamund Clifford at her house in London. (It was a house that Henry had rented for her so that she might be conveniently accessible to him.) She was, of course, most surprised to see me. Still, the wench, to do her justice, had been brought up with certain amenities and so made a proper curtsy and bade me welcome.

She summoned a servant. Tea was served. The servant was dismissed. She passed the sugar. She smiled nervously. I smiled more calmly. I let her ponder the purpose of my visit for a few moments, and then I came to the point.

"I thought that we should meet face to face," I told her. "Wife to mistress, and mistress to wife, as it were."

"Oh." Fair Rosamund was clever enough to say no more than that. She made no denials. Nor did she confirm the relationship of which I spoke.

"You are very attractive," I told her.

"Thank you." Her smile was tremulous. "And you are just as beautiful as they said you were."

"*Merci.*" I sipped my tea. "It is easy to understand my husband's infatuation with you."

"Infatuation?" Suddenly the smile, no longer tremulous, turned triumphant. She said no more than that. It was enough. Her hold on Henry—so testified her lack of words—was far more firm than mere infatuation. But then she was unexpectedly gracious. "It is likewise easy to understand why Henry challenged the power of France itself to snatch you from the French King,'' she said.

"Shall we be friends then?" I smiled my most convincing smile.

"But of course!" How naive is youth. She warmed to my warmth, relaxed, neglected to remain wary.

"My husband is a satisfactory lover, I hope." My tone was light. It said we were just girls chatting with no men present to inhibit us.

"Most satisfactory."

"Do you take him into your bed?"

"Why of course." My question obviously puzzled Rosamund.

"It's just that my experience with Henry has been most varied," I explained. "I have found him to be a husband of sudden appetites, and we have frequently satisfied them in such places as barns and gardens, ship's holds and behind the roadside bush."

"I too have known some variety with him," Rosamund admitted, blushing slightly.

"You blush most becomingly," I told her. "But you do not blush when you do it with Henry in your boudoir, do you?"

"Why, I'm not sure." And she blushed the more.

"I have a favor to ask," I told her. "I would very much like to see the boudoir in which you and my husband make love."

Rosamund stared at me, caught off balance. "Why?" she asked finally.

"I have no adequate reason," I acknowledged freely. "I can only beg you to indulge me."

She thought about it a moment. "Why not?" she decided finally.

She led me from the sitting room where we were having tea. We mounted a broad staircase to the second floor of the sumptuous house. We entered an anteroom, passed through it, and came into a boudoir with a canopied bed.

Casually, I swung the door shut behind us. "So this is where you do it," I remarked.

"Yes."

I studied the room a moment. Then I turned my attention back to Rosamund. She was wearing a demure beige afternoon gown trimmed with lace. It had a very high neckline. It accentuated her youth, but not her allure.

"Does Henry ever come here in the afternoon?" I inquired.

"Some times."

"And you make love here in this bed in the daylight, with the sun shining through the window as it is now?"

"We have."

"Does Henry undress you on these occasions?" I wondered.

"Sometimes."

"Does he undo the stays of your gown in back?" I moved closer to her.

"He has."

"Like this?" I reached my arms around Rosamund and opened the top clasps of her afternoon dress.

"Yes. Like that." Her little pink tongue appeared and disappeared quickly. Her blue eyes narrowed and looked sharply into the green depths of mine. "What are you doing?" she asked in a low, husky voice.

"I like to share my husband's interests," I told her,

quickly unbuttoning the rest of the buttons down the back of the gown to the waist. "Do you mind?"

"I'm not sure if I mind or not." She caught her breath as I slid my hands inside the gown and around to the sides of her naked breasts.

"What lovely breasts you have," I exclaimed, squeezing them and weighing them in the palms of my hands. "So young! So round! So firm!"

"No woman has ever fondled them before." Now Rosamund's face mirrored her confusion. She had not stopped me when she should, and now she could not stop me if she would.

"It feels different from Henry's caresses, I warrant." I stroked and teased the flesh.

"Yes." She was panting now. "Quite different."

"I must see them," I declared. I pushed down the front of her gown and her naked breasts sprang free.

They were unexpectedly large for such a slender girl, really outsize in comparison to her small-boned frame. They were quite flushed and rosy and damp with perspiration. With each deep gasp she took, they rounded marvelously. The aureoles were large and of an unexpectedly golden hue—bronze, really—and of a roundness that covered the entire tip of her breast. The nipples were not hard and were indistinguishable from the aureoles. The cleft between her breasts was deep and narrow and a bit more red than the rosy-pink breasts themselves.

"Does my husband like to kiss them?" I inquired.

"I believe so. Yes."

"Like this?" I bent my head and bestowed a long, lingering, sucking kiss on one bronze aureole.

"Ahh! Yes! Yes!"

I traced the circle with my tongue. I dipped my tongue in the cleavage and ran it up and down, licking deeply, hotly. I sucked the other nipple.

"Better than Henry." Rosamund giggled. "Don't tell him."

How nice! We really were getting to be such warm friends! So close, indeed, that she was making me her confidante—little English ninny!

"Perhaps he is only different," I replied, "with your breasts than with mine because your breasts are different from mine. Look you! I will show you." Quickly I unlaced my bodice and took out my naked bosom for her to see.

"Your nipples are so long and red and hard!" Rosamund was impressed. "And your breasts are more oval than round, and point to the ceiling in the fashion of a man's cock when he is aroused." She licked her lips. "Truly Henry must enjoy sucking on them."

"Would you like to test the enjoyment for yourself?" I offered. I lifted one of my breasts and pressed the nipple to Rosamund's lips.

In a trice she was kissing and licking, nibbling and sucking. I fondled her own naked bosom, soft as butter, and she bent devouringly to mine. When she raised her head, her small mouth was swollen and moist with the pleasure she had found.

I put my arms around her then. My hard red nipples stabbed into the soft pink mounds of her bosom as we embraced. I kissed her on the mouth and our tongues went wild with the titillation of breast pressed to breast, aureole rubbing aureole, nipple stabbing nipple.

When the kiss was over, I pushed Fair Rosamund gently toward the bed. While doing so, I located the stays to the skirt of her gown and opened them. It fell around her ankles and she stood at the edge of the bed and stared at me with wide, worried, hungry English blue eyes.

I loosed her long black hair so that it tumbled free to her waist. I tangled my fingers in it and swept it ticklingly over her panting bosom. We kissed again, and she fell back onto the bed, wearing only her chemise, her bloomers, and her stockings. As for myself, I was bare to the waist and panting quite as much as she from my exertions.

"Do you not take off your chemise for my husband, Henry?" I teased her. "Do you not remove your bloomers?"

Fair Rosamund did not answer. Instead, her hands went to her waist and she removed her chemise. A moment later her feet pointed toward the ceiling and she slid free of the bloomers.

"And what of the stockings?" I inquired.

"Henry prefers that they remain."

"Very well, then." I turned my attention to her naked body. It was, I must admit, exquisite in its small boned English way. The pinkness of her cheeks was echoed by the roundness of her thighs and of her high, small, pert bottom. Her waist was very narrow and she was slim hipped, but this served to accentuate the pronounced rise of her mons veneris, which was cleft quite neatly and redly beneath the curly black triangle of hair enhancing it.

I stroked the insides of her thighs, which while slightly athletic were nevertheless quite girlish. I slid my hands underneath her and she rolled back and forth over them, laughing, and bounced in response to their probing intimacy. When I touched the moist and trembling lips of her young girl pussy, she gasped and clutched at my naked breasts and licked her lips greedily at my long nipples nestling in the palms of her hands.

"Does Henry kiss you here?" I inquired, sliding a finger up and down lengthwise in the cleft of her pussy without actually entering the deep hole.

"Yes!" Fair Rosamund gasped. "Yes, he does!"

"Like this?" I bent and ran my pursed lips lightly over the curly black triangle. "Or like this?" I quickly stabbed my tongue in and out between the swollen portal of her pussy entrance.

"Yes! Yes!"

"Which?" I used both my hands to spread her lovely pink thighs farther apart.

"Both!" she moaned. "Both!" And then, unable to contain herself any longer, she let go of my naked breasts and tangled her hands in my auburn hair and pressed my head down over her quim. "Do it!" she pleaded. "Do it!"

I pressed my lips to her honeyed pussy. I kissed gently, then not so gently. Fair Rosamund's lower body rose to meet my lips—slowly, then not so slowly. I licked the honey from the squirming lips. I pushed my tongue up the tight, hot, twisting tunnel. I sucked deeply. Her clitty pressed against my tongue insistently. I licked it and sucked again and again. I fell into a rhythm of clitty licking and cunt sucking.

Fair Rosamund's thighs vibrated around my ears. Looking up from the delicious quim I was sucking, I could see her too-large breasts bouncing wildly against her small rib cage. Her whimpers had turned to moans, and now they were turning to animal grunts.

"Oof! I'm going to come! . . . Ugh! . . . In your mouth! In your mouth! In your mouth! . . . Wump! . . .

Suck me! Lick me! Eat me! . . . Grrrr! . . . I'M COMING! I'M COMING! I'M COMING . . . AARRGGHH!''

My mouth was wide open now and her pussy was actually inside it. I was sucking with all my might using my tongue like a rudder to try to maintain some kind of control over her wildly tossing pussy. It went on for a long time and it excited me tremendously.

I had planned that Fair Rosamund's orgasm would be but the prelude to my own, but even with the planning, I had not anticipated how really and truly raunchy it would leave me feeling. Her coming made it an absolute necessity that I come too. And once her spending had run its course, I made it clear to Fair Rosamund that this was my expectation.

Still all aglow with her hot spendings, she was nothing loath to cooperate in mine. Naked save for silken stockings, she scrambled to the floor beside the bed and knelt between my knees. She rested her chin on the edge of the bed, licked her small red mouth, and looked up at me with blue eyes that were sparkling and expectant.

Gazing back at her, I licked the last of her syrup from my lips. I sat up, naked pear-shaped breasts jiggling, long nipples beckoning redly. I pulled my skirts above my waist and dispensed with my own passion-soaked bloomers and chemise. Then, sticking my long legs out at wide angles from my hips, I thrust my gaping, pulsing, chestnut-haired pussy to the very edge of the bed where Fair Rosamund's mouth was waiting to receive it.

Heaven! Her tongue touched first, a tickle, a probe, a thrill. She reached up with her hands and fondled my naked breasts. She licked the entrance of my pussy widely. When I shivered, she dropped one hand from my breasts and put it between her legs. Toying with her own so-recently-abraded pussy, she took her first deep suck of mine.

"Ahh!" I smoothed her ebony hair and pulled her face into me. "Suck! Lick! Kiss! Taste! Eat!"

Fair Rosamund did all those things with a vengeance. She raised me up a bit off the edge of the bed, and in this position she sucked at each of my most sensitive and intimate orifices by turn. I slid my long, shapely thighs around her cheeks and guided her lips, her tongue, her wondrous mouth.

It was not long before I felt my passion building to that explosive ecstasy which is the pinnacle of all sexual experience, no matter what the gender of those involved. This was the moment for which I had been waiting. This was the moment for which I had so carefully planned.

I widened my thighs and pressed in hard to Fair Rosamund's face until I was sure that my pussy quite covered both her nose and her mouth. Then I quickly tightened my thighs and locked them around her head. In this fashion was established the maximum contact, and the sensation this contact provided was truly excruciating and blissful.

And this contact also insured that Fair Rosamund could not draw further breath! No air could reach her nostrils or her lips! Those too-large lungs, denied all inhalation, were blocked from life!

Oui, mes amis! It was true! That was my plan! My rival would die by this most sensual suffocation. Locked in a death grip of lust, her fists flailing futilely as I pantingly approached the pinnacle of life's experience, she breathlessly approached her end.

As I came, Fair Rosamund would go!

Chapter Twelve

She struggled, of course. I, however, had the advantage both of surprise and of having established the superior position. In the most classic sense of military strategy, I had taken the high ground. I was up on the bed, Fair Rosamund on her knees below me on the floor. I had contrived to lock her arms with mine so that their flailing was of no use to her. At the same time, my palms were clasped firmly atop her head, pinning it firmly in place. My powerful thighs—the inner muscles developed by horseback riding since infancy—formed a classic pincers trapping her face. And my writhing, climaxing pussy itself was the instrument of her suffocation!

Even as my orgasm peaked, the struggles of Fair Rosamund to save her life grew weaker. No breath was reaching those large, round, oversized breasts. Their rosiness was paling, the flailing of arms a mere flutter now as life was being wrenched from youth with each delicious spasm of my strangling pussy.

"Die!" I moaned, coming. "Die! DIE!"

And so she would had not untoward circumstance chosen that very moment to intervene. A voice sounded from the stairs outside the doors to the apartment. "Rosamund?" Closer now, in the anteroom. "Fair Rosamund?" And then the door to the bedroom itself flung open and the doorway filled with freckles and flaming red hair and bowed legs. "Rosamund, what action is this I find my love performing?"

She could not, of course, answer. She could not breathe, and therefore had not breath to make reply. What words she might have found were choked off by the death grip of my grinding thighs.

"Eleanor?" His mistress not having answered his question, my husband turned his inquisitiveness on me. "How came you here?"

"On long, strong Aquitainian legs!" I gasped, my belly vibrating with lust.

"What are you doing?" He moved into the room from the doorway to the bed. "What are you doing to Fair Rosamund?"

"Only that which she herself did when our positions were reversed!" A long drawn-out spasm seized my pussy and I pressed down hard over Rosamund's lips and nostrils, sure that this would write finis to the fair Anglican's last gamahouche.

"You are killing her!" Suddenly Henry realized the true effect of my orgasm on his mistress. "You are suffocating her between your legs! Stop at once! I command you! Stop spending!"

It is a wife's duty to obey her husband in all things,

great and small. Still there are some matters, *mes amis,* in which she may not so easily bend to his will. This was such a one. Murder quite aside, the journey of orgasm is one which once embarked upon cannot be halted ere its destination is reached. Coming is an active verb!

"I said cease and desist!" But even Henry realized that I was beyond the ability to do as he commanded. And so he took matters into his own hands. Literally. He bent over, grasped my naked thighs in his large, strong, round hands, and pried them apart. Fair Rosamund's raven-tressed head fell from between them like the floppy top of a rag doll.

My honey was still on her lips, but her eyes were closed and her cheeks were white and as cold as fresh-fallen flakes of winter snow. Breath was no longer denied to her by my grinding pussy, and yet she breathed not. So still was she, indeed, that it seemed my murderous purpose was accomplished.

With an oath, Henry fell to his knees at her side and felt her ashen temple for a pulse. He found some sign of what he sought and an instant later was pushing on the ribs below her oversized breasts in an effort to urge air into her lungs. Finally there was a cough and a sputtering, and Fair Rosamund's long lashes fluttered and the color returned to her English cheek. She lived!

"You tried to kill her, Eleanor!" my husband growled as he helped his naked mistress from the room. "I shan't forget that!"

I made no reply. Still, I could not. Rapture held me even yet. All I could do was squeeze my burning, climaxing quim and grunt and watch the door close behind them.

*   *   *

The incident, I must confess, put a strain on our marriage. Henry found it extremely inconvenient to have his wife running around seducing his mistress and attempting to murder her. It offended his old-fashioned notions of what the institution of marriage should be. Needless to say, this attitude took the form of extreme displeasure with me.

"Anjou!" I found myself reacting to that displeasure loudly the next morning. "But why Anjou?"

"Because that is what I have decided!" Henry may have been younger than I, but his will had been tempered by generations of masculine privilege.

And so I was forced to pack my bags, leave England, and return to France by myself while Henry stayed in London to continue his dalliance with Fair Rosamund and wait for the death of King Stephen. I suppose he chose Anjou to punish me, since it was his land, not mine, and within teasing distance of Aquitaine while yet removed from it. Nor was the Anjou castle at Angers where I was to live anything like as lavish as the accommodations I had been used to in Aquitaine.

Nevertheless, once I was ensconced there, I determined to make the best of it. There was little social life to speak of, no tourneys, no jousting—only the dullness of an agrarian countryside. Very well then! I would arrange my own amusements.

Thus, from the determination brought on by this ennui was born the Court of Love!

The first thing I learned at Angers was that the ladies of the aristocracy there were as bored as I faced being. The second thing I learned was that they relieved this boredom as noblewomen have done from time immemorial—by engaging in love affairs, cuckolding their husbands if they were married, betraying their lovers if they were not, seducing the clergy on slow days, and opening their scabbards to the swords of passing knights on nights both short and long. The third thing I learned—no surprise!—was that these activities resulted in a great deal of friction (and not just the physical friction of lovemaking) between the sexes.

Husbands and wives, confessors and penitents, lovers and mistresses were constantly at odds over the ways in which they treated one another. "A forum of arbitration is needed," I realized. "There should be rules governing the behavior of lovers as there are rules governing all other human activities. These cases must be heard before they are acted upon instead of after, when it is too late, as is now so often the case. I am Countess of Anjou"—I invoked the title I had gained by marriage to Henry—"and so I shall declare a court and sit in judgment myself. And besides," I added sotto voce to a woman friend, "it will do much to relieve that tedium which seems to be the chief harvest of the soil of Anjou."

My proclamation of a Court of Love created great excitement among the Anjou aristocracy. There were grumbles from some of the Barons, and some of the priests as well, that being a woman my judgments might be weighted too much in favor of the distaff side. My ladies, on the other hand, were quick to see the opportunities to enlarge upon the sport of gossip so dear to their hearts. On the other hand, a few privately raised the question of discretion with me.

It was, of course, a most delicate question. Once a matter was brought before the Court of Love, its privacy was automatically sacrificed. That might suit the one who had brought the case, but suppose it did not suit the other party to the dispute? And suppose the Court of Love found for the party who had not wished the matter made public in the first place? Obviously the judgment rendered would have to compensate for consequences beyond the original suit. The very first case I was called upon to judge was a good example of this dilemma.

A lady charged a knight with swearing eternal love to her whilst plowing her field and then subsequently breaking the vow by furrowing another. She asked that the Court enforce his original vow and bar him from consorting with his second love. The knight, most loath to have the case heard at all, would say only in his defense that his behavior was most natural manly behavior, that it was only polite to vow eternal love whilst sinking one's shaft in fertile soil, and that pledges made in such circumstances were not meant to be literally construed as permanent.

I found his argument convincing. To hold lovers to each word they utter in heat would be to impose too great a constraint on one and all. We may all be God's creatures, but we all of us know Satan's wanderlust as well. I held for the knight and dismissed the lady's charge, remarking in my opinion that the enjoyment of her lover's flesh did not entitle her to shackle his soul with fidelity.

That was not, however, the end of the matter. The knight, it seems, was a married man—a circumstance he had neglected to mention to both his first and second lady loves. Now his first lady love, by her suit, had revealed his adultery. This much displeased his wife, who petitioned the Court for his punishment. At the same time, the unfortunate gentleman's second lady love came forth to accuse him of seducing her under false pretenses, having led her to believe that he was unwed and eligible, therefore making her more cooperative in spreading her thighs.

"A hornet's nest this Court of Love has stirred up for me, Countess Eleanor!" the poor fellow protested, with justification.

I deemed that he had been put through enough. I dismissed his wife's claim with the advice (hard learned in my marriage to Henry) that fidelity was not natural to husbands and therefore its lack not punishable. And after ascertaining from his second lady love that she had indeed enjoyed the passion of the moment when they had made love, I advised her that she had no right to return pain for pleasure by splitting the hair of his marital status which was, after all, irrelevant to the activity in which they had both willingly engaged.

One of the more interesting cases was brought by a Baron who was having an affair with one of my unmarried ladies-in-waiting. He came to her one day and spoke as follows: "You say you love me, but I require proof. Demonstrate your love by willingly granting me permission to make love to another."

"I love you more than life!" the silly goose replied. "Go and dip the wick of your candle elsewhere with my blessing."

A month passed before she saw him again. On this occasion, he knelt and spoke these words to her: "I was only testing," he confessed. "I have remained faithful to you."

"You have not dipped your wick in the tallow dish of another?"

"I have not."

"Begone!" She was furious. For one thing, she did not

believe him and thought the lie an insult to her intelligence.
For another, if by any wild chance it was not a lie, then he
had been (and here only the Sicilian patois will do) fucking
with her mind, and that was unforgivable.

"You don't understand, my love. I have been faithful.
Yours is the only tallow dish in which I wish to dip my
candle wick. And never so much as now, and ever so
better sooner than later!" Saying which, he raised his tunic
and moved to fit his action in his words.

That, as was later testified to, was when she kicked him
most painfully in the groin and sent him on his way.

And so the hapless fellow, gonads still sadly swollen,
brought suit before the Court of Love where I, Eleanor,
Countess of Anjou, sat in judgment. I heard him out and
found him not unsympathetic. Also, I heard behind the
testimony of his lady a song quite different from the one
she sang aloud. My verdict was rendered accordingly.

"It is the nature of love," I pronounced, "that a lover
may falsely pretend to desire fresh experiences in order to
test the steadfastness of the partner in amour. Because it is
natural, a woman sins against love itself when she with-
holds her flesh from her lover for any reason save that of
clear evidence that he has in actuality been unfaithful to
her."

Thus did I sentence them to a night of lust—the first of
many such, I hoped.

Not all the cases I heard required great insight. Some
merely called for experience. And although I was scarce
thirty years old, God knows I had had my share of that.

One comes to mind of a knight with a particularly
woeful countenance who told the Court of Love a tale of
how his lady had taken another lover in his stead. When he

protested, she soothed him by promising that if she ever lost her present lover, she would once again take the woeful knight into her bed. Subsequently, she and the lover were married. When the knight heard of this, he filed his claim with the Court that she had lost a lover when she gained a husband, and therefore should make good on her promise to him.

The decision was obvious to me, as was the reason for it. "Love cannot exist between husband and wife." I declared for posterity. "The lady did indeed sacrifice love to marriage and can no longer be said to have a lover. Therefore she must honor her promise to the plaintiff. She is hereby ordered to make said plaintiff welcome to her bed."

To hear such cases was amusing. To ferret out the details was titillating. To pronounce judgment was ego gratifying. (Where would judges be without the judged?) But then one day I was presented with a case like none other!

"I had a love affair with a woman of very high station," said the petitioner before me. "She was married to a very powerful man. Nevertheless, we were most deeply in love."

Although he paused, I had no words. He continued.

"It went on for some time. Finally circumstance dictated that we take a trip together. In the course of this trip, I happened on my lady naked, in the arms of another, also naked. The situation could not be misconstrued. They—"

"Could it not?" I interrupted. "Are you certain?"

"What the eyes see, they see." He shrugged.

"Perhaps she was tempted," I granted. "But perhaps her love for you was such that she would not have succumbed. Perhaps you interrupted at the very instant she was about to change her mind. Perhaps she was about to refuse to grant her favors, about to put her clothes back on, about to leave the naked man in whose arms you discovered her, about to flee back to your arms. Perhaps—''

''Perhaps—'' He shrugged again. ''It was a very long time ago. Perhaps. But how shall we ever know?''

''Is there no way then that this Court of Love can resolve your doubts?'' I pleaded with him.

''I fear not.''

''Then what is it, good sir, that you want from this Court?''

''To hear me out. No more than that.''

''Continue, then.''

''My love betrayed, I left my lady,'' he continued. ''Time passed and I did not see her. I heard tell of her doings, though. She embarked on a great cause, and it was rumored that she had affairs with mighty men, Princes and Emperors, Christians and infidels, countrymen and aliens—even, so they say, a Sicilian!''

''Get to the point!'' I held my head high, although I could not keep my lower lip from quivering.

''I will. And quickly too. One day not so very long ago rumor reached me that my lady, my love whom I could never forget, never renounce completely no matter what she had done, was divorcing her husband.''

''This circumstance affected you?'' I was touched.

''I rushed to Paris, believing her to be there, ready to forgive all, wanting only to claim her for my own.''

''But she was not in Paris.'' I sighed.

''No. She was elsewhere. Elsewhere, remarrying before I could so much as give voice to the endurance of my love." Now it was his voice that quavered. "And then she was not in France at all," he added.

"But she returned," I prompted him.

"She has returned. And so I have come to this Court—this Court of Love—to ask—to inquire—"

"Oui?" Oh, how my heart was pounding.

"If it is possible under the rules being promulgated here that—that—"

"Oui!" The aristocrat onlookers gasped as I descended from my throne and embraced the petitioner. "It is possible! The Court has decided. She loves you! She has always loved you! I trust that this decision is satisfactory to you, Monsieur Bernard de Ventadour?"

It was. As soon as our bodies touched, the years fled. More, they evaporated as if all that had happened since last I had lain in his arms had never been. And that, *mes amis*, while we were still fully clothed!

There was only one thing that remained to be done. "Restitution must be made!" I announced to the Court of Love, and then dismissed court for the day.

And when we were alone, restitution was made. Our clothes fell away like leaves in a gale. I took my poet as befit the recovery of a long-lost love. And he took me with a pentameter no other man had ever equalled, nor ever would!

Hallelujah!

Bernard de Ventadour was back in my life!

Hallelujah!

We had three blissful months together before I received word from Henry, summoning me to return to England. King Stephen had fallen ill. His doctors said that he was dying. In order to insure a smooth succession, it was necessary that Henry have his Queen by his side when the old King breathed his last.

It was also necessary to quiet the doubts of the English Lords. That Henry should take Fair Rosamund for a mistress was acceptable, but that the future Queen of England should be so estranged from the King as to live on French soil was not. Indeed, this circumstance could prove an impediment to our securing the throne. Despite the fact that King Stephen had signed a paper designating Henry his successor, the English Lords still had to approve before Henry and I could actually be crowned. Traditionally, this approval could only come after the old King's death. It would have been quite automatic had not the question been raised of whether it was fitting to crown a King of England whose Queen might live in France.

And so I went to London.

Bernard de Ventadour accompanied me. I would not have had it otherwise. We were in love more strongly even than we had been years ago. So much so that it was difficult for us to keep our hands off one another. I would brook no separation from him, neither English Channel nor any other. Having my lover with me was my price for smoothing my husband's way to the English throne.

I made this very clear at my first meeting with Henry after our arrival in London. After allowing a decent interval for unpacking, he came to my chambers, expecting to find me alone there. Confronting Bernard instead, he raised one fiery red eyebrow. "Who is this fellow?" he demanded.

"He is my lover," I told him defiantly.

"*Oui*. Well, I write poems too," Bernard added with what was meant to be an ingratiating smile.

"Poems?" Henry growled.

"Would you like to hear one?" Bernard offered.

"I would not!" Henry roared, drumming his fingers on the hilt of his sword. "You are in my wife's bedroom!" he reminded Bernard. "That is reason enough to call you out!"

"I don't duel," Bernard told him. "I write verses."

"You don't duel!" Henry stared at him.

"He is a coward," I told Henry.

"A coward?" Emotion rendered Henry's face a freckled sea of confusion.

"A coward," Bernard confirmed. "It's a matter of religious conviction with me. I prefer life to death."

"What manner of man is this?" Henry wondered in a tone of complete disgust.

"The best I have ever experienced, including husbands!" I assured Henry.

"In a poetic sense!" Bernard backed away from the purple wrath that flooded Henry's face. "She means poetically!"

"I mean physically," I clarified sweetly.

"Are you trying to get me killed?" Bernard moaned.

"He won't kill you," I assured Bernard, "because he knows that if he did, I would behave in such a manner as to be sure to cost him the Crown of England."

Henry snorted, brought himself under control, and started for the door.

"By the way," I called after him, "how is Fair Rosamund? Be sure to give her my regards."

The door slammed after him so violently that a mirror fell from the wall and shattered.

"Now we shall have seven years' bad luck!" Bernard groaned.

"Not if we counter the curse with the proper spell," I assured him.

"The proper spell? What is that?"

"This," I told him, raising my skirts to the highest. "Just this."

Shortly thereafter, on October 25, 1154, King Stephen died. Immediately the English Lords went into conference behind closed doors to confirm his successor. This should have been accomplished with some immediacy, but it wasn't. Instead, it dragged on for over a month. Finally, one Saturday in mid-December, Henry and I were notified that a decision had been reached, and we were invited to Westminster Palace, adjacent to Westminster Abbey, to hear it.

We proceeded there by separate coaches. I arrived first with Bernard de Ventadour among my entourage. A little later I was on the balcony of the boudoir to which I had been shown and observed the arrival of Henry with Fair Rosamund Clifford. A few moments passed, and then Henry, Fair Rosamund still in tow, as was their baggage, was led through the doors of the boudoir proper.

I started to open my mouth to inquire as to the meaning of this intrusion. Henry, reading aright the indignation on my face, silenced me with a glance. He dismissed the majordomo, covering over the tension with an expression of gratitude for the arrangements. Only when we were alone did he address the awkwardness of the situation.

"Protocol demands that we share the same bed tonight, Eleanor," he informed me. "It would not do to demand separate arrangements. Even now the Lords are free to alter their judgment of our fitness, mine and yours, to be crowned. We must not risk losing the throne for reasons of marital discord.''

I did not dispute the point. The truth is, *mes amis,* that I put as high a value on the English crown as Henry did. I had been bred to power, had relinquished much of it with my divorce from Louis, and this was my opportunity to embrace it once again. As to how it might be shared between myself and Henry, why, the forecast was stormy of course, but I had faith in my ability to weather the tempest of our royal marriage.

"There is but one bed," I replied. "We will have to share it."

"So be it." Henry shrugged.

"What of her?" I leveled a finger at Fair Rosamund.

"I sleep with my love, or do not sleep at all," Henry told me.

"Then stay awake!"

"Half the bed is mine," Henry pointed out. "If I choose to share it, that is no concern of yours."

"And if I share my half," I snapped back, "neither is that any of your affair."

"So be it! So long as these arrangements and what occurs here go no farther than the walls of this room."

"So be it!" I echoed.

And so it was agreed. . . .

That evening, Henry and I, dressed in our finery, dined with the English Lords. The announcement of their decision regarding the throne would come the following day and would be followed by the appropriate ceremony. It would not have been politic to inquire about it this evening, nor for it to be mentioned in our presence. Instead, we were entertained.

There were jugglers and dancers, acrobats and a troop of players performing excerpts from translations of Greek dramas. The dinner consisted of many courses, and while the food tended to be meaty and heavy in the English fashion, there were many delicacies from far-off places as well. Where the French would have drunk wine, we were presented with tankards of ale. This peasant slake was at least backed up by a most potent mead. Its effect was marked, and the occasion soon turned quite wild and even risqué. Serving girls and even noblewomen were fondled and pinched, and kisses were stolen openly.

Henry and I naturally had to hold ourselves somewhat aloof from these activities. Our position dictated this. Nevertheless, we both drank quite a bit of the ale and the mead with the result that when we finally rose to go to our room, we were more than a little unsteady on our feet. Loathe each other though we did, it was necessary to put our arms around one another's waists in order to navigate the stairs. And if in our lurching Henry inadvertently palmed one of my breasts and I cupped a buttock 'neath his tunic, there was little of lust in the contacts. We were each of us committed elsewhere.

When we entered our boudoir, we were each relieved of the burden of the other. Fair Rosamund was quick to lead her lover away from his murderous wife, and my beloved poet, Bernard de Ventadour, moved just as swiftly to catch me in his arms as I turned from my husband. Henry being in his cups, Fair Rosamund set about undressing him.

Recognizing my tiddliness, Bernard performed a like service for me.

His love stripped Henry nude. Like most men of our time, this was the condition in which he preferred to sleep. Bernard removed all of my clothes except my camise. Like most women, I often slept in this garment in lieu of a nightdress. Bernard then quickly stripped nude himself and joined me beneath the coverlets of the bed. On the other side, Fair Rosamund, clad only in a chemise similar to mine, slipped in beside my freckled husband.

"You take up too much room!" Henry growled at me.

"Less than my due, for it is you who overlap your half!" I replied.

"Your Aquitainian presence spreads unconscionably!"

"It is your Norman seizure of territory that violates the division!"

"Aquitainian invader!"

"Norman conqueror!"

"I do wish that you two would try to get along," Fair Rosamund whined. "I can't get any sleep with you bickering this way."

"I try to be reasonable, love," Henry told her. "But Eleanor keeps thrusting her hip over on my side of the bed."

"That's not her hip, it's my hip," Fair Rosamund informed him.

"Oh."

There was silence for a moment. Then—

"Oh!" This time the expostulation was Rosamund's, and it most decidedly was a squeal.

"What are they doing?" Bernard whispered in my ear.

"What do you think?" I slid my hand down his belly. Why should Henry have all the fun?

"Squeeze them harder!" Rosamund murmured.

"God, I love big breasts!"

"Ouch!" Bernard exclaimed. "Why did you bite me?"

"Sorry," I told him. "It was an accident. I was distracted."

"Your hair is so red and curly," Rosamund commented. Her hands were deep under the blanket. Henry's head was not.

"Kiss the other one now," I told Bernard. "That's it! Suck it hard!"

"You're squirming over onto my side of the bed!" Henry complained.

"Forget about her, can't you?" Fair Rosamund sighed. "Kiss me."

Out of the corner of my eye, I saw her small mouth open wide and her red tongue beckon an invitation. Then Henry kissed her, his flaming red hair tumbling over her slightly flushed brow. An instant later he changed position and butted me with his hard left buttock.

"Oof!" I slapped up against Bernard and felt his big, thick, Gascon prick against my belly through the material of my camise. "Be careful, you oaf!" I snarled at Henry.

"Did I hurt you, darling?" Bernard was solicitous.

"No. I wasn't talking to you." I stroked the hard shaft.

"Ahh, Eleanor!" His hands stroked my bottom until the cheeks were flaming and squirming wildly to his caress. He licked my nipples with his tongue so expertly that it felt as if he had ignited them. And his balls swelled in my palms whilst his prick throbbed hotly against the camise over my furry pussy. "Ahh, my Queen, my love!"

"Not yet a Queen!" Henry snorted from my other side.

"Bastard!" I snapped my elbow into his ribs.

"Bitch!" He pinched my bottom viciously.

Somehow Bernard and fair Rosamund managed to get us apart. We subsided. We each went back to what we had been doing.

"Kiss it!" Henry ordered a few moments later, and I saw Fair Rosamund's ebony curls disappear under the covers.

Not to be outdone, I licked my way down Bernard's hard body to his groin. I furrowed the crinkly hair there with the tip of my tongue. I caught one swollen round ball between my lips and gently sucked it. Then I sucked the other one. Finally I licked deep between his legs, up his shaft, and engulfed his prick in my mouth. Sucking, I gauged its throbbing and felt the honey dampening that portion of my camise that I had trapped between my fevered thighs.

"Look at that!" There was a certain amount of awe in Henry's voice which belied his words. "That's disgusting!"

"What do you mean?" Rosamund took exception. "Wasn't I just doing the same thing to you?"

"Not like that!"

"Could you two hold the conversation down?" Bernard requested. "You're interfering with my concentration."

"Do you believe that?" Henry asked Fair Rosamund. "I don't believe that! Do you believe that?"

"No." Fair Rosamund straddled him and I felt her thigh brush my hip. "I don't believe that!"

"Hmm." Bernard was looking over my shoulder. "She is rather attractive, isn't she?"

I carefully removed his penis from my mouth. "You

should always be very careful what you say when I'm performing fellatio on you," I advised him.

"I didn't mean to offend you, my darling."

"Men have found themselves castrated for less!"

"A lover's quarrel!" Henry was delighted.

"I just couldn't help noticing how very large and well shaped her breasts were." Trying to explain, Bernard dug himself in deeper.

"Like a cow!" I opined succinctly.

"Henry!" Fair Rosamund was insulted. "Did you hear what she called me?"

"Ignore her, my sweet! Ignore her and keep right on doing what you're doing!"

Curious, I craned my head over my shoulder to see what that might be. What I saw was Henry lying flat on his back with his freckled face perspiring whilst Fair Rosamund rode up and down on his erect penis. Her pink breasts were bouncing energetically and her blue eyes were staring as if focused on some wondrous prize soon to be reached if she would gallop fast enough. And so she galloped. . . .

"Put it in me!" The sight quite stripped me of any shreds of modesty I might have had left. I pulled off my camise and scrambled to mount my throbbing, tumescent poet. "All the way!"

I rose up high, my pear-shaped breasts gleaming, the nipples red and hard and terribly aroused. I positioned the wedge-shaped head of Bernard's thick Gascon cock between the swollen lips of my pussy, and slowly, enjoying the sensation, I settled down over him. His prick filled me and his balls trembled against my pussy lips and the crinkly hair of his groin tickled me so that I laughed uncontrollably. Spreading my sensitive inner flesh over his groin, savoring the hardness of the shaft buried in me, I bent to stab his firm chest with my breasts, to kiss his warm lips, to lick his tongue with my tongue.

Bernard grabbed me by the hips and rose up high and hard under me. I was propelled toward the boudoir ceiling at the same time that his hands held me down so that I might feel the full force of the head of his cock striking against the entrance of my womb. When he began to move in hard, tight circles, my clitty felt as if it would explode against the hot shaft of flesh. I whimpered and at the same time I began forcing my way up and down his cock with long, deep fucking movements.

"That's it!" Beside me Rosamund spoke. "Fuck me, darling! Fuck me hard!" Like me, she was moving rhythmically up and down and moving in circles around the cock buried inside her.

Our eyes met. We were enemies, and yet we smiled. And then, as if simultaneously, seized by an impulse we could neither of us deny, we embraced. Her large, soft breasts overwhelmed my smaller, uptilted ones, but it was my hard, long, pointed nipples that dug into her aureoles. We kissed, our tongues entwining. And prolonging this embrace, we squeezed our lovers' cocks deep inside us and communicated to them the urgency of our desire. Soon our message was that we were coming and that we wanted nothing so much as for them to come with us while we continued to kiss and merge our bosom flesh.

Deep inside me I felt Bernard explode, and my cunt was bathed with hot male nectar. At the same time, Fair Rosamund stiffened in my embrace, and I knew that Henry must be spending inside her. Together, we shuddered and let go. Our climax was mutual and had as much to do with our arousal of each other as with the hard malenesses discharging into us.

After a long, long time we all four of us collapsed, exhausted. We may have dozed then. I'm not sure. I only remember being roused by Bernard's voice making a lazy observation. "This was not such a bad arrangement after all," he said.

"No. It wasn't," Fair Rosamund was quick to agree.

"An aristocratic arrangement," I granted. "Too good, as my father used to say, for the peasants."

"A royal arrangement." For once Henry did not dispute me. "And when I am King, I shall so decree it."

"And what will you call it?" I asked him.

" 'Open marriage,' " Henry decided. "I will call it 'open marriage.' And I will restrict it to royalty."

"Call it what you will," I told him, speaking out of my vast experience in the Court of Love. "But you will never restrict it. Never!"

I was right, of course. Still, it is interesting, is it not, that open marriage had its beginnings in Westminster Castle on the eve of a very, very important day. *Oui.* The following morning the English Lords informed us that they had decided to follow King Stephen's wishes and grant Henry the crown. The coronation was to take place right next door in Westminster Abbey that very afternoon, December 19, 1154.

It was the afternoon that I, Eleanor, Duchess of Aquitaine and Normandy, Countess of Anjou, former Queen of France, just thirty-two years of age, was crowned Queen of England!

And that, *mes amis,* was only the beginning.